THE OFFICIAL ZOMBIE HANDBOOK (UK)

THE MINISTRY OF ZOMBIES

www.severedpress.com

ISBN: 978-0-9807996-1-3

This book is dedicated to my wife Constance for her tireless support and to my nephew Frank.

Stay alert and keep your eyes peeled for when the zombies finally come to Ashford…

CONTENTS

Introduction

This book is about survival. It's about staying alive when all about you have turned into bloodthirsty ghouls. It's about equipping you with the knowledge, skills and techniques to say – I will survive the coming zombie apocalypse and will not become an easy snack for the teeming dead.

The genesis of this book was the realisation that our country is sleep walking towards a catastrophe – that is the day when an outbreak of zombies will reach critical mass and turn our green and pleasant land into a grey and shambling wasteland.

Don't get me wrong. Some sterling work has been completed in the field of zombie research, much of it presented in fiction but developing some superb 'what if?' scenarios providing those aiming to survive with masses of data to work with.

Through my own research however, I became convinced that the average Briton could, despite our lack of access to virtually any type of firearm, greatly increase their chances of survival through some proactive action provided we act now.

Much of this activity is based around what I have called the "90-day survival plan" which, not surprisingly, is a blueprint to help you and your family survive the opening chaotic phase of the zombie outbreak, plan your next steps then either expand your current location or move to a better long-term location. To cut a long story short, to survive a true zombie apocalypse.

The challenge will be far from easy and there are some scary facts to consider but I hope that on reviewing this volume and others, readers will develop into real 'zombie survivalists' by making some of the recommended improvements and changes in lifestyle.

The messages in this book also fit well with today's green agenda. For example, thinking about how much food, water and energy you use is the first step to taking control and managing what are finite resources. Knowing where your food comes from can help you realise how very dependent we have become on imported and increasingly exotic foods. And finally, getting your home shipshape is always good practice and projects such as insulating your home will help keep your costs down.

To answer one question which may be lurking in the back of your mind: is he insane?

No, I'm serious; I just plan to see the whole ghoul invasion through and forewarned is forearmed. No one can say when the ghouls will rise but the evidence says they are coming so get yourself sorted before they are drooling at your window . . .

Sean Page.
Ministry of Zombies
London, 2010

A Survivor's Guide to Zombies

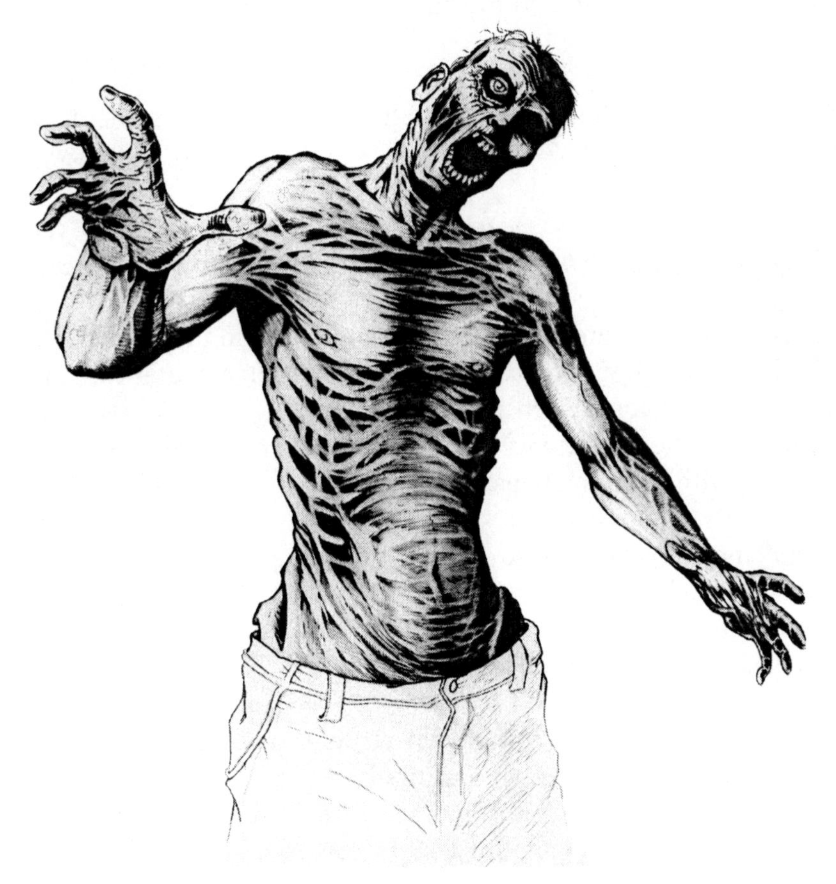

The following section is designed to provide you with the basic information you need to help you survive a zombie outbreak. If you like, see it as a Zombie 101. The emphasis throughout is on practical action but having a good awareness of the developing science of zombiology will certainly help you prepare and may keep you alive once the shuffling grey masses arrive – so this is also addressed. Crucially, this section will help you determine what a zombie is, how one is created and most important of all, how to stop them.

The chapter concludes with a set of case studies detailing confirmed zombie outbreaks in history. Hopefully, these will demonstrate that a possible ghoul incident in the UK today is not such a remote possibility.

What is a Zombie?

The term 'zombie' as it is used today is both broad and diluted and can mean anything from a traditional African voodoo god to a modern slogan for an apathetic person. A real weakness in the zombie fighting community is an inability to pin down a precise definition. However, in any war, and the battle against the living dead will be a war - it is essential to know your enemy.

For the purpose of this volume, the best tactic is to go for the lowest common denominator:

A zombie is a dead body that has been brought back to life by an as yet unidentified virus which leads to the body to behave in a low intelligent and cannibalistic way.

Collective terms for these creatures range from "zombies" to the "living dead", although in the politically correct UK we may soon find ourselves referring to them as the "mortally-challenged" or some such nonsense. But, this is no joking matter, for once there is a black and white answer, well, a grey one. Zombies are the dead returned and they cannot coexist with living humans.

The term 'ghoul' may also be used to describe such a creature, although in history this term has often been used to infer a creature from the underworld or from some other evil source. In fact, zombies are not 'evil' as such, they are not demonic and they are not, as most experts now agree, supernatural in origin.

The concept of the recently dead turning up at unexpected moments permeates many cultures of the world. Be they known as jumbie, kongo, nzumbe, draugr, revenant or zombie, the theme is the same: that in some way, the dead have come back to life and in most cases with an unhealthy appetite for human flesh.

Although the origin of the term "zombie" itself is shrouded in some mystery, it is generally accepted to originate from the Caribbean island of Haiti. Here, around a mix of indigenous and African religious traditions, a "myth" was created, with the zombies being the recently deceased who had been returned to life deliberately through witchcraft and that once returned they fall under the spell of their tormentor. This therefore conjures up the image of zombies as undead slaves, doing the bidding of their master, normally, some evil deed or murderous task. The important point is that the zombie is under the control of a living person. As with most folklore, this is a mixture of truth and myth. For instance, we in the zombie fighting community owe much thanks to the islanders of Haiti for bringing the issue of the living dead to the world's attention. But, the idea that they can be controlled is a dangerous myth which could get people killed. The living dead do have a motivation but it is not to carrying out various tasks for living controllers.

A high profile study in the 1960s by anthropologist Dr Roger Winters pointed to a possible link between Haitian zombies and a deadly neurotoxin called tetrodotoxin which can be found in native puffer fish. In the correct doses, this substance can render a victim in a 'death-like' state and may reduce reactions to external stimuli, in effect creating zombie-like symptoms. It may be that cases of deliberately poisoned people and genuine zombie outbreaks blurred such that the two very different states became confused.

As with many innovative and radical free-thinkers, Dr Winters's work was widely criticised in the United States and allegations were made that he had observed the desecration of graves whilst gathering ingredients for his studies. It is perilous for anyone working with the living dead, that digging up the odd corpse is an unpleasant modus operandi and can leave researchers open to much police attention. Some of this scientific criticism was published in the late 1970s in the reputable British science magazine, the *Lancet*. For open minded sceptics, it is always an eye opener to realise that the subject of the living dead and work pertaining to this troubling phenomena has been discussed in formal journals.

This pioneering work into zombies continues to be developed by researchers around the world but is largely ignored by both academic institutions and the media. Most notable in this effort has been the discovery that whilst the chemical tetrodotoxin can cause a zombie-like condition, it is not the cause of zombism in its wider context which we now know is caused by a viral infection. This virus will be discussed in more detail later.

Much work is now freely available on the internet and through specialist forums. This includes everything from how to recognise the living dead to a detailed description of the zombie virus by medical experts. However, calls for increased funding in this area of research have gone largely unanswered in the university communities of the world. Few correctly qualified researchers would dare to submit a proposal based on investigating the living dead, fearing their careers would suffer, and in the current climate they may be right. Much of the research has therefore been completed by gifted but still amateur researchers. We are thus presented with a raft of works of varying quality and insight which only serves to add confusion to what should be recognised as the fledgling science of "zombiology".

In the media, films such as *28 Days Later* and countless volumes of 'end of the world' fiction, have created new myths around zombies and their capabilities, further complicating the misty nexus which is our next subject of discussion - exactly how a zombie is created and the various theories around zombiology.

Zombie Creation

More has been written as to why zombies exist than has ever been written on survival tactics and trying stay alive once the ghouls take over. This academic, even theological debate has dominated the emerging science of zombiology for almost a decade and in some cases has set serious scientific investigation back. Whilst the viral origin of zombies is accepted by virtually all major figures in the zombie fighting community, zombie creation theory continues to spark debate on the fringes.

Those planning to survive any zombie incursions face a wide range of possible causes including everything from an engineered airborne virus to a supernatural-inspired apocalypse and the many weird and wonderful ideas in between. Standard military doctrine states that the more intelligence you have on an enemy - in this case the corpselike zombies - the better prepared you will be to face them in combat. Once the ghouls actually emerge, it won't make too much difference where they come from, but for now a brief outline of the main origin theories may be useful. It should be noted that these 'schools' overlap and merge in certain areas but on the whole, zombie experts tend to fall into one or other of the two camps.

The Supernatural School

As the name implies, this theory of zombie creation sees zombies as a product of supernatural intervention such as a vengeful act of an angry deity or some kind of black magic spell to create these living dead monsters. Basically, the origin of the ghouls, be it a single zombie or millions, is from beyond the natural world.

The classic zombie outbreak location for this school is normally the cemetery or morgue where any unfortunate witness will see the grisly ghouls digging their way out of the grave, resurrected by anything from voodoo to devil worship.

The resulting creatures may possess supernatural powers or skills, even the ability to 'lead' the living dead or communicate with other of the countless wandering corpses. More often than not, these zombies are found in works of fiction in which various 'super-ghouls' are presented as being either more intelligent or even able to converse. These supernatural talents may also include seeing into the future, sensing humans or controlling a ghoulish army of the undead. This seems to be a device convenient to facilitate plot development rather than one based on any factual research. It should be noted that to date no zombies have ever tested positive for any powers which could be considered 'supernatural'.

Supernatural zombies are often described as the 'living dead', but in this context this has a spiritual implication, for example, the creature may be assumed to have no soul or to be damned in some way. Frequently, a mass rising of supernatural ghouls is also linked to stories of the end of the world or classic 'opening the gates of the underworld' legends. There is often an overarching "mission" at work, such as the destruction of mankind or a cleansing of the earth to rid it of sin, etc.

In the cold light of science, it may be easy for readers to scorn the ideas of the supernatural school but many of these beliefs have developed over long periods of human history and are deeply embedded in our psyche. Whilst now very much a minority view amongst experts, once the dead rise, panic may lead many into believing the central themes of the 'supernatural school'. One can easily imagine cults developing around an 'end of the world' belief and that if organised, these communities could become as dangerous to survivors as the zombies themselves.

The Scientific School

As a general rule, the origin theories of the Scientific School have grown in prominence in the zombie fighting community over the past 50 years, maybe longer. Central to this theory of zombie creation is that some "external" factor, most commonly a virus but also including factors such as chemical poisoning or even alien intervention, has deviated the human form into something which can be best described as a "zombie". Definitions of whether the subject is actually dead or not are to a large extent academic but in virtually all cases, the 'person' is gone as is the conscience and in most cases, any memory to be replaced by a single-minded desire to feed on living flesh. This is the very essence of what is meant by the term 'ghoul'.

The creature which remains is effectively 'undead' in its new state but this is not a supernaturally-induced state and is best described as a medical condition, albeit an irreversible one.

The most important difference with the Supernatural School is that these living dead are very much governed by the laws of nature. For example, although a zombie may under some circumstances sprint, it cannot exceed the basic restrictions of the human body – there is nothing supernatural at work here.

An Assessment on the Schools

Recent research published in both academic journals and across the web has all but dismissed the concepts of the Supernatural School. Certainly, there are areas of zombie biology we still do not understand but the origin debate has been greatly enlightened by the work of mainly US-based zombie experts. Microbiologist and anthropologist Dr Khalid Ahmed, formerly of a prominent American university, has published several papers following an intensive period of research between 1997 and 2001, in which he had direct access to zombies or suspected zombies. All of Dr Ahmed's field work was carried out in remote villages in north western India and centred on the study of a limited ghoul outbreak which was quickly brought under control by police and local militia. During the incident, several villagers thought to have caught a "madness" were locked up and Dr Ahmed had the unique opportunity to study the zombification process in near control conditions. In years to come, his time in India will doubtless be seen as important to the science of zombiology as was Charles Darwin's voyages on HMS *Beagle* to the theory of evolution.

Importantly, Dr Ahmed claims to have isolated, if only for a few seconds, what he believes to be the cause of zombism in humans – that is a complex RNA virus which creates what he refers to as Zombic Condition in those infected. Dr Ahmed noted that in nine patients he investigated, eight showed signs of obvious human bite marks, missing limbs or other large open wounds. One patient was discovered to have been a mute carpenter from another village and was therefore clear of the virus when brought in by the local authorities. Unfortunately, this individual had been kept near to the other zombies and received a bite shortly after testing.

Dr Ahmed recorded that the virus induced a death-like state on the mute villager but without access to more advanced medical equipment, he was unable to confirm which parts of the body were still functioning. The subject lay perfectly still for some four hours after which he began to exhibit signs of movement. Dr Ahmed was able to document the full transformation process which will be detailed later in this volume but like so many medical breakthroughs it was the accidental and tragic infection of a human being in which he was able to see clearly the stages of infection, clinical death, incubation and transformation.

His research is controversial to say the least and he was deported from India before his research was published. Since returning to the USA, Dr Ahmed has been unable to secure a research position at any of the leading institutions his qualifications and experience should entitle him to. However, his short period of research highlighted for the first time the viral origin of the Zombic Condition and suggested strongly that it is spread by a blood to blood or other fluid to blood transfer.

As with most areas of research, it also creates a whole new set of questions which demand further research around subjects such as spread patterns, whether there are any humans with a natural resistance or immunity and even whether there is the potential for a cure or a vaccine to be developed.

The Zombie Virus and the Zombic Condition

Whilst we still know frustrating little about the actual biology of the zombie, thanks to the pioneering work of Dr Ahmed we at last have a useful medical framework to outline the key symptom stages of the Zombic Condition.

Most trusted sources, including Dr Ahmed's research, identify four stages in transformation from human to zombie. This information is core research for anyone planning to survive a zombie apocalypse.

- If infected by bite, scratch or fluid exchange, within three to four hours the victim will begin to feel flu-like symptoms which may include raised temperature, vomiting, and tiredness. More noticeable will be the psychological symptoms such as panic and an irrational desire to run. There are no recorded cases of infected humans being cured even after amputating limbs in attempts to isolate an infection. The transformation to zombie is 100%. This 'living dead' sentence is obviously a massive psychological trauma and patients will sometimes become violent.

- The second stage occurs within two to eight hours of infection and will see the victim suffer a loss of verbal and hearing functions. The skin will become noticeably paler as they move towards a comatose death-like state. Hallucinations and drooling may affect those who maintain consciousness. It is also worth having some air freshener handy as you are likely to face some fairly noxious and stale vapours. Some reports have mentioned a milky film over the eyes or a whitening effect over the eye similar to cataracts. (The latter symptoms were not in Dr Ahmed's study but are from reliable South American sources).

- Apparent clinical 'death' will occur six to twelve hours after infection. This rate depends on factors such a patient age, health, size and the dose of infected fluid. The victim will turn a deathly pale colour – almost light blue in some cases. Life signs are minimal if there are any at all; heartbeat will slow and eventually stop. This 'dead time' is the calm before the storm before the virus 'creates' the living dead creature and if you have been humanely caring for an infected member of your party, this is the time to get busy with the axe. It is imperative that the brain is destroyed. Most experts say the head should also be removed as a precaution. The body is no longer your loved one or your team member. They are vulnerable so take action and get hacking whilst they are inactive.

- The human to zombie transformation is complete when the victim rises from death, starts to lumber emitting moans, groans and generally taking an unhealthy interest in eating your flesh. Crucially, no human at Stage 4 has ever managed any verbal communication so this can be a useful differentiator between an earlier status. At Stage 4, you are dealing with an inhuman cannibal which is both aggressive and driven by a desire to feed. We can never see into the mind of a zombie but some writers such as David Wellington have aptly described this all-encompassing, desperate drive to feed on living flesh and suggested that to a ghoul, anything living is perceived as a 'golden energy' source which must be consumed. There is no scientific evidence for this but it is useful if only as a framework to understand the single-minded motivation of these creatures.

With strict safety protocols in place, such as constant vigilance around any wounded parties and prompt action at Stage 3, survivors should never see Stage 4 in a victim within their own compound. Some experts advise dealing with victims as soon as they are infected. However, this brutal approach although sensible would be deemed too extreme for most survivor parties. Therefore it is imperative that strict quarantine procedures are adhered to and that most importantly of all, the victim is monitored at all times and dealt with at the moment of death without hesitation. It's far easier said than done if it is a close friend or family member.

One experienced zombie survivalist passed on a particularly useful warning when dealing with recently transformed zombies. "They are the ones to watch, the new ones, they look human, dress human, and they even sometimes smell human." The message is clear. Whether they are already a member of your party or a stranger, be very cautious until someone is clearly identified as human, such as a verbal response or a clear gesture. Until then, be on your guard or you risk becoming a snack for the newly undead.

So, even with the medical research which has been completed so far on the zombie virus, our knowledge of the zombie transformation process is by no means complete. We know that it is spread by fluid, normally saliva-blood transfer. We know the horrific symptoms which develop in those infected and that although the timeframe may vary, the transformation to ghoul is 100%. The speed of the transformation seems closely linked to the volume of fluid exchange and the height, weight and age of the victim.

The transmission of the zombie virus effectively creates a voracious and single-minded predator. Unlike many other viral outbreaks which, although horrific, will not lead to their victims joining the ranks of a living dead army, there is potential for vast numbers of these creatures to literally overrun our society, creating ever greater numbers as they feed. Indeed, a zombie outbreak will tend to grow exponentially with the constant addition of new victims.

However, contrary to myth and legends of the Supernatural School, zombies are not immortal. Ghouls may well be clinically dead but their bodies are riddled with parasites and bacteria who continue to live and prosper after the victim's death. In fact, some experts suggest that the majority of zombies will simply fall to pieces or rot within 12-36 months of an outbreak.

One of the most wonderful things about living tissue is its ability to regenerate and heal itself. The living dead have no such capacity so be prepared for some awful sights as the zombie uprising fades into one messy, rotten pile. The damp weather in Britain and our reasonably temperate climate may help to speed up this process.

The 12-36 month zombie 'fall to pieces' window is by no means universally recognised within the zombie survivor community but most scientific studies agree that a wider 18-60 month timeframe is reasonable for these creatures to survive without the benefit of the body repairing damaged tissue. There have certainly been examples in history of ghouls surviving for more than two years and still being able to function and feed.

There are no official studies into the longevity of those suffering from the Zombic Condition so the zombie survivalist must plan for the worst case scenario. We simply do not know how long these creatures will last, no one does. It is safest to assume that most zombies have an operating 'lifespan' of at least 36 months and that many will survive longer in their dormant state, trapped in rooms or in other closed off areas. This means that even if you have managed to survive the first few years of the zombie apocalypse, ghouls will be an ongoing threat and members of your party will be constantly uncovering these dormant zombies. Of course, any new zombie is capable of creating a new outbreak even within a community of limited numbers. In basic terms, the zombie menace will remain for many years to come.

According to Dr Ahmed's work, it is an RNA virus we are dealing with and one which seems immune to any anti-viral drug so as it currently stands, there is no known cure. Developing effective anti-viral drugs often takes years of research and is made more difficult as all viruses use host cells to produce copies of themselves so any 'attack' can easily damage these cells. Recent rumours were circulated on the internet that a possible vaccine was being produced by the Russian military but no concrete evidence or research has yet been released. With the current state of zombiology, it is extremely unlikely that any anti-virals or vaccines will be developed in the next few decades.

How to "Kill" a Zombie and Zombie Capabilities

To survive a zombie apocalypse you need to have a clear idea of what the living dead are capable of, their strengths, abilities and weaknesses. You must be able to separate fact from fiction and so base decisions on which life may depend on the best information available. Make no mistake; many will become easy pickings for the ghouls in the opening weeks of the crisis as they try anything from holy water or a crucifix to drugs or silver bullets to stop the living dead. Knowing your enemy is the key to success in any battle.

First things first, you can slow down a zombie by taking off limbs or pinning it to, say, a wall or fence. You can trap the living dead by locking them in rooms or blocking their path. You can even slow them down with carefully laid traps or simple obstacles over which unbalanced ghouls will stumble and trip. But, none of these techniques will 'kill' a zombie. Zombies without limbs have been known to crawl for miles after their prey. Equally, the cleanly severed head of a ghoul can still do fatal damage as it can snap with jagged teeth. What we know of zombie biology is limited but we do know that as long at the brain is in any kind of condition, the ghoul will continue the struggle to feed on live flesh.

The only way to stop a zombie permanently is to destroy the brain, in effect, to smash it completely and thus take out the infected organ which drives it. Scientists have suggested that at least 80% of a zombie's brain must be destroyed to ensure that it is retired for good but as a rule of thumb in the field, go for a complete brain smash to be sure. Glancing blows with a spade or a bullet graze will almost certainly not be enough.

Broadly speaking, zombie physical capabilities are similar to those of living humans although individuals can display amazing strength when closing on a prey. One main area of difference is that the dead have significantly diminished motor neurone skills. This ensures their movements are slow, lumbering and sluggish. Beware of urban myths around tales displaying superhuman strength and remember that as creatures they have the same restrictions of the human body they now occupy although fewer of the weaknesses such as pain response.

Another crucial difference from the living is that zombies do not breathe or need oxygen to power their biology. The Zombic Condition results in massive chemical changes within the body, most of which are still not yet fully understood. Blood ceases to circulate and transforms into either a blue-grey sludge or a very thick purple paste-like substance. This is thought to be linked to the duration the body has been reanimated.

So, importantly, zombies do not need air to breath, their lungs are mostly inactive and they are therefore immune or unaffected by any tear gas or smoke. Equally, no drugs such as tranquillisers have been shown to have any impact on ghouls.

Whilst the zombie ability to feel no pain, operate with missing limbs and their apparent immunity to any known drugs may seem like super-human qualities, the living dead have some serious limitations which offer mankind a chance of survival.

First, although driven by an all-encompassing desire to feed on living flesh, ghouls lack the intellectual capacity to solve problems or plan in any realistic sense. Zombies could never be described as mentally dextrous and lack the IQ to use tools or develop any tactics. Debate has raged in the zombie expert community over the level of intelligence possessed by the living dead. Case studies have sighted everything from an ability to open closed doors to the use of simple tools but most of these have largely been debunked. For sure, zombies can push open unlocked doors, collapse fences or walls through sheer weight of numbers but they cannot 'plan' an attack.

Some of the confusion may be to do with what zombiologists describe as 'retained behaviour' which sees the living dead apparently mimicking tasks they previously did as living humans. This behaviour could include congregating in town centres or repeatedly bumping up against a car, even gathering at a local supermarket. The best explanation currently available to explain this phenomenon is that some traces of human memory have been retained after death but this should not be confused with any traces of humanity.

Second, even if they had the mental capacity, their fingers lack the dexterity to use any kind of tools. Tests have shown that the subject appears to suffer almost complete motor neurone failure during the transformation process.

The Weapons of a Ghoul

No matter how slow and cumbersome a zombie is or how disgusting, foolish or even comical they look, the living dead are flesh-hungry predators at the top of the food chain and are armed with a range of weapons which you will need to consider and treat with respect. Numbers will always be a zombie's greatest advantage but the individual living dead are also armed with some dangerous weapons of their own.

Teeth are a zombie's primary attacking weapon as these are used to take bites out of live flesh. But depending on the age of the ghoul, zombie teeth are frequently torn, jagged and much sharper than live human teeth, turning them into far more effective tearing and piercing weapons. Zombies do not seem to chew or grind their food to any great degree. They prefer to force any ripped chunks of flesh they can get down their throats as quickly as possible. The digestion process of a zombie and how this meat is transformed into energy is a complete mystery to modern science. Zombies do not seem to pass any waste but have been known to vomit. Most experts believe that some form of altered chemical reaction occurs in the gut of the living dead, something very different from human digestion.

Zombies cause death to their victims primarily through blood loss as they are particularly drawn to major arteries as well as fleshy areas such as the thighs. The living dead do have a taste for brain but are often distracted from it by the lure of the more obvious flesh in front of them.

It is a well-known fact that nails continue to grow after death and this provides them with powerful slicing weapons in their fingernails which typically grow up to an inch. The normal rough and tumble of ghoul life often leaves fingernails broken and sharp, further increasing their potential as almost sword-like slashing weapons.

A zombie-inflicted fingernail wound will not in itself transmit the Zombic Condition. There has to be a transfer of body fluid such as saliva or blood for this to occur. But any such wound almost always becomes infected and may lead to various forms of blood poisoning which in themselves can prove fatal in a world with limited medical care. Zombies are home to thousands of different bacteria and any direct wound must be treated quickly to avoid the living dead's secret weapon - bacterial infection.

As a final note, it is worth repeating that zombies don't feel pain or emotion. You cannot 'wound' a zombie, you simply diminish it. A walking corpse without limbs will still come at you grinding its teeth and with jagged nails if it has them. The opponent you face may not be intelligent but it is relentless and very robust from a physical perspective.

It is vital that in your battle against the ghouls, you never underestimate this and that you never get complacent with such a single-minded opponent, particularly now you know something of the arsenal of weapons at a zombie's disposal.

A Guide to Zombie Outbreaks

There is no universally agreed upon scale such as the Saffir-Simpson Hurricane Scale which rates a hurricane's intensity, with which to judge zombie outbreaks. Experts sensibly warn concerned citizens to monitor the media for unusual crimes involving cannibalism or outbreaks of 'madness' in towns but there will be no official warning of the zombie apocalypse. Your local council is too busy issuing parking tickets and worrying about the next round of wheelie bin pickups to be concerned about any living dead activity. Equally, as we will discover in the next chapter, central government has few if any mechanisms in place to detect an outbreak.

One rating which has been adopted by the zombie fighting community is the so-called Zombie Condition or "Zed-Con" Rating - a "Zed" being American slang for a zombie. Designed to help survivalists assess and manage risk, it is a general system to gauge the intensity of a zombie outbreak. Various forms of the system are available but most are based on the four standardised 'condition' emergency levels used by the military with Zed-Con 4 being a minor outbreak and Zed-Con 1 being the most serious. The terms may change but the following section breaks down these phases.

Zed-Con 4

This is a localised outbreak or ghoul infestation which is typically, a village or urban outbreak with fewer than 100 confirmed zombies. It is estimated that more than 90% of Zed-Con 4 outbreaks fall below the radar of any central authorities. Most are dealt with by local authorities and in remote locations may fizzle out with ghouls simply rotting away and the local population avoiding the area. In effect, the world has always been at Zed-Con 4 with an estimated 100 outbreaks a year and many more unrecorded ghoul incursions. Although minor, some of these incidents such as the destruction of the Patagonian village of Puntas la Corunna in 1964 can make the global news. In this case, some 130 villagers were reported to have been killed in an oil spill fire.

The zombie virus and the associated Zombic Condition have never been eradicated and therefore may become an epidemic at any time. As has been previously noted, there is little research into how the virus exists between outbreaks, whether it is dormant or even if there are carriers of the virus. Most outbreaks involving the Zombic Condition fall into the Zed-Con 4 rating.

Zed-Con 3

This phase is classified as a 'regional level' outbreak and often involves several villages or larger towns with between 100 and 200 zombies. In urbanised societies, any outbreaks at transport hubs such as airports or stations would immediately be graded a Zed-Con 3 incident by authorities as things could easily develop into a more serious situation. Most Zed-Con 3 incidents would see some response from the military and with any impact being felt outside the immediate area. For example, one would expect to see important roads closed, military checkpoints established and normally a curfew. An important condition for the Zed-Con 3 rating is the existence of a 'dead zone' normally at the epicentre of the outbreak. In this area, authority and control breaks down under the pressure of the ghouls and local police stations will be over-run. Unless the authorities re-establish control things will escalate but at Zed-Con 3, the dead zone of lawlessness at which zombies roam and feed will normally last less than a few days.

Not surprisingly, Zed-Con 3 outbreaks are more difficult to conceal and some explanation such as a plane crash or nuclear accident is typically used to explain the disappearance of an entire town. The Soviet authorities have been accused of covering up Zed-Con 3 incidents in the early 1980s in Afghanistan. The official explanation was a military plane crash but experts see excessive Soviet military action around the town of Turkut as a response to a zombie outbreak. Local tribal leaders fought side by side with their Russian oppressors fighting what was officially reported to have been an extremist breakaway faction. Several ex-servicemen from the Russian Special Forces interviewed in 1991 for a documentary on war-induced stress disorders, described a brutal campaign involving the decapitation of anyone captured and widespread stories of madness, enemies who could not be stopped by bullets and above all rampant cannibalism amongst the local population.

Decisive and often brutal action at Zed-Con 3 is vital if a zombie outbreak is to be contained. With erratic and unpredictable spread patterns, complacency can easily lead to the widespread horrors of a full blown zombie crisis particularly in heavily populated areas. There is always a chance that even a Zed-Con 3 outbreak will die out by itself but in today's global village, these incidents are more dangerous than ever.

Zed-Con 2

This rating sees a Zed-Con 3 outbreak or outbreaks move out of a contained area to become a nationwide emergency. One can expect to see martial law being declared and even a national quarantine enforced as central government battles to control a growing number of living dead. Although the modern world has never experienced a Zed-Con 2 incident, ancient historians have suggested that the collapse of the well-developed Sudanese Empire around 3000 BC may have been linked to a national-level zombie outbreak. The powerful African kingdom virtually ceased to exist over a period of around five years and this rapid demise is seen as the outcome of a massive zombie outbreak. The region remained relatively cut off for the next 100 years or so possibly enabling the millions of zombies to rot away in the desert wilderness. Stone tablets discovered in neighbouring Abyssinia offer a short commentary on the massive upheavals which must have gripped the Sudanese kings. They speak of a war against the dead and how the kingdom was overrun after the gates of hell were opened. These foreign commentaries hinted that a brutal king had angered the gods by taking their place in the eyes of the people, so they wrought a supernatural punishment on them and destroyed the kingdom.

The archaeological record is frustratingly incomplete with further investigation made more difficult by the current political turmoil in the region. But, in the dry and arid desert, skeletal remains may still exist and be in good enough condition for analysis for any bite marks or patterns.

Typically, any central authorities will need to use draconian force to suppress a Zed-Con 2 outbreak. Ironically, less developed civilisations with more regional autonomy and covering large distances have traditionally had more resistance to these outbreaks.

Zed-Con 1

The world has never experienced a Zed-Con 1 zombie event in recorded history. This stage is characterised by a pandemic outbreak of ghouls and a multi-national and even global struggle. In this doomsday scenario, the zombie hordes have grown beyond the control of a single nation and swarmed across national boundaries. The ghouls may still be contained in a specific geographic region particularly an island, peninsula or continent but one can expect to see millions of ghouls during this phase which may also be characterised by other seemingly unconnected lower level outbreaks. These outbreaks may then combine to create a global zombie pandemic; a scenario dreaded by all of the zombie community. Some ancient historians see the collapse of the well-developed pre-Incan civilisations in South American as the result of a Zed-Con 1 zombie outbreak with ghouls swamping the then known world but contained on the South American continent. From archaeological surveys of the ruins, it would certainly seem as if the empires disappeared within a few years and recent discoveries of both gnawed human bones and numerous corpse pits in which all of the bodies have had the skulls crushed, have fed speculation that it was the zombie virus which destroyed this culture. Rumours and legends of ghouls wandering lost in the Amazon persisted into the time of the Spanish arrival with many villages completely barricaded.

Recently, a well-known zombie research group has added a Zed-Con 0 or Zero rating to model a fully blown global outbreak in which the ghouls effectively replace humans as the dominant species on the planet leading to an extinction level event or "ELE" in which small communities of the living fight an increasingly desperate battle against massive and growing hordes of living dead. The history of the earth is littered with extinction level events and some have pointed to the fact that the eclipse of humans in favour of the living dead may be seen as a clear example of natural, or this case, 'unnatural' selection.

The history of zombie outbreaks as far as has been recorded suggest that a majority of outbreaks are at Zed-Con 4, that is, they are localised and dealt with by whatever forces are on hand. This indicates that whilst the zombie virus is at least as old as mankind, certain conditions are required to create a real outbreak. This area of zombiology demands further study as currently there is simply not enough validated information to draw any conclusions. Some researchers have projected that the massive growth in world population and increasing mobility of people is creating the conditions for a major outbreak particularly with the growth in air transport and other forces of globalisation. Both national governments and international organisations such as the UN should use the Zed-Con rating to monitor and manage outbreaks in different parts of the world but currently there is no official monitoring in any part of the globe. It is a worrying situation for all of us.

A Personalised Zombie Outbreak Scale

Terms such as a "Zed-Con 1 outbreak" or "major zombie incident" are often discussed in zombie expert circles but it is strongly advised that any survival planners create their own monitoring system to help track zombie activities even if based on the generally accepted 4 stage model. The formal outbreak scale outlined above was designed to help local and central authorities manage the zombie virus. Those of us planning to survive the zombie apocalypse require a more personalised and localised system to help us manage risk and our preparations.

This could be something as simple as 'traffic light system' which may be arranged on a convenient wall or even with fridge magnets with 'green' being all OK and 'red' appropriately being the flesh eaters are coming. By carefully monitoring the media, internet and a few other more specialised sources, the average citizen could audit the level of zombie activity with a few hours of study a week.

Hot points to look out for would include any incidents of cannibalism, unknown illnesses with flu-like symptoms, suspicious accidents wiping out small towns and bluish-grey recently deceased corpses walking around eating close friends or relatives.

A personalised warning system undoubtedly requires more time and effort but there will be no government warning of the zombie apocalypse or letter from your local council. It is your responsibility to watch for the signs and you will be able to 'calibrate' your own system to suit your own needs. For example, there is no need to start bricking up the windows and destroying the stairs because of one suspicious murder. But if a pattern emerges or a set of suspicious incidents occur, it's time to prepare you and your family for the trials ahead. You may wish to include more regional information such as the situation at any transport hubs close by or the status of any local emergency services. In effect, you create your own personalised Zed-Con system which you may share with your family and close friends.

No system of monitoring zombie outbreaks is foolproof and the sea of misinformation around ghoul incidents makes the task seem nigh on impossible. A robust personal system will support your survival planning but the golden rule is to assume every day will be outbreak day. You should always be prepared and never rely totally on any warning system—zombies don't follow agreed rules so stay alert and stay vigilant. A well thought-out warning system will certainly give you an edge and may enable you to start stocking up before a major crisis erupts. This crucial head start could mean the difference between survival and getting eaten or starved out of your home once the zombies arrive.

Zombie Controversies

Divisions within the zombie-watching community go far beyond the original debate and can generate a significant amount of confusion for survivalists. In fact, virtually the only area of zombiology which seems to have some degree of agreement is that they are despatched by inflicting a significant amount of damage (estimated to be at least 80%) to the brain. And, even in this case, there are some groups which still believe that simply decapitating a zombie will destroy it.

The following section examines some of these controversies but is far from exhaustive and focuses on the five key areas of debate within zombiology.

(1) Zombies Rebranded: Speed

The internet forums and zombie community at large are thick with discussion and opinion on the physical capabilities of their living dead counterparts as a result of the reinvention of the zombie in the late 1990s and early 2000s. Even the untrained viewer could easily contrast the monumental difference between the zombies of Romero's movies and the new Brit-Zombies of *28 Days Later* or viral super-ghouls of the *Resident Evil* series. Hours of email time were taken up with how current plans, which mainly focused on the traditional shambling zombie type, could be obsolete in the face of this new, faster and more powerful threat. Zombies were no longer lumbering, slow and awkward; they had been rebranded to become the agile, vicious and lightning quick 'infected'.

Fierce debate and disagreement continue to rage over this issue although no significant changes have been made to the orthodoxy of zombiology. A new generation of sci-fi horror movies and other written fiction were created for entertainment and this entertainment now demands a level of speed and action which seem to have made the classic living dead obsolete. It is as if zombies needed to be rebranded and reinvented to terrify the modern day audience.

Current research confirms the zombies of the coming apocalypse will be of the "classic type"- that is, they will be in the ultimate stage of the Zombic Condition, in other words, bloodthirsty, relentless but shambling killers. The living dead are still capable of lunging forward to grab humans and can still move with some speed over very short distances but speed is never going to be their main weapon. It is possible but unlikely that a new virus could create "infected" humans along the lines of these films so in terms of preparation, less time needs to be spent on these super-zombies and more on working with the scientific knowledge we already have. The best preparation is to ensure any plans, defences or weapons are robust enough to cope with both the shambling dead masses and those more intelligent and agile human enemies likely to prosper in the immediate aftermath of the collapse of civilisation. These are more likely to be roving bands of bandits rather than the new darling-zombies of British cinema.

(2) Zombie Animals

A question often asked is whether the Zombic Condition can spread to members of the animal kingdom. This could have massive consequences for the survivor community in terms of the threat faced with the prospect of living dead dogs, cats and even birds, adding a frightening new vector to the zombie menace

Current research indicates that the Zombic Condition only develops in humans, although the virus itself can be present in animals. A serious lack of research in this area does leave the possibility that other animals, particularly primates, may be prone to the condition but there are no documented examples. With the number of primates in the UK, even if the condition did develop, it would pose little real threat to any remaining humans. Far more dangerous will be the wandering packs of uninfected dogs which will grow increasingly desperate and wild as they are left to fend for themselves.

The most feared and discussed zombie animal online is the so called Z-Shark or any large man-eating shark infected with the Zombic Condition. Whilst sharks may be considered the perfect killing machine when alive, there are no reported sightings of a 'Z-Shark' and because an undead shark would lack the cognitive powers to use its sensitive detection or direction sensing, any such creature would seem to be less of a threatening prospect.

A final question to consider is whether zombies would be attracted to the fresh meat of other living creatures other than humans? Would our innocent pets be as much in danger from the shambling masses as we are?

Current orthodoxy is that the living dead have a strong preference for human flesh and that they show little interest in any type of animal. They seem to be drawn to living people with a drive and passion which overwhelms any other food source and would ignore any other life form close by. Whether they would ever start to eat other living creatures is not clear but a witness to an outbreak from the 1920s in what is now modern day Iraq reported seeing ghouls in the desert scooping up large black beetles and clumsily putting them in their mouths. These zombies had been wandering the desert for some time and it may be they were using whatever life was available until they could once again reach their preferred food source - humans. No other documented examples of the living dead eating animals exists so for the moment this issue, as with many others in zombiology, must remain open.

(3) Zombies and Water

Due to their lack of co-ordination and manual dexterity, the zombies cannot swim and often demonstrate something approaching hesitancy when confronted with large stretches of water. With their extremely limited mental capacity, ghouls can just about manage to put one leg in front of the other and simple obstructions or an uneven surface can easily topple a lumbering zombie. What they lack in skill of movement they make up for in persistence and zombies will often slowly make their way through any obstacle as long as they are not trapped, held back or trampled on by the living dead masses following behind.

However, water does seem to have a special effect on the living dead and they have often been seen pausing on the banks of rivers or canals, almost as if they are trying to take their next steps. Some cultures, such as the Sioux native Americans and native Australians, perceive the living dead as having a 'fear' of water due to its traditionally purifying properties. Both peoples see water as a cleansing force in nature which repels the rotting dead. Modern zombiology interprets this simple behaviour rather as some form of very basic survival instinct by the ghoul using its low level of intelligence.

Whatever the answer is many witnesses have reported that ghouls paddle clumsily across short stretches of water, particularly if driven by the hunt for live meat. It is also common to see the living dead wading through water to reach their goal so rivers or canals should not be seen as hard barriers against the living dead.

Medical evidence indicates that most undead bodies will float and are capable of travelling over significant distances washed along by river flows, currents or tides. Ghouls do not need to breathe and are immune to cold, so it is possible that any living dead who somehow end up in the water will be a danger to survivors for years to come. This has significant implications for any survivors planning to use boats or islands as refuges; there will always be the threat of stray sea-ghouls washing up alongside your location.

If the living dead are anything, they are persistent and given their numbers, may simply block any rivers or canals with their bodies as they stumble over each other to move forward.

(4) Zombie Sociology and Intelligence

Although a group of zombies is frequently described as a horde, the living dead lack any kind of social order which is seen amongst wolves or other pack animals. Zombies simply lack the brain power to team up and work together to achieve any objective so will therefore operate solely based on their own overwhelming instinct to feed. This can produce symptoms which at first glance can appear like pack behaviour. For example, living dead activity will often attract additional ghouls so that a small crowd will often appear where food is smelt. Similarly, a feeding frenzy will bring ghouls from the immediate area shambling in search of food. It would seem that they have just enough intelligence to correlate activity or movement with food.

No scientific study has yet assessed zombies in terms of intelligence against, for example, an IQ rating or other benchmark. What we do know from case studies and previous outbreaks is that ghouls have a very low ability to solve problems, so whilst they may be able to push doors open or force their way through windows, they will not demonstrate any discernible co-operative behaviour with other zombies.

Contrary to what some experts would have you believe, the dead do not gather together for any form of community or communication. Once the transformation into zombie is complete, all bonds of family and location are broken. The living dead are often witnessed demonstrating 'remembered behaviour' so locations such as local shops, stations or shopping centres may become relatively crowded with ghouls. The reason behind this retained memory is clouded in mystery but it seems that a fraction of human memory is carried over even after the process of zombification is complete. It is important to note that they are still the living dead. The most dangerous element of any human-like behaviour is that it can confuse or distract the living from the very real threat these creatures represent.

(5) The Taming of the Ghoul

Some observers suggest that zombies can in some way be tamed and perhaps even trained to do our bidding. It is certainly a theme which has been explored in recent zombie fiction and this claim is not as outlandish as it sounds if one considers many of the myths surrounding the origin of zombies. For example, in places such as Haiti, 'zombies' were traditionally brought back as slaves to do their tormentors evil tasks. Indeed, in some legends, the living dead were kept in subservient service for years on end, trapped in a kind of ghoulish slavery. The image of busy ghouls tirelessly worked at our command on anything from basic labouring to tilling the fields does have its attractions. Here would be a workforce which does not rest, sleep or strike.

In reality, attempting to tame a ghoul in any way is an ill-advised and dangerous pastime and so far there has been not a single documented case study of a zombie being 'taught' anything from a human teacher. Research has shown that even months of attempted training had no impact on the behaviour of the living dead. Basically, ghouls will lunge to take a chunk of your living flesh at each and every opportunity and there is considerable danger in bringing an infected human or zombie into your home or compound. This is a massive risk you should avoid at all costs as the living dead have an uncanny knack of finding a way out of restraints. Remember, they are remorseless, they will not stop and they cannot be taught. A particularly dangerous scenario would be keeping a zombie close or trapped, not to train it but due to some emotional attachment to the "body". Whatever the temptation is to view these creatures as humans or even the friends and relatives they once were, it is vital to understand that they are human no longer. They may be humanoid in form but the similarity stops there. If you forget this in waves of emotion, you could easily end up on the menu.

Zombie Case Studies

Stories of the dead coming back to devour the living are as old as human civilisation with tales of zombies in various guises popping up in virtually every major culture. This pervading myth or fear of the "hungry ghoul" seems to be buried so deeply into the human consciousness that it is now impossible to determine a real origin but it is almost certainly in pre-history. What is for sure is that the dead seem to have been wandering round in various forms since records began and that our ancestors have faced the challenge of zombies for thousands of years.

The section outlines some of the most well-known zombie case studies from history. Although not exhaustive, it is hoped that this will provide a historical perspective to mankind's ongoing struggle against the ghouls–a battle which, as we shall see, is set to become a fight for our very survival against a background of the population explosion in recent decades.

Prehistoric Ghouls

The earliest known record of a zombie attack was discovered in a network of underground caverns in southern France at the turn of the last century. Since the late 1890's, over 350 sites with cave paintings had been found in various regions, some of which have now been carbon dated as being over 30,000 years old. The most common themes in these simple paintings are wild animals such as bison and abstract patterns which may have held some religious significance to the cave dwellers.

Researchers were, however, shocked when in 1901, French archaeologists discovered a sequence of cave paintings which seemed to show misshapen and hairy characters they assumed at first to be bears. With better light, the figures were judged to be humanoid in form and seemed to be stalking or chasing other men. Subsequent paintings show these lumbering figures feasting on a still struggling human. Whilst cannibalism is sometimes offered as the most plausible explanation or some form of inter-tribal conflict, recent research using infra-red technology has revealed that each of the attacking figures has an unusual symbol painted above it which academics suggest may have been how our distant ancestors highlighted that these people were different, or to some observers, were prehistoric ghouls. It possible that the zombie virus has been with mankind from the very start and several studies have been proposed to search for the zombie 'missing link' which would be evidence of early humanoids or even primates infected with the zombie virus.

One of the earliest pieces of written evidence of zombie activity comes from the ancient Sumer story, *The Epic of Gilgamesh*, which clearly indicates a belief in both zombies and just as importantly, the fact they love nothing more than to feast on the living.

"I will knock down the Gates of the Netherworld,
I will smash the doorposts and leave the doors flat down,
And will let the dead go up to eat the living,
And the dead will outnumber the living."

Several clay tablets are still in existence but from a much later period and detail how contemporary forces battled what they referred to as "ghilan", which is the plural of the ancient word from which the word ghoul is derived. These fragments are frustratingly incomplete but provide the first written guidelines on how to deal with the living dead.

In ancient Egypt, hieroglyphic translations have indicated the existence of what can loosely be described as "dead warriors" which served the various Pharaohs in the underworld. Rather than being an organised military force, they seem to have been a 'force' to be unleashed should the world of the living break certain creeds. Although no text clearly specifies whether this army of the dead would feast on the living or not, the inference is more that they are along the lines of a plague or curse on mankind rather than a military force. Some observers believe one of the curses on mankind mentioned in the Bible, that of the locusts in the book of Exodus is in fact a mistranslation, and that it actually outlines a plague of the living dead on the Egyptians. Academics now suggest the Hebrew word "locuti" is a corruption of the Egyptian verb "loci" which means to die or be dead. In this context, the empire of the Pharaoh was subjected to several days of loci or a living dead plague – most likely a regional zombie outbreak taken to be a sign or warning from God.

Roman Province of Atlas, 55 AD

One of the best documented references to the living dead in the ancient world is to be found in the written records of the Roman Governor of the town of Atlas which is found in modern day Algeria and was at this period a thriving Roman colony. The records show Governor Decimus Fortunis, a veteran military leader from the famous Tenth Legion and now in his fading years, began to issue a series of increasingly draconian edicts from the summer of 55 AD onwards to deal with an unprecedented outbreak of bloodthirsty violence in what was previously a peaceful trading town. The guidelines, issued directly by the governor to his local forces included the instant beheading of any murder suspects and cremation of any remains. The latter edict caused particular issues as the local population practiced a pre-Islamic tradition of drying bodies in the scorching sun before placing them on a funeral pyre. Despite a reputation for brutality which included crucifixion, most Roman Governors would only have enforced such controversial and dangerous edicts in the most extreme of circumstances. For the most part, the governor's job was to keep the peace, keep the taxes flowing to Rome and allow the local population to manage themselves as much as possible. At virtually the end of his career, the last thing Governor Fortunis needed was a local rebellion requiring additional troops from Rome.

The crisis began when a commercial caravan party arrived several weeks late with four Nubian slaves who appeared to be suffering from heat exhaustion. It would seem that by the first morning of their stay in Atlas, all four had turned into bloodthirsty zombies and murdered several merchants and the local taxation legate. Things quickly got out of control and several quarters of Atlas were overrun and the hungry dead began to fan out into surrounding villages.

Over an estimated three to six month period, the besieged governor and his forces battled to take control back from a town besieged by ghouls. The small town was isolated as a 'plague town' and merchant records back in Rome show exports from Atlas fell significantly and did not recover for a further 24 months. The town was effectively taken off the map for some two years and historians have suggested the absence of the town's main export, which was iron ore, caused something of a panic in Rome, particularly as this commodity was of prime importance in manufacturing weapons for the army.

Only through seemingly cruel and despotic action did Governor Fortunis take back the town and one can easily imagine it was only through the action of his battle-hardened veterans that he was able to stamp out this zombie outbreak at source. He was removed from his post after this event, leaving his successor to manage famine and an additional uprising by the various semi-autonomous villages which had survived alone in the chaotic past year.

The origins of the outbreak remain a mystery with the only reference being that the slaves originated south of the Sahara. With the frequency and range of caravans at this time, this means the virus could have been transmitted from any part of Africa including the Nubian kingdoms or Abyssinia.

Lithuania, 1230

In Europe of the Middle Ages, it was commonly accepted that the 'souls' and bodies of the deceased could return from dead, typically on a vengeful quest of some sort or a mission to right an injustice inflicted on them when they were alive. Stories and myth were commonplace and persist to this day in folklore and fairy tales but a well-documented factual case study of this comes from the memoirs of Baltic merchant Lechter, who was based in modern day Gdansk and ran a very profitable amber import and export business out of Sweden around 1230. Records preserved in the Finnish Institute of History show his regular business trips took him to the Lithuanian town of Silute on the Eastern Baltic. Despite its prominent position, the feudal state of Lithuania was still a strongly pagan nation resisting all attempts at conversion to the prevailing Christian religion. Indeed, later, there would be years of bloody war to enforce this conversion led by the merciless Teutonic knights order. But, for the moment, Lechter found Silute to be a melting pot of ancient superstition and religion that in no way inhibited his business dealing which in this case were new sources of timber, the demand for which had gone through the roof following a series of wars between an aggressive Swedish Kingdom and the re-emerging kingdoms of Poland and Norway.

It was on a business trip some 20 miles inland to see a new timber station that Lechter noted loggers dealing with what he first presumed was . . . "merely a simpleton".

"Theye hounded and goaded him. This unfortunate wretche who was pale grey in colouring and seemed to be less blessed by the Lorde in his faculties."

What Lechter had taken for a ". . . cruel jeste . . ." turned out to be far more serious as one of the loggers beheaded the confused ghoul they had captured. Throughout the ordeal, there had been a white haired monk-like figure guiding the work of the mob. Lechter later discovered this mysterious instigator was a form of local religious leader known as a Magj.

Religious persecution was not such as shocking sight for this experienced medieval trader who was quite accustomed to adapting to or steering clear of any delicate issues which may affect his commercial business. But, Lechter was later told there were entire villages of these ". . . death-made folke" and that the loggers had been dealing with one which had apparently escaped from a sealed-off area.

"Theye were indeed pitiful, with falling skin and a pinched discoloured face," he wrote after a further encounter. "For most of the days they were lifeless and limp, staring for long hours only to be driven to an insanity not from the Lorde when seeing the chance to feed on men," he recorded in his journal.

Lechter's record is frustratingly incomplete with much of the text focused on his financial transactions. Researchers have been unable to locate the exact location of the villages mentioned in the text but it would seem that one of the last pagan kingdoms in Europe was clamping down mercilessly on a Zed-Con 4 outbreak during his visit. Indeed, some observers have suggested that this violent and bloody conflict of which Lechter was on the periphery, was one of the factors weakening the kingdom against the future crusades of the Christians.

Tse Village, Imperial China, 1360

Manuscripts from China in the mid-14th century offer us a tantalising glimpse into how a zombie or "Kuang Shi" outbreak was dealt with in what was probably the most advanced civilisation on earth at the time. Although now in fragments, a set of parchment documents formally record how a regional administrator called Lin Ji Wun battled the living dead in a deeply superstitious and mainly Taoist province.

In this very traditional society, the widely accepted belief was that when ancestors died away from home, if not returned to their ancestral villages within eight days, they would make their way back along the dusty rural roads as reanimated walking corpses known to the local population as "Jiang Shr" or more commonly in China as "Kuang Shi". Thus when an extended wedding party from another village succumbed to what was most likely cholera, it was accepted by the villagers that after a series of funereal rites, the Taoist priest would guide the bodies to their own land for final burial - in this case on several ox-drawn carts.

Whilst applying charms to the corpses, the priest was bitten by a small child and quickly lost consciousness. Another priest was sent for but he would take two weeks to arrive from a neighbouring province. Meanwhile, the corpses were anointed and left in an open building on the edge of the village. Some of the more superstitious locals expected the bodies to quietly make their way back to their home village and its ancestral burial places but for most of the population, this was not a literal process. The dead did not actually walk home; it was more a guide for their spiritual path.

The village was thrown into chaos during the night as the ghouls began to rise in a very real sense and rather than hitting the road home, the reanimated ghouls turned back towards the people and started to feast on whoever they could grab. The superstitious villagers were torn between their Taoism and its deep respect for the dead and the ruthless need to take down these walking corpses to prevent a much wider outbreak. The confusion was made worse as local Taoists could not understand why the bodies had risen as Kuang Shi but were behaving in this violent and cannibalistic way.

As the chaos developed, Lin Ji Wun, then a regional administrator led a force of some 200 militia from nearby villages against the living dead and soon requested further imperial troops to suppress what was then a major Kuang Shi outbreak. Little is known of the battle itself as these documents were destroyed in a raid by British and French troops in the 1860s, but the official death toll was recorded as 40 men and their families, or two entire villages. It must be remembered at that time that such documents would only have listed registered land-owning villagers. One could probably factor in up to 200 other landless peasants and workers.

Venice, 1576

A significant zombie outbreak in Venice during the 1570s shows how easily a major ghoul infestation can be overlooked by historians against the backdrop of an even greater historical event, in this case, the arrival of the bubonic plague in Europe. There is no doubt that the sheer volume of plague dead and poor precautions taken for dealing with the recently deceased corpses contributed to a serious outbreak of ghouls in the Cannaregio district of this cramped city. By late 1576, this former residential and trading area had become a ghost town of empty homes and burnt out warehouses, populated only by wandering ghouls and the few remaining humans barricaded in their homes. Fellow Venetians sealed off the quarter by blocking several of the narrow connecting streets but incidents continued to occur as floating corpses moved around the city via the canals only to spring into life at the scent of a human. Demand for action began to boil over into the threat of a major civil disturbance.

The Venetian Doge convened a meeting with the Bishops of St Mark's and even a visiting Papal Legate but church guidelines forbade the destruction of the unfortunate victims left in Cannaregio, preferring instead to exile the creatures to a walled cemetery island about half a mile off Venice. Here, surrounded by a four-metre wall and cut off from the mainland, it is estimated that some 200 zombies were left in isolation. The Doge had pushed for firmer action on the ghouls but because of the serious crisis in the Church caused partly by the impact of the plague and its effects on a previously devout population, the Bishops refused to sanction any execution order.

A zombie clearance by the local militia was successful but the Cannaregio area was still subjected to several minor outbreaks as ghouls were discovered trapped in basements or other locations. With each incident, pressure mounted on the Church to sanction a formal cull of the cemetery islands' inhabitants. Indeed, it was said that on a clear night, the living residents of Venice could hear the low moan of the ghouls of the island. The Doge insisted the island was the source of the outbreaks and that if it was not dealt with, one day an incident would threaten the whole city once more. It is also rumoured the cemetery island was understandably bad for trade with several important Eastern spice traders threatening to go elsewhere to avoid what they saw as a cursed place.

Finally, sometime in 1578, the church authorities agreed to allow the Doge's troops to "free the souls" of those imprisoned on the island but only after a Mass was held at the locked gates to the cemetery islands. Interestingly, several years later when the great Basilica di Santa Maria della Salute was completed to recognise the delivery of Venice from the plague, the consecration prayers included a section in which the Bishop faced the cemetery island and offered prayers to deliver the city from disease and the evil forces which dwell on the earth.

The cemetery island was cleared and effectively abandoned for the next decade or so. After being re-consecrated in the 1700s, burials once again took place on the island which is now open to the public. Indeed, visitors can catch a boat to the island to inspect the many fine tombs and can also still see evidence of the deep scratch marks made by the ghouls on the northern wall and near the giant gate posts.

Lucknow, 1858-9

The 19th century is peppered with small localised incidents as the imperial forces of mainly Britain and France expanded into new territories in their bids to build truly global empires. One of the most detailed records of a British Army encounter with the living dead comes from the military documents of the 4th Sikh Rifles which saw significant action in the uneasy years following the great mutiny on the subcontinent.

Between 1858 and 1859, an English Lieutenant Richard Wakefield, encountered several villages which had completely succumbed to what was believed to have been be cholera or some similar plague. However, as the Sikh forces moved into the region, it became obvious this was no cholera outbreak as they defended themselves against frenzied attacks by seemingly possessed villagers. The regiment dealt swiftly with any survivors found and it is likely that at least some living humans were dispatched in this enthusiast cleansing.

The son of an Anglican Bishop, Wakefield was a fervent Christian and his letters to his father reveal the level of relish which he seemed to have in facing what he considered to be " . . . the evil hordes . . ." once the disease explanation had been discounted.

"They come at us father like wild men, but they are not just men, they are the whole of the people. They move like those driven by darkness. Shuffling with empty faces which soon fill with desperation to reach us when they see our well-ordered lines."

Lacking any real experience in combat, Wakefield had only arrived on the subcontinent once the uprising had been subdued; the young Lieutenant rushed his troops into action. The battalion made short work of the villages concerned. Interestingly, no protests seem to have been received from any of the local princes as would have been expected after such brutal action and, when much of the country was still smarting from the harsh punishments meted out after the rebellion. In a region well-known as a seedbed of discontent, it would seem that one inexperienced but effective junior lieutenant was given a free hand to stamp out a zombie outbreak with the kind of ferocity which can only be driven by religious zeal and inbuilt belief in his own superiority.

"These creatures are not like us, they are not even like the natives. They are sullen and lack the devious smile of the Asians. They seem to come alive when they sense a living man, then their bedevilled urges drive them into frenzy. I feel father like I have seen evil and defeated it."

Once subdued, the area saw further bloodshed as the dominant Hindu community turned on its Muslim neighbours, blaming them for bringing the sickness with them from the trading cities of Gujarat. Shamefully, Lieutenant Wakefield did little to intervene in this massacre and kept his troops in garrison during the three-night riot which followed.

Burma (Myanmar), 1986

A more contemporary but equally controversial zombie outbreak occurred in 1986 in Burma and involved the corrupt and despotic ruling military junta apparently using an outbreak of the living dead as a pretext to clamp down on the Karin people's independence movement which had been growing since the late 1970s. Living in a semi-autonomous region in the east of the country, the Karin, ethnically different from the Burmese, followed their own traditions and way of life until reports came into the central authorities of insane, bloodthirsty rebels raiding Burmese villages well into government-controlled territory. These kinds of pillaging raids had gone on for years but the savagery of these specific attacks in which bodies were mauled and dismembered proved too much for the ruling junta who despatched military forces in a punitive action.

It would appear from what journalists reported that the Karin rebel leadership tried to intercede with the junta insisting they had not carried out these raids, but a substantial Burmese military force continued north swamping any resistance. Many western governments accused the junta of using excessive military force with thousands of loyalist troops flooding into the Karin provinces but little international action was taken, partly because the regime was a major customer for the British arms industry, in particular for light aircraft and other weapons.

Journalists from neighbouring India reported that the army cut off large areas of the countryside and despite some apparently fierce fighting, the aid stations to which they were restricted with their accompanying guides, saw few casualties other than the odd traffic accident. Indeed one experienced US war journalist said he had never seen anything like it. It seemed to be a war with no wounded.

Dissidents and deserters who later appeared in India spoke of the Burmese Army being engaged to contain a major zombie outbreak. The action started as a punitive expedition against Karin rebels but developed into first containment then an extermination campaign against the ghouls. The Burmese Army had actually uncovered a major zombie outbreak emanating from one of the Karin villages. No one really knows how many ghouls were involved but numbers are certainly estimated to be in the hundreds if not thousands. We have no record as to the tactics the army employed to fight the ghouls but with a government which cares little for human rights, the campaign was said to be bloody, thorough and decisive.

Any soldier bitten or infected was instantly executed as the military junta feared this outbreak was potent enough to engulf the entire country. The army's brutal but decisive action effectively de-populated several Karin provinces and the junta seems to have taken the opportunity to terrorise the local human population as well as deal with the living dead. But the outbreak was contained. Again, frustratingly, little information is available on this zombie incident but in years to come and with a change in government, we may learn more about how a regime, cut off by much of the world, defeated the ghouls in what experts consider to be a Zed-Con 3 outbreak.

Why Now?

Reviewing even this brief historical survey seems to suggest our struggle against the ghouls is by no means a new phenomenon and that the war between the living and the living dead has been raging since prehistory. So, if the living dead have been among us for so many years, why the urgency now? If our ancestors have successfully dealt with these low level outbreaks throughout history, why with all the resources of our modern world should we be concerned now?

Well, several factors have changed over the last hundred or so years which seem to make our society and many others across the globe more susceptible, not to local zombie outbreaks as these have always occurred and been dealt with, but to the chance of a local outbreak developing into a Zed-Con 1 or global pandemic.

Possibly the most significant factor is the massive growth in world population in recent years which will soon see our numbers reach seven billion. Whilst the zombie virus has always been around, this growth in population density has greatly increased the chances of a low level outbreak taking hold. In addition, for the first time in our history, the number of densely packed urban and city dwellers will exceed the rural population, making growing city slums and super cities such as Mexico City, Rio de Janeiro and Cairo, the perfect locations for a serious outbreak. Poor living conditions, weak police presence and a transient population offer an ideal seedbed for the zombie virus to take hold in the slums, then spill over into the city.

One driver for this book was the realisation that much of the survival literature currently available was based on heading out into the wilderness or escaping the rat race of urban life. Well, with the UK population soon to be knocking on the door of seventy million, there are few if any truly remote locations left in the UK and what islands and highlands there are, will soon be swamped in any crisis. In short, at least in the UK, we have run out of places to hide.

The pattern and speed of movement in our global society also now means that our island geography presents little real defence against an outbreak in any part of the world. With key UK transport hubs such as Heathrow handling well over 20 million passengers annually, the chances of infection being brought in from another country have grown exponentially in the last decade or so. This effectively means that the spread of any worldwide pandemic is now spoken of in terms of weeks rather than months or years. Basically, even if we see a Zed-Con 3 or national level outbreak in another part of the world, it is likely the UK will not have the time to either enforce quarantine or prepare for the zombies.

All of these factors must be laid alongside the fact that we have a scientific community which largely refuses to acknowledge the existence of a zombie virus and its associated condition. The impact of this uninformed stance is that no serious research is either sponsored or completed and that none of the mathematical models used to help with disaster or disease planning have factored in a virus in which the dead move around infecting more people. For example, much of the Health Protection Agency's data model on disease spread is based on the flu and smallpox pandemics of the 20th century. Now, as bad as these outbreaks were, the crucial factor was that the dead tended to stay still. Those suffering from the Zombic Condition will be very active agents in spreading the virus and unless specific preparations are made to deal with the 'victims'. Our current structures will simply be insufficient to deal with a zombie crisis.

The Survivor's Perspective

The debates will rage on right up to the zombie apocalypse itself or until the groaning dead push their way into teenage bedrooms and stop them posting any more sharp, witty theoretical posts on the internet forums. Healthy debate has undoubtedly moved the cause of zombie awareness and theory forward but the current level of disorganisation within the community is not helpful and means activists are incapable of drawing the attention of the public to this important issue.

For those planning to survive, a general lack of consensus on the zombie threat means different scenarios must be taken into account. The following sections briefly examine these debates with particular reference to their potential impact on survival practices and preparation.

First, it is possible to get completely hung up on the term 'zombie' and what actually classifies as a zombie. From theological discussions over the term 'living dead' to vigorous debates over the reason for outbreak in the halls of our best universities, the talking won't stop until the hungry ghouls are breaking through the college window. As a rule of thumb, if it looks like a zombie, walks like a zombie, sounds like a zombie and seems more interested in eating your flesh than discussing the weather, then it is a zombie.

The term 'zombie' should be used as a blanket term to cover all of the walking dead intent on snacking on the living. In terms of their origin, when our civilisation breaks down and chaos is all around, will it really matter? Background reading around this issue will offer the researcher every explanation possible from radiation through to divine-inspired apocalypse. In the end, you make your own decision. However, in terms of survival, it is important to see through the fog of misinformation to understand the implications of what is widely accepted to be the direct cause of zombism even if we never understand the big questions around why. It is generally agreed that a zombie is created through the transmission of a virus. We simply don't know all the details but it is good enough for now to understand the implications of this in terms of infection, transmission and containment. Whatever the medical community calls this virus, the facts on the ground are what matter to those planning to survive the coming trials.

A Zombie Apocalypse in the UK

So, if it is really just a matter of time until a major zombie outbreak, how exactly would the UK respond if the dead began to rise? How would our government and local authorities battle the zombies and can we depend on them in what is after all their primary function, to protect our way of life?

The objective of this section is to lay out the blueprint of a major zombie outbreak in the UK. As you will see, there is no official preparation in this country to deal with the zombie menace so assumptions have to be made as to how our key emergency resources would deal with an uncontrollable and growing wave of hungry ghouls. The sad truth will become clear because although we have some of the finest, best equipped and dedicated professionals at every level, they are simply not armed to deal with zombies and will in most projections be over run within the first weeks of a major outbreak. This has real implications for those of us planning to survive, the most important of these being that the forces for which we depend on for protection in our everyday lives, are going to crumble under the weight of the ghouls. They may buy us some time with their heroic work but at the end of it all, we will all be on our own.

What is the Threat?

Before assessing our nation's defences, it is important to grasp the nature and scale of the threat the country faces and here the numbers alone tell a disturbing story. With a population of some 65 million, zombie experts project around 20% will be lost in the first chaotic month of a major zombie outbreak, with another 20% either seeking refuge or fleeing our urban centres. It is estimated the remaining 60% or up to 40 million could realistically be transformed into bloodthirsty ghouls – if we take a conservative estimate, our emergency and armed forces could be looking at maybe 10 million ghouls in the first weeks, steadily growing to the 20 million-plus figure within the month. None of our country's emergency planning is designed to deal with these kinds of numbers, indeed, recent anti-terrorist planning in London has revealed that central London hospitals are poorly equipped to deal with hundreds of casualties from an incident, let alone thousands or even millions.

Most of the factors which influence a nation's propensity to resist the living dead point to a grim future for the UK with many zombie experts highlighting that, despite having a well-developed network of health and emergency services, this country will be one of the most dangerous places to be in any major ghoul outbreak.

One simple fact which makes this country so unattractive in terms of zombie defence is the relatively high level of population density. The UK has an estimated 246 people per square kilometre compared to 31 for the USA and 2.6 for Australia and recent projections for Britain only see our population increasing. Many Western European and other industrialised countries such as Japan share similar statistics, but this will be scant comfort, as any survivors of the initial attacks are likely to be overrun by the sheer number of hungry ghouls on this crowded island.

Another factor shared with most other European countries and Japan is a relatively low ratio of firearms amongst the general population. In most of Europe, firearms are tightly regulated in contrast to the USA and this means that in places such as Britain and Ireland, there are barely 8 guns in civilian hands per 100 of the population compared to an unbelievable 97 per 100 in America and an estimated 60-70 in war zone countries such as Afghanistan and Somalia. The almost dogmatic insistence of US citizens on the right to bear arms has often been heavily criticised in the past but in this instance, access to firearms of all descriptions will at least give our North American cousins a fighting chance in the upcoming apocalypse.

Whilst firearms training is available at specialised gun clubs in the UK, a majority of the population have never handled let alone fired any kind of gun or firearm.

Beyond the numbers and a general weakness in the availability of weapons, there are certain cultural and macro-economic issues which make the UK a dangerous place to be when the ghouls rise. As one of the richest and most developed countries in the world, most of us enjoy the full benefits of consumerism with access to a bewildering variety of luxury goods and services. We can go to any supermarket and pick up even the most common items such as tomatoes or apples which have been flown into this country from as far afield as New Zealand and China. Few if any of us grow our own food and much of what we do eat is imported. We have enjoyed the benefits of cheap imported food and rely heavily on imports more now than at any point in our history.

A downside to this is our reliance on international trade for even our most basic needs, leaving us inextricably linked to a fragile network of imports and international trade. Simple world events such as the occasional closure of a major sea lane or strike in a distant land seem to have an instant and very real impact on our supplies of not just food but medicines, engine parts, oil and the list goes on.

It is interesting to contrast the UK with regions such as Somalia and Afghanistan which are normally regarded as dangerous parts of the world. Their de-centralised set-up, highly armed population and small localised economies will put these countries in a good position to survive the zombie apocalypse with each region or village quite capable of growing most of its own food and defending itself. The iron rule of a local warlord and the force of his disciplined militia may prove to be the best form of government to deal mercilessly with the living dead menace.

What are your Chances of Survival?

With all of this in mind, experts estimate that without the thorough personal preparation outlined in this and other guides, your chances of surviving more than eight weeks during a major zombie outbreak in UK are less than 5%. In other words, two months into the crisis and not factoring in any international rescue as it is unlikely to come, the population of Britain will be hovering down at around three to four million.

In 1999, Dr Raymond Carter, a virologist from a prominent American University's Medical Research Centre, constructed a computer model which has been used to plot the path of a virus through the population, taking into account factors such as whether the virus is airborne, other modes of transmission and incubation period. In 2002 he developed a mathematical add-on to the model which enabled zombie researchers to factor in a unique feature of the zombie virus, that the recently deceased actually come back and actively continue to spread the virus. He referred to the living dead phenomena as an additional 'vector of transmission' and programmed its impact in accordingly. Dr Carter's model was run on an American state but one with a similar profile and population distribution to the UK. The results startled the research team.

The research projected that the state would be overrun with zombies within four to eight weeks and that over 57% of the population would be "converted" into ghouls. What struck Dr Carter most was the exponential and unpredictable spread pattern of the zombie virus. Although not airborne, the model took into account the chaos caused by the recently dead returning. Not surprisingly, locations such as hospitals, major transport routes, airports and religious buildings quickly became 'hubs' of the virus with ghouls spreading in every direction. Interestingly, other locations such as city centres and police stations followed the same pattern. It was also observed that any transport 'black spots' also held up the spread of the ghouls. The computer model for example showed thousands of ghouls massing at the entrance to a major river tunnel. One can only imagine the Dartford tunnel or Forth Bridge causing the same pattern. In one fascinating graphic display, researchers could see the panic of a relatively small zombie outbreak, leading to increasing numbers flocking to some of the sites identified above. Equally, the model then demonstrated increasing numbers of ghouls heading away from these sites looking for fresh meat. The chaos and panic in effect fed an exponential spread of the zombies.

By week 12 of the simulation, the living population of the state had been reduced by over 97%.

Although controversial and far from accepted in many parts of the zombie community, Dr Carter's work illustrates how a country like the UK could be overrun in a matter of weeks. But what are the real implications of this theory for those planning to survive this zombie apocalypse in the UK? We have one of the finest armies in the world; won't they be able to defeat the zombie menace?

UK Anti-Zombie Capability

As one of the richest and most industrialised nations in the world, the UK benefits from multi-layered emergency response resources including hundreds if not thousands of back up organisations and decision-making bodies which could if correctly targeted; provide us with a formidable anti-ghoul force. Each area of the country has well-established local authority organisations and each of these has dedicated bodies such as county ambulance services, police forces and other support mechanisms.

This well-developed network of agencies is set up to deal with most emergency situations, the most visible in our current climate being the high-profile anti-terrorist response simulations held in various cities across the country to help the authorities plan for a possible biological weapon attack. In fact, we have emergency preparedness frameworks and policies in place ranging from major floods to nuclear accidents.

However, a trawl through any local or central government documents on all of this emergency planning will leave the casual observer facing a bewildering range of frontline organisations and central committees, none of whom have any official policy on dealing with the zombie menace.

As one MP outlined in response to a query on the country's zombies preparedness:-

"Nice films but not covered by government policy."

It is interesting in contrast to note that the possibility of the earth being hit by an asteroid was deemed a real enough threat to be highlighted by Welsh MP Lembit Opik during a long campaign on the dangers of near earth objects such as meteors. There is no such sponsor for plans against the living dead and until there is one at the highest level, central government and its direct emergency planning bodies such as the Civil Contingencies Secretariat will not produce a single pamphlet or literature on how to deal with zombies. They leave our frontline medical, police and military forces blind to the living dead menace. If the motto is 'knowledge is power' then we are woefully unprepared for the shuffle of the ghouls.

Our First Lines of Defence

In the absence of any directives from central government, our local NHS, medical, police and fire services will form the backbone of any response to an emergency. The very early days of an outbreak in the UK will be characterised by confusion as zombies overrun things and our brave emergency services struggle to contain a challenge they do not understand. Therefore it is vital that your home is a fortress, not for a few days, but a good 90 day survival window, which gives you a chance to survey the landscape and decide your next move.

The Police versus the Living Dead

In the UK, we are lucky enough to have one of the best police services in the world in terms of reputation, honesty and overall crime clear-up rates. Although they may lack the glamour of other police forces in the world, the local bobby still survives in the form our community officers and new organisations such as SOCA (Serious and Organised Crime Agency) are starting to give a more edgy feel to the set-up. Their fearless devotion to public duty will see the police become our first line of physical defence against the ghouls.

According to official figures, there are 200,000 serving officers in the UK and Northern Ireland with an additional few thousand "community support" roles, with the latter growing particularly in our city centres. Although some forces have suffered recently from some high profile incidents, the overall reputation is still considered strong when compared to international police forces where corruption and dishonesty seem to be order of the day. But, whilst our police may be well-respected and effective in crime prevention, they are in no way set up to deal with the kind of onslaught they would face in a major zombie outbreak.

The first thing any observer learns about policing in the UK is that there is no single 'police authority' and that the country is in fact split into numerous divisions, county authorities and even separate forces. For example, most forces are organised along county lines, each with their own recruitment process and traditions. In other cases, such as the British Transport Police or the Port of Liverpool Police, the forces operate as virtually independent bodies with their own officers and supporting structures. If the complexity of different legal systems between the various countries in the union are factored in, the policing landscape becomes even more complicated with blurring lines of authority and frequent friction between forces during investigations.

This fragmented policing structure in the UK means that our local and to some extent central police forces are in danger of being paralysed during the initial chaos of a zombie outbreak. If the outbreak started in one of our major city centres, it is unclear how ready each police constabulary would be to make tough decisions such as implementing curfews or even shoot-to-kill policies. Experience shows that where organisations are fragmented, key decisions in times of stress are often delayed.

Another feature for which the British police are well-known is that they continue to be mostly unarmed which bucks the trend of most other countries including many in Western Europe. The UK's lack of an armed police force removes the backbone from our "Bobbies" as an effective anti-zombie force.

For example, despite our "Armed Response Units" and their vehicles being well-armed with sub-machine guns and semi-automatic weapons, they are in no way set up to 'go to war' with fewer than 5% of current serving UK officers being trained and licensed to carry firearms. The fact they are not ready to engage in a protracted, armed conflict against the living dead could be made against most policing forces in the world, possibly with the exception of the LAPD (Los Angeles Police Department) but other forces at least have a strong cadre of firearms trained officers who may be able to adapt quickly to the challenge of the living dead.

In summary, the fragmented set-up of policing in the UK combined with the fact that it is mostly unarmed will limit the impact of the British police in anything beyond a Zed-Con 4 incident. Unclear operating guidelines from the government will restrict decision-making at force level, with no chief constable willing or able to instigate a 'shoot-to-kill' policy on the infected until it is too late. Perfectly designed to keep the peace in a civil society, our police forces will quickly be overrun in the opening weeks of the crisis by sheer numbers and will be unable to stem the widespread looting and chaos let alone battle the ghouls. Few doubt the courage of our thin blue line but in terms of anti-ghoul force, there are serious shortfalls which mean survivalists will not be able to depend on them in any capacity as the chaos develops.

MI5 and MI6 versus the Living dead

The UK has one of the most well-developed "secret services" in the world which operates both at home and abroad to protect our country's interest. Honed in the Cold war era and in the struggles with the IRA, this force is mainly based around MI5 and its shadowy sister organisation MI6, and continued to develop in recent years in response to the growing threat of international terrorism.

MI5 or "Military Intelligence, Section 5" is responsible for counter-terrorism, counter-espionage and for protecting the democracy within the country while MI6 or the "Secret Intelligence Service" mainly operates abroad on external threats. Much respected internationally by our traditional allies, these security forces are a significant force at the government's disposal but how geared up are they to defend us against the living dead?

Well, the first factor which needs to be considered is that despite its relatively high-profile, its sparkly London headquarters and the arsenal of high-technology weapons, it is estimated that the two agencies have fewer than 3,000 employees in the UK. So in terms of numbers, with projected zombie numbers in the millions, it is clear that once an outbreak takes hold, these 'secret' security forces will have only a small role to play other than maybe protecting key surviving government members or the Royal Family. Although both MI5 and MI6 have good access to firearms and some of the best training in the world, their limited numbers will negate them as a real force in the battle against the ghouls

The real value of these organisations lies in their analysts, after all, they are both primarily 'intelligence' organisations and often work closely with the army and police to target operations. As such, they were never designed to be a fighting force – they have always been more subtle than this. The key point here is the battle against the living dead is going to be far from a subtle affair. For example, there won't be any place for secret listening devices or mobile phone tapping - it will very much be about taking out as many hungry ghouls as possible. However, both these agencies and particularly MI5, have teams of analysts looking at mountains of information and data in an effort to detect any threat to our country. Currently, these analysts simply have nothing to assess, as they do not recognise the threat from the living dead. This has led to what is termed in the security industry as 'threat' blindness'.

One former serving member of MI5 recently leaked to a zombie forum that in the 1960s service analysts had developed a scenario which was codenamed "Trojan Day". This provided a model and established protocols to deal with a deliberate viral release and outbreaks. In one of the scenarios, infected individuals were being transported into the country in containers through our main ports. It is easy to see how this situation could easily be adapted to factor in groups of the living dead effectively being imported into the country, dormant during transit, only to spring into action when the container is first opened. Each container would create a Zed-Con 4 level outbreak with the deadly plan that at least one of these would escalate.

Sources at MI5 have always denied that the service has ever specifically considered any living dead scenarios and deny the existence of the Trojan Day project but, former agents insist they developed computer-modelled scenarios using so called "VCI" or Virally Compromised Individuals up to at least 1984. After this date, many cold war projects were cut and any results from this research buried but there is at least a hope that somewhere in Whitehall there is a dated version of what could be considered to be Britain's only official plan to survive an outbreak.

In summary then, once a zombie outbreak occurs, our secret security forces will be of limited value. Their numbers, tools and core competencies are simply not geared to face a no-holds barred fight against the ghouls. Their potential value in defending our country is in their traditional role of recognising the potential threat posed by the living dead. But as we have seen, they need intelligence flowing in and strategic leadership from government to build this scenario and neither of these is on the agenda in the near future.

The British Armed Forces v the Living Dead

So, the ghouls are very much in town and the country is facing a major zombie outbreak. As the chaos quickly grows beyond the control of the police, our armed forces will be the next line of defence but how will they measure up to the hungry hordes? Will the British Army reach its own Waterloo as millions of former Britons are transformed into bloodthirsty ghouls? Will the RAF bomb the living dead into oblivion? Will the Royal Navy sail to our rescue?

Well, it is important to remember that any projection on how the British armed forces would respond to a major zombie uprising would only be an estimate at best. Nothing is certain and we can only overlay our current armed forces against the violent background of a country flooded with zombies.

The following sections review each of our main armed forces in turn to offer a balanced assessment on the kind of protection, if any, you can expect.

The British Army

Britain has a professional but very small army compared to many other countries in the world. Historically, this has been the case possibly as a result of being an island. In fact, it may surprise some readers to learn there are more therapists than soldiers in the UK, with an estimated 150,000 therapists of various descriptions compared to less than 100,000 frontline troops.

Although the British Army is ably backed up and supported by an additional 35,000 Territorial Army soldiers, our country cannot fall back on the millions of trained numbers who are available to many of our European neighbours. For example, whilst conscription may now be deemed poor preparation for modern warfare and a drain on funds, it does provide a core of potential soldiers who are at least schooled in the basics of military discipline. The battle against the ghouls won't be a high-tech war and numbers will make a difference. Being able to raise thousands of armed troops quickly will be a key advantage in countries where conscription is still in force, enabling some cities to create militia-type units to defend urban areas quickly.

The British Army is currently deployed in over 80 countries around the world, on various assignments ranging from diplomatic duties, training assignments and even open warfare. Current government policy has stretched the army structure to breaking point and has in some cases resulted in our troops doing 'back to back' tours in dangerous parts of the world. For example, the highest overseas deployment numbers in the 1990s saw some 10,000 troops in the former Yugoslavia and at one point over 45,000 -- not far off 50% of our frontline troops -- in Iraq and other parts of the Middle East.

As any soldier will be able to confirm, the growing worldwide role of the army has not been matched by either an increase in manpower or budgets. Indeed, some analysts estimate that since the end of the cold war in the late 1980s, both have been cut by up to 40%. These cuts have bitten deeply into ammunition and ordnance stocks. Although much of these are still manufactured in the UK for security reasons, stocks are often said to be kept as lean as two weeks' supply.

Bearing all of these factors in mind, and that current models predict a major zombie outbreak could easily see ghouls in the millions in under a week, it is clear our brave armed forces would quickly be overrun given both their limited numbers and resources. In the most basic terms, we simply won't have enough trained soldiers or bullets to kill the millions of ghouls in a major nationwide outbreak.

However, as most military historians will attest, numbers are most certainly not the whole picture in any war and sound strategy can also play a decisive role. Unfortunately, this is also an area where our armed forces are woefully prepared to battle the living dead.

For example, most zombie experts agree that the first battles against the living dead will be the only chance to contain the virus. These actions will demand ruthless and firm action if the country is to have any hope of containing the ghouls. This will be like no war the army has fought before. There will be no prisoners, few wounded and every single 'enemy combatant' will be unarmed, mostly civilian and certainly deadly.

In addition, as a direct reflection of the government's lack of any central policy for dealing with a zombie outbreak, our military forces do not have a single pamphlet on how to deal with the living dead.

Confused attempts to capture and quarantine the infected, poor tactical information on how zombies operate and restricted numbers will lead to some brave but desperate last stands as the army battles the sheer weight of the living dead. Lay these brave but mostly futile defences over on to a background of a poorly armed police force and no overall strategic direction and things start to look very bleak indeed.

One very specific concern regarding the British Army raised by qualified observers is of the basic infantry weapon, the SA-80. Since it was introduced almost a decade ago, the weapon has struggled to shake off its reputation as fragile and unreliable. It is considered by some infantry to be more akin to an 'air fix kit'. Recent tests and new versions are said to have rectified this and it will be the main infantry weapon against the ghouls but even official reviews still highlight laughable faults in the rifle, such as its propensity to damage if over-cleaned! What is certain is that in the upcoming war against the ghouls, the army will need a simple, accurate and robust gun with plentiful ammunition. It also needs to be something non-military people such as civilian militias can be trained in quickly. It doesn't need to be the highest-tech rifle on the planet; it just needs to be able to hit a ghoul in the head at say 50 metres with enough force to take him out. One can't help feeling we should order two million AK-47s from the Red Army in China and mothball them. The ordering of these infantry weapons should be a central pillar of any military anti-ghoul policy.

Another significant weapon in the army's arsenal is their fleet of some 350 Challenger Two tanks and almost 800 lighter but equally deadly Warrior vehicles. Providing both of these vehicles are deployed correctly in the UK and with the right support, they could inflict significant damage on the ghouls. This would undoubtedly be helped by the army command's insistence on keeping far more high-explosive rounds than other armed forces, many of whose armoured vehicles carry a significantly higher proportion of armour piercing (AP) rounds. To clarify, AP rounds of any description, including rifle ammunition, are largely ineffective against the living dead. Whilst it is true that the sheer power of some shots will decapitate a ghoul or blow a significant enough hole to stop it permanently, many rounds just go straight through their rotting flesh. Modern weapons such as tanks and machine guns could inflict a large number of zombie kills if supported with the right tactics such as funnelling the living dead into a blockaded area and creating a 'kill zone'.

With limited numbers, inadequate resources and non-existent anti-ghoul training, it is estimated by experts that the British Army would be quickly overrun and between four to eight weeks after a major outbreak, the hordes of zombies would very much have the upper hand on mainland UK. There may be pockets of resistance but as a nationwide fighting force, the army will cease to function, swamped by a bloody tide of the living dead.

The Royal Navy

Most Britons still have romantic visions of the Royal Navy with hundreds of warships scattered across the globe ready to come to our aid but this has not been the case for some time. Indeed, despite major naval operations, most notably the Falklands War in 1982, the Royal Navy has suffered ongoing cuts to its fleet in recent decades such that it now has less than 30 major ships with 50 or so support, patrol and supply vessels. Crucially, it is short of ships in key areas such as aircraft carriers and frigate (there are 3 and 30 vessels respectively in these classes). The number of ships overall has declined by almost 50% from 172 in 1985 to 82 in 2007.

Add into this the 'lean' operations policy operated by the navy which carefully manages the quantities of stores, fuel and ammunitions supplies, then it would seem that in its current orthodoxy, the Royal Navy would quickly be reduced to a role supporting the army and a possible evacuation role in any battle against the ghouls.

However, our naval forces have a long tradition of defending the UK against any threats and several features in the service could play a prominent role in anti-zombie operations if correctly deployed. With the number of anticipated ghouls being in the millions, it is unlikely the navy will be able to stem the inevitable grey tide, but in crucial areas they may provide invaluable assistance. First, far from being restricted to seaborne operations, the Royal Navy is capable of extending its operations inland, keeping a sizeable force on constant standby for operations. This mix of marines, support ships and other vessels is collectively known as the UK Amphibious Force (UKAF). It is a balanced expeditionary force ready for instant deployment and most importantly, it can survive without supplies for around 30 days. In addition, built around HMS *Ocean*, our one major amphibious support craft, it can supply rely on up to 18 helicopters of various descriptions to support operations in addition to up to 2000 combat troops, mostly Royal Marines.

One projected scenario would see that whatever government remains in London after the first wave of zombies, ordering UKAF and whatever remaining military units still remain, to create a "safe zone" which citizens could make their way to. The most likely locations would be around the Royal Navy's main dockyard and port facilities on the south coast in Portsmouth and Devonport. It is possible this force, supported by others, could establish and hold a perimeter, at least for a few months, providing it was limited in size.

A second crucial service of the Royal Navy could be in its evacuation role. Having already noted UKAF's helicopter resources, it is worth noting that the navy's other ships particularly their giant Sea King and Chinook helicopters could be put to good use evacuating people to an offshore location, most obviously, the Isle of Wight or other cut off location.

With its limited resources, the Royal Navy would need to focus its strategy on one survival plan. For example, it may be that the UKAF is deployed on the Isle of Wight and the Portsmouth area creating an evacuation path for those fleeing the zombie hordes. This tactic would require all the navy's resources not just in defending the area on the mainland but in enforcing quarantine around the island itself and purging any ghouls already there. It is also questionable how long their supplies would last. UKAF may be able to hold out for one to two months at a push and most of the navy's larger vessels can last up to 7,000 miles without refuelling but there will be a time when operations begin to become affected by the need for fuel, suppliers or spare parts.

The role of the Royal Navy's submarine fleet, which numbers some 14 operational vessels, is more problematic to assess. These nuclear-powered craft operate mainly out of their base in western Scotland but can be deployed anywhere in the world. Despite being some of the largest submarines ever operated, they only have a crew of around 120 and can scarcely take more than this number so in terms of any evacuation duties, their role will be limited. However, they can stay at sea for virtually an unlimited period of time, coming in only for food and water as required.

With these factors in mind, two real scenarios develop. The first is that our submarines serve to evacuate a few important people to a place of safety or are used to monitor developments in other parts of the world. The second is that their crews and whoever else is on board head out to sea, where they will effectively be able to stay in isolation for months, even years. This would at least guarantee the survival of some humans.

A final note on our submarines would be that many carry a complement of nuclear missiles which could be used to take out huge concentrations of zombies. For instance, if our large metropolises such as London or Leeds are completely overrun, a decision may be taken to simply devastate these areas to prevent our rural areas being swamped by urban ghouls driven out of the cities by hunger. This doomsday scenario certainly lends more weight to the survivalist argument rather than fortifying an urban dwelling. You would be better off moving lock, stock and barrel to a remote and rural location before the ghouls arrive. In the case of a nuclear strike, not even a fortified dwelling will be safe.

The upcoming zombie apocalypse would probably see a mixture of all of these plans, with factors such as desertion or ships being deployed in remote locations, having an impact on the naval response to the ghouls. What is certain is the Royal Navy's current lack of preparation to face a zombie menace. As with the other areas of the armed forces, this leaves any response they make open to some serious miscalculations as to the threat they face.

For example, one can imagine one of our brave vessels taking on hundreds of refugees in a Dunkirk-style evacuation, including wounded, only to realise their mistake as zombies emerge from every dark corner aboard their crowded ships. Once again forewarned is forearmed and although it has the potential to at least keep the ghouls at bay, without a sound strategy, any resistance will be piecemeal and ultimately doomed.

The RAF

Few Britons will doubt the steely determination of the RAF in defending both our country and our interests. Perhaps more than any other of our armed services the struggle of the RAF on the early 1940s has come to define what many see as the British drive to survive against the odds.

Although the RAF of today is still a highly trained and motivated force, there are some serious questions marks over its role in any struggle against the living dead. With fewer than 1,000 operational aircraft and less than 40,000 personnel, those planning to survive the zombie apocalypse in Britain should not be depending on the flying boys in blue for any great help.

Several factors make the RAF particularly vulnerable to any significant ghoul outbreak. First, as with the other military arms, the service has been severely hit by budget cuts over the last few decades and whilst both the planes and the supporting equipment have become more complex, the technical infrastructure of the force has been slashed. Remember, the zombie apocalypse will see a rapid breakdown in lines of supplies and it has been estimated that the RAF would last less than one month in continuous action separated from a source of high-tech components, oils and fuels. A combination of lean fuel supplies, perilously low ammunition and ordnance supplies mean that the force could not maintain operations for a serious length of time without immediate resupply.

In addition, the RAF has also been in active service across the globe in recent years, with extended commitments in Iraq, Afghanistan and also still in south-eastern Europe. Many senior commanders in the RAF have argued that the service has been stretched to breaking point, with both aircraft and men feeling the strain of continuous service.

Another major factor which will negate the RAF's role in the zombie apocalypse is its complex operational structure, which sees a confusing mix of units such as groups, wings and the traditional squadrons, spread out across the country. No doubt, this wide distribution made sense to planners during the cold war era by ensuring that the RAF could not easily be knocked out on the ground in a single series of raids, but the sheer distance and number of bases which probably number anything up to 30, make the guarding and security task of the RAF Regiment nigh on impossible.

As mentioned previously, few of us would doubt the courage and training of our pilots but in terms of zombie defence, there are serious concerns around the effectiveness of their weapon systems in the upcoming struggle against the ghouls. For example, the mainstay combat aircraft of the fleet, the Tornado and its up and coming replacement, the Euro Fighter, are certainly some of the most advanced fighter aircraft in the world. However, they are also aircraft which require notoriously careful maintenance and back up which will be increasingly difficult as the ghouls take over. Their main armament, such as high-tech laser guided weapons, whilst not useless in terms of anti-ghoul operations, will be a significant 'overkill' in the zombie war. The level of technology in these planes and their weapons is simply not required to hit the ghouls where it hurts.

And, bearing in mind the numbers of living dead which will be faced, cheap and effective weapons will be the order of the day rather than multi-million pound missiles. Even the Fighter's top speed, which is over 1,500 mph, will be wasted in a low-tech war against the grey masses. It is likely that these sparkly aircraft will be reduced to reconnaissance roles in the war against the zombies in stark contrast to their immense tactical value in current combat theatres.

So, a combination of budget cuts, operational stresses, structure and inappropriate weapons systems is in danger of making the RAF virtually irrelevant in ghoul defence. However, there are some areas in which the force may be of great service provided it can maintain operational effectiveness as the living dead swamp parts of the country.

One important RAF-led but multi-service organisation is the Joint Helicopter Command or "JHC". This group brings together many of the nation's operational helicopters under one command group and can provide an estimated 230 helicopters at any one time into a theatre of action. This force includes a range of aircraft but is mostly made up of Merlins, huge Chinooks and the lighter Pumas. The JHC could provide our emergency authorities with the massive lift capacity to not only move supplies and key personnel around but also potentially to evacuate hundreds if not thousands of stranded humans. Recent conflicts and humanitarian disasters in different parts of the world have demonstrated the immense value of choppers and as a country and mainly through the work of the JHC, the UK has a significant and action-ready group which could play a key role in our defence against the ghouls.

An additional and invaluable service from the RAF could be the ongoing provision of up to date intelligence on the movement of any ghoul hordes or in the search for survivor communities. The force operates a large number of unmanned aerial recognisance craft which can travel over large distances constantly feeding back information to operators. These drones are also used by the army and have proved their worth in the Afghan conflict being able to scout ahead of patrols, checking for any potential ambushes or enemy concentrations. It is possible that in the Britain overrun with zombies, these unmanned craft could provide the same invaluable service.

In war against the ghouls, the RAF, like the Royal Navy, must focus its strategy and resources very carefully. For example, one sensible and cost-effective policy would be to reduce the number of operational bases and to better fortify current sites to improve their resistance to the ghouls. In truth, whilst most RAF bases now have a tight security perimeter, few have the capacity or basic supplies within this perimeter to cope with the hundreds of panicky refugees who would rush to these sites as the living dead run rampant across the country. Each military base must plan for this as it will happen and these desperate people cannot be turned away or left to the hungry zombies.

In a wider context, the RAF needs to focus at least some of its resources on developing 'ghoul-busting' weapons systems. One example here would be to ensure stocks of basic high-explosive bombs and ordnance is maintained as in the ghoul war, the old weapons may well be the best. In addition, the RAF would do well to expand its fleet of training aircraft such as the Tutors or the Vikings, which, due to their low speed and ease of use, would be ideal.

In a final review, the RAF shares the same institutional weakness of our other armed services. It has failed, at either a strategic or operational level, to prepare to face an army of the living dead. And, whilst some elements of the force such as the JHC, could play an invaluable role, without the planning and guidelines in place, a rapid descent into chaos is a likely outcome for the RAF.

The British Criminal Underworld versus the Living Dead

If the outlook is bleak for the police and our armed forces, it is worth also looking at the various other organisations which may stand against the shuffling grey masses. This could be any organised group with sufficient numbers, loyalty and some element of force. This could include any organisation from the Scouts to shooting clubs but the most likely candidates to be able to wield the kind of force needed to really hold their own against the zombie horde are the various illegal crime syndicates and gangs which blight our country. Only these organised groups combine the structure, the will and the downright brutality to fight the ghouls.

By far the most potent of these organisations are the various paramilitary and criminal groups which are particularly strong in our troubled inner cities or in regions such as Northern Ireland. In some cases, they can better be described as 'gangs' or collections of mainly younger people, grouped together for mutual protection and for other criminal purposes. In the case of paramilitary groups proper such as the Continuity IRA, they can have complex command and control structures supported by secret caches of weapons and various sleeper units across the country.

But, how would these illegal organisations respond to the menace of the ghouls? Would they seek to take advantage of the situation or simply evaporate into the panicking masses along with a general breakdown in any social order? More importantly, what are the implications of this kind of gang activity on those planning to survive in their own homes?

A key factor in the success and long-term survival of any illegal group is loyalty. This is ranked above all else and binds the group together in a bond which has seen them through tough times and violent encounters. This loyalty to the group is often backed up by excellent levels of organisation which may extend to shared transport, safe houses and command structures which, together with the threat of violence, maintain strict discipline within the group.

Something frequently cited by gang experts is that members of crime groups are often driven together by fear more than anything. They frequently come from divided or crime-ridden areas in which the police authorities may not be trusted. In some ways, individuals are driven into these organisations by external threats, a factor which will only be stronger as the zombies ravage our cities and things begin to breakdown.

Finally, in the UK today, these gangs have relatively easy access to firearms, particularly if they are involved in the drugs trade. Indeed, even if they do not keep a large stock of weapons, most can find reliable contacts who are able to procure them anything from a hand gun to a laser guided missile. One only has to look at the weapons the Metropolitan Police in London have confiscated in the last few years to see that semi-automatic weapons such as the AK-47 assault rifle and gangster choice, the Uzi, have already made their way into our country in significant numbers.

Modern urban history in the UK has shown us that as the police retreat from trouble spots or lawless inner cities, various illegal organisations, be they the IRA, mafia-type or street gang, develop to fill the void. In some examples they even begin to take on some of the ‘law and order’ duties, carrying them out in their own style which may include beatings or protection money. But, would any of these organisations seriously look to take power as our police and other authorities crumble? Would the violent street gangs of our inner cities see this as their chance to seize power?

Well, the evidence would seem to suggest that as police retreated and were replaced by the shuffling grey mass of the living dead, these organisations would seize this chance and attempt to take control. It is likely the illegal gangs operating before the zombie apocalypse will continue and will adapt as criminal organisations have always done. Bound together by their shared values and with numbers ranging from the smallest gangs of around 20-50 youths up to major crime syndicates running into hundreds, they will be in a good position to defend themselves and possibly even prosper. It is certainly true that any humans who can organise, particularly in the kinds of numbers these gangs can, will greatly increase their own chances of survival. Add into these the discipline, local knowledge and access to firearms and it is likely that our much-maligned underworld may stand fast against the zombies for significantly longer than our armed forces.

Crime frequently flourishes in a crisis and the opening months of the zombie apocalypse will be no different. With thousands of very desperate people around, it is most likely these gangs will move into areas such as people trafficking to help the lucky few escape the country. Once this avenue closes down, they may seal off areas or even entire districts of cities and offer "protection" to the population – remembering that none of these services will be for free. Also and most importantly, there will be no local law and order authority to stop them.

Zombie survival theorists predict any gang which can muster more than 20 members and meets some of the above pre-conditions such as loyalty and access to firearms has the potential with the right leadership to carve out a niche for themselves in a country dominated by ghouls. How long these groups will survive is a complex question. It is estimated that the smaller, less well-organised groups will evaporate along with many other of society's structures within the first month or so of the zombie outbreak. However, the more developed operations are thought to be capable of surviving for much longer, possibly years given the right conditions. It is feasible in time that these extended survival groups effectively become the authorities in the land, seeing us return to the days of the robber barons and possibly a feudal style society.

The implication for the home zombie survivalist of these organised and dangerous communities surviving is significant. Immediately images of carefully prepared home fortifications being wrecked and laid down supplies looted spring to mind. Equally, survivors and their families may be forced to join these groups regardless of their own preferences. With the police and any central authority gone, these robust and powerful groups may come into their own with the force of a small army and even firearms.

The lesson here for those planning to survive in their own home is obvious but worth repeating. A Britain overrun by zombies will be a dangerous place but not just because of the ghouls. Gangs and other criminals will seek to survive like everyone else, the difference being that they will be prepared to do it at anyone else's expense. So, running silent once the zombies take over is standard operating procedure along with the other techniques to deter bandits or opportunist thieves, such as making your home look derelict rather than a well-stocked home fortress. Equally important will be discretion in your preparations before any zombie outbreak. If you are known as the local zombie survivalist expert, guess where the first stop will be when the first ghouls show up? So, any purchasing of food supplies or building materials should be discreet and over time. Your defences should be solid but look 'average' and not in any way 'out of place'.

Remember, with the collapse of law and order, the ghouls won't be the only threat out there -- organised gangs, unruly mobs, increasingly desperate loners and even packs of hungry dogs will be every bit as dangerous as the zombies. Your primary weapon will be 'running silent' but make no mistake, you must be able to defend yourself, your family and your home if required against human as well as inhuman opponents.

Would the British Government Cover Up a Zombie Outbreak?

Conspiracy theorists argue the government has already covered up several zombie outbreaks in the UK, with Zed-Con 4 incidents in south Wales in the late 1950s and the north west of England in 1967, being mostly widely discussed. In each case, the theorists maintain a cover story was fabricated and leaked out to the media: in these examples, a mining accident and a nuclear leak respectively.

In recent years, British governments have been accused of being less than honest on a wide range of important issues ranging from going to war in Iraq to the outbreaks of BSE across the UK's farming sector. These controversies will not comfort those who fear the government's first and default position will be to deny any problem or attempt to cover up a zombie outbreak at precisely the time it should be dealing with crisis with firm action.

However, from another perspective, it could be argued that there may be very pragmatic reasons for our central authorities to 'manage' any zombie crisis, hoping to minimise the panic and quietly regain control. One may expect news blackouts, misleading statements, police enquiries bogged down in legal details, all designed with the best intention, to keep everything quiet as the authorities deal with the incident.

No British government could cover up anything more than a Zed-Con 4 outbreak for long and the most likely scenario is that we will be subjected to weeks of speculation and rumour before efforts to contain a living dead outbreak are finally overrun and it becomes a national crisis. How the drama will play out will very much depend on the nature of the outbreak. For example, if a virus carrier or zombie comes through one of our major airports and things start getting nasty there, then warnings will be in hours not days. For those planning to survive, you need to keep your ear to the ground and maintain your personal early warning system at all times. Remember, if the authorities decide to keep things quiet, you will need to look even harder. Monitor the press; scan some of the discussion boards cited in the reference section of the volume and talk to other zombie survivalists. You must be ready to believe an outbreak is imminent or in progress once the signs are there and more importantly, be constantly ready for action. Days, weeks, even months of denial will cost millions their lives as they cling to a belief that zombies do not exist, right up to the point when the living dead themselves start clawing at the door.

Rather than any deliberate conspiracy on the behalf of our beloved politicians, it is most likely that a mixture of ignorance, good intentions and ineffective decision-making will ensure no real action is taken in the event of a zombie crisis. One only has to look at the various crises faced by British agriculture in the last few decades as these are littered with cases of misinformation, 'don't panic everything is fine' statements and mismanagement at a local level.

When you consider all the facts, it's hard to be optimistic about our government's response to a ghoul outbreak in the UK.

However, not all threats will come from within our government jurisdiction. One dangerous scenario to consider would be an outbreak in a state abroad, possibly in a draconian state such as the People's Republic of China with its restricted media, vast size and tendency to see any request for international help as a sign of weakness.

As for global defence against the living dead, a ghoul foothold left unchecked in a populous location such as China could easily grow into a significant outbreak which could quickly engulf the world with zombies. The living dead could number in the millions before the crisis even crosses any international borders. One can then easily imagine ghouls being accidentally locked in containers and being shipped around the world or people exiting the area through every main airport in the world including Heathrow. Equally, lawless backwaters would attract little media attention as they are overrun by ghouls, only noticed once the problem spills over into more populated areas or cities.

The UK is poorly prepared to face an internal zombie attack and its poor border control and major transport hubs make it particularly vulnerable to an imported threat. The fact we are an island is at least some defence but our major airports and their position globally negates any advantage the sea may have given us. Most experts believe whatever the level of preparation by our authorities, the most likely Zed-Con outbreak scenario is the virus and zombies are 'imported' into the country. The fact our government has no co-coherent anti-ghoul policy just leaves us even more exposed.

The measures in this book are designed for the individual, family or group but facing a major outbreak in another country would mean the government needs to translate these survival plans into national policy. For example, our borders would become a line of defence and would need to be closed. Our nation's stocks of food, water and other essential supplies would need to be controlled and, rationing would need to be implemented as soon as possible. However, whichever administration is in power, the zombie survivalist must prepare a barrage of misinformation and cover up, most likely done with the best intentions but that will mean it will basically be up to you to look for, and defend against the living dead.

A Note of the Legal Position of Zombies – Zombie Rights

The zombie apocalypse will present the British government with a plethora of problems in its opening weeks not least of which will be the legal status of the living dead. In an age where human rights legislation is mentioned daily in the media, initial attempts by the police to respond to the crisis will be hampered by an inability to confirm or deny zombies as the "living dead". The British police or armed forces will not be able to shoot from day one, and hesitancy and a lack of clarity will dominate decision-making as legal teams wrangle over definitions. Some of the emergency planning already in place will serve to create further chaos as the authorities' battle with a new and deadly menace.

In March 2007, the London Resilience Partnership, a collection of emergency providers such as police, military and heath authorities, published a grim but comprehensive guide to how they would cope with emergencies in the capital, called the London Mass Fatality Plan. This document provides an overview of responses to catastrophic events in London such as a flu pandemic or bio-terrorist attack which would result in significant casualties in the city. The plan fits into a wider London Strategic Emergency Plan which was published in 2005 by the same organisation. Although most parts of these weighty reports are available to the general public, the consequences in terms of our preparation for the zombie apocalypse are only just being understood. The key factor is what can loosely be described as 'zombie rights'.

Filled with good intentions and the best motives, the authors have re-enforced the legally recognised rights the deceased have. For example, Interpol Resolution AGN/65/Res/13 (1996) recognises that for legal, religious, cultural and other reasons, human beings do not lose certain rights after death. It does not mention the rights of the living dead but the legislation is clear enough to create uncertainty and confusion. This may be fine when the dead are stationary but when they walk around and start to feast on the living, the guidelines may have created a confusing nexus of rights and guidelines which will slow down response and reaction to the ghouls.

A further complication to the legal status of the living dead may be around the human rights and associated legislation designed to protect people with particular medical conditions such as those in what is called persistent vegetative state. In this context, zombies could be viewed as having a syndrome and rather than being the living dead, we may well need to refer to them as the "livingly-impaired" or the "mortally-challenged". Terms such as ghouls or zombie may be deemed offensive if not to the living dead themselves certainly to the friends and family of the deceased.

In the UK, it is rightly illegal to discriminate against an individual for many reasons including those who suffer from various medical syndromes. As has been discussed, this is not always directly linked to whether the victim is dead or living dead – even after death, humans maintain certain rights. One possible loophole being explored by the anti-zombie community is the legislation around health and safety which may enable survivors to deal with the living dead under the remit that as walking corpses they present a serious health and safety risk to people.

In this complex area, it may well be illegal under current guidelines for the police or survivors to despatch zombies. This presents us with the alarming scenario that in the crucial opening weeks of the zombie uprising, we will find our police forces paralysed into inaction by our own well-intentioned guidelines and unable to implement any cull of the ghouls whilst there is still a window of opportunity to contain them.

So, what does this mean for those of us planning to survive the ravages of the ghouls? In some scenarios, it could mean that we see survivors being arrested in the chaos for 'abusing the dead'. Whilst it is unlikely the ghouls will insist police acknowledge their rights, our well-meaning authorities may try fervently to enforce what they see as the law. We could therefore face a situation of arrests based on offences against the ghouls and even the police attempting to detain any living dead. For sure, many of our frontline medical and police teams will be overrun as they try to intervene or restrain zombies.

Self-defence legislation in the UK is a confusing minefield much of which focuses on the legal phrase 'reasonable force' and in the case of a zombie attack it could be argued that the living dead suffer from diminished responsibility. It is therefore sensible to advise caution in the early days of any crisis. As always, avoid combat where possible and obey the laws.

The authorities will be extremely busy trying to maintain a semblance of law and order so run silent and keep a low profile. It is also worth remembering that under some emergency guidelines, activities such as looting may be subject to a 'shoot-on-sight' policy. In many ways, the first few weeks of the zombie crisis will be the most dangerous times.

UK Scenarios

Following extensive research into zombie outbreaks in the last 25 years, a series of scenarios have been developed to offer our best projection of how a zombie apocalypse could start in the UK. With this kind of 'war game' planning, we simply do not have enough data from this country alone to provide a realistic analysis of exactly how a zombie outbreak could happen.

It should be noted that all of these scenarios are fictional but set in real locations and have been based on the reports of similar outbreaks across the globe and on the collective experience of the zombie fighting community. For those planning to survive the zombie crisis, they will make chilling reading, showing how the zombie virus can enter the country and then reach a critical outbreak stage very quickly. Understanding this backdrop will give a new impetus to any emergency planning as you realise this could easily happen and at any time.

Using a panel of zombie experts and advanced plotting software similar to that used by the Health Protection Agency, the scenarios were developed specifically to help those planning to survive a zombie incident in the UK. The panel, which included several well-known academics from human and urban geography, a military historian and a microbiologist, all of whom have asked to remain anonymous, was presented with an outline of the location of the incident, any local resources and the starting point of the zombie crisis. The team then proceeded to develop a most likely scenario based on this information with updates at various points. This kind of 'war game' is very common in the military and designed to help with contingency planning and preparation by exploring most likely scenarios.

Our experts did not always agree and certain assumptions had to be made but overall, it is believed these case studies represent some of the most likely zombie outbreak scenarios. Each will start with a background outline based on the 'sit rep' (situation report) briefing given to the experts. The point of infection is also highlighted in these accounts but the panel was not made aware of this during the scenario building. The text below summarises how the scenarios developed based on decisions made by the key players on site. These were judged to be 'reasonable' actions based on the available information.

Case Study: Milford Haven Oil Port

Background

Situated in the rural Welsh county of Pembrokeshire, Milford Haven Oil Port (MHOP) is a major oil and gas terminal, handling an estimated 20% of the UK's total fuel. There are about 1,000 people working on site including numerous contractors and specialised engineers to service the extensive port and several major refinery facilities as well as numerous outbuildings and offices.

Point of Infection

An overseas tanker docked at MHOP and immediately contacted the port authorities requesting a doctor as one of the crew had been struck down by some kind of infection and was now becoming violent. With its massive cargo of oil and already delayed on its next job, the ship was berthed and the oil extraction process began.

Scenario

A local GP from the small town of Milford Haven was brought in and with two security contractors from the port authority was led on board. They found the former first engineer standing in the corner of the medical bay. He was emitting a low moan and had been locked in this room for at least 12 hours. The on-board medic reported that once he had become violent, the door had been locked as they were so close to port.

As the doctor and security entered, the patient slowly turned and moved towards them. The doctor spoke to the patient but he didn't respond. His movements were slow and not particularly menacing but once close enough; the moaning figure lurched forwards towards one of the security guards. Both men were ex-military police, and quickly went into autopilot to restrain what they perceived as an aggressor. However, whilst restrained in a well-recognised judo-style hold, the patient managed to close his jaws around one of the guard's arms and take a deep bite of flesh. The guard pulled back in shock but the second guard managed to adjust his lock as the former first engineer chewed on his mouthful of flesh.

The patient was carried to the port medical facility where he was placed under further restraint whilst the guard was immediately taken to the local hospital, certainly needing stitches and antibiotics. With a temporary bandage and although shaken up, the security guard wanted to drive himself and so left whilst the rest of team contacted the hospital for further help with the still delirious first engineer.

Unknown to the port authorities however, the security guard did not make it out of the port compound, passing out in his car unnoticed or logged out by either the CCTV or gate guards.

On the advice of the doctor, the first engineer, port security guard and the local GP himself were quarantined and all ship's crew restricted to the ship. Unsuccessful efforts were made to contact the guard who had been bitten. The port authorities were unable to locate the guard's home address details as he was employed by a third party contractor. They assumed he had gone directly home and were busy trying to locate his number from colleagues.

The security guard had in fact lost consciousness as he was about to start his car. Two of the port's engineers heard banging from inside the car a few hours later and opened the door, assuming whoever was inside was having some kind of seizure or fit. Instead, a newly created zombie launched itself from the vehicle biting one man on the thigh. As the bitten engineer pushed the creature away, the ghoul fell on to the second man and took a deep bite out of his neck and continued to feed.

Resulting Outbreak

The expert panel reviewing this scenario projected a 60% chance that it could be brought under control. The actions of the bitten engineer are crucial. If he panicked and left the port complex then the zombie virus would be uncontrolled but whilst kept within the perimeter, there was a realistic chance of bringing it under control. Even if he had made it to the local hospital, this would have created the chance of a further outbreak at this vulnerable location. Meanwhile, the isolated crew on the ship were unable to contain the outbreak as further infected zombies emerged from the many dark corridors within the huge vessel.

Three of the five expert panel believed that given the current state of knowledge and resources on site, this zombie incident would be restricted to a Zed-Con 4 outbreak. Our media expert projected it would most likely be managed as some kind of tropical disease outbreak as the local authorities would be very reluctant to admit they had no idea about the virus they were dealing with.

The key turning point in this zombie event was the failure to recognise the mode of transmission. The panel's medical expert explained that in many cases it is best practice to quarantine anyone who has been in close contact with an infected patient with such pronounced symptoms from an unknown vector. The bite victim should therefore fall under this category.

In a brainstorm to conclude this scenario, the panel pointed out a complete lack of any information with reference to the zombie virus would contribute greatly to the threat of an outbreak. For example, it was pointed out that in recent outbreaks, it had taken medical authorities over a week to identify patients with the 'bird flu' virus. They concluded that fateful decisions made by on-site personnel, such as the decision to send the guard home, could have disastrous consequences in this scenario.

Case Study: Clinical Research Facility

Background

This is at an advanced clinical research facility at an unnamed leading company in central London. The facilities main research projects are based around nutrition and cancer research but the Ministry of Defence has previously used the laboratories for more advanced biochemical research. There are four fully equipped labs within the complex and 24 researchers on site, with a further 400 staff in the building.

Point of Infection

A project for the MoD under the umbrella of allergy research for the army sees volunteers tested with small doses of known but non-classified viruses. Ten volunteers are tested along with a further four control patients. During the delivery process, at least two of the volunteers are unknowingly infected with the zombie virus in addition to the test virus. None of the volunteers showed any reaction to the known virus and through follow-up tests, the researchers concluded the virus was not effectively transmitted. Therefore, all 14 volunteers retired to a 'cool down' area where there was a TV room and cold drinks.

Scenario

After an hour or so, front desk security was alerted by a nurse who reported the patients in the recovery area had gone insane. She had briefly entered the room to be faced with something akin to a bloody abattoir. Several volunteers were leaning over, apparently tearing a victim apart.

The nurse understandably panicked and dashed to make a call to security. She did not seal the cool-down area as is standard protocol in these cases. As soon as she replaced the phone, she was mauled by a ghoul.

The zombies, now numbering around eight, swamped the floor. Several other researchers who had been in the various meeting rooms on the floor, emerged only to be grabbed and attacked by the hungry dead. The floor was effectively overrun but the zombies were contained. The lift doors were closed. The stairwells had particularly fiddly and heavy doors.

The security guards on the front desk did not contact the police immediately as they had only recently received a memo about the authorities possibly charging companies for any inappropriate use of resources. In addition, their roles were under review and possibly due to be outsourced. The two unarmed guards therefore decided to try and handle what they suspected was a patient fight themselves.

As the guards emerged from the lift, the floor was silent confirming their belief it had been a minor incident. As they entered, a crouched figure slowly turned and moved towards them. It was one of the researchers they both recognised. She looked lost and was babbling but showed no external signs apart from a cut or graze to her forehead.

One the guards rushed forward to help as she looked as if she was about to collapse and as he held her, the dribbling ghoul sank its teeth deep into his neck.

At this point, further zombies emerged from the various meeting rooms and the second guard was swamped as they clawed at him. During the scuffle, one of the ghouls was pushed back into the open lift and did not move as the doors closed and the lift was called to the ground floor.

The police were not called to this site for another hour, when zombies began spilling out on to the streets. Many staff had panicked, assuming some sort of terrorist attack and had exited the building via the two authorised fire exits. Several infected individuals were swept up with these crowds and as the police battled to control the situation in front of the building, reports came in that a similar scenario was developing further along the road and at the entrance to the tube station.

Resulting Outbreak

All the experts on our panel concluded the outbreak in this scenario would be extremely serious with London being under threat within 48 hours of the first incident. A combination of central location, high population concentration, poor security and a slow police response, would mean that zombies could easily be overrunning nearby streets and stations within hours.

One point our medical expert noted in this scenario was the possibility of some factor driving the ghouls to spread as quickly as they could. He pointed out that the 10-15 zombies in this scenario could easily have been kept busy feasting on the people within the building. It is possible they chased their prey as office staff and fellow patients dashed away from the outbreak but there is some research which suggests zombies, as with other creatures, have some form of survival instinct deep within them. In other words, ghouls ‘perceive’ in some way that by creating numbers – in effect breeding represents the best chance of survival. In zombiology, this is known as the Linggs Impulse after a Norwegian scientist of the 1960s. In this theory the living dead have an in-built instinct to infect others as well as feed. Professor Linggs’ revelation shook the fledging science of zombiology as it seemed to question the whole premise that zombies are purely driven by a desire to feed. He modelled two outbreaks in the very north of his country in the 1940s and noticed a tendency for new zombies to take only one or two chunks out of victims then move on, leaving the human still alive but infected. The virus develops into the condition creating a more intact ghoul than if say a leg had been bitten off.

Dr Linggs’ theories remain very controversial and have been challenged by most voices in the zombie community. However most will agree that any scenario building or planning must include an element of the unknown and for the moment we simply do not have enough research to completely dismiss Dr Linggs' findings. If proven correct, the Linggs Impulse would certainly challenge our current models of the spread of zombies.

Case Study: Manchester Airport

Background

Manchester Airport is the UK's largest airport outside London and is a major international and nation hub handling some 22 million passengers a year. The airport handles well over 100 inbound flights per day from destinations across the world and directly employs almost 20,000 people on site.

Like any modern airport, in addition to the terminals, there are hundreds of shops and other facilities on site to service an estimated 50,000 passengers per day. The airport has an armed police presence at all times. Worryingly, it has estimated that around one third of the UK population lives within a travelling time of two hours from the airport.

Point of Infection

An infected subject coming to the UK on a scheduled flight from Malta displayed no symptoms before boarding but steadily became more lethargic as the flight progressed. He ordered several alcoholic drinks and so the flight attendant assumed he was sleeping when they landed at Manchester.

As the passengers began to exit the plane, the subject became 'excited and uncontrollable'. Two male stewards tried to restrain him and security was called within minutes in accordance with the airline's protocol for dealing with passengers behaving in a violent or abusive manner. By the time the security team arrived, two passengers were helping to hold the infected man down, whilst the two attendants had each been bitten by what they now assumed to be someone with serious mental health problems.

Scenario

Shortly after security arrival at airport, chaos erupted from within a scheduled flight from Malta, with passengers rushing to exit the aircraft. Most of them were too panicky to report anything but one did tell the security guards not to enter. Cabin staff reported a drunken passenger had needed to be restrained during the flight. He had passed out around an hour ago but now was wide awake and violently lashing out to break free of his restraints. Other passengers confused the situation by reporting that a woman had been injured and that they had seen blood stains.

The security guards instantly escalated the incident to their command centre at the airport and the on-site police armed response unit. The nature of the incident was unclear so maximum security protocols were issued. It was assumed they were dealing with a drunken tourist but they did not rule out some sort of terrorist threat.

The crowd of some 20 passengers forced their way through the exit desk to the waiting lounge where they had been held by local authorities. The civilian guard there was simply overwhelmed and the crowd too panicked.

The police were unsure of the threat faced and so set up a perimeter around the waiting lounges. They grew tense as they heard somebody coming down the link way but were visibly relieved to see it was a member of the aircrew.

As the leading policeman walked forward to get a 'sit rep', the air stewardess seemed to be in shock and didn't respond. Before he could react, she surged forward as if to collapse but bit deeply into his neck, leaving blood gushing from him. The police followed standard operating procedure and shouted a verbal warning to the infected stewardess but she was by this time bent over the fallen officer feeding.

Other members of the crew and several passengers started to emerge from the connecting tunnel, in all around 12 zombies. A couple went straight for the fallen officer whilst the others ran towards the thin line of waiting police.

One officer opened fire with his assault rifle on semi-automatic. Two zombies dropped to the floor but his shots had been low and they continued to drag themselves towards him. The other four armed officers opened fire but were soon overrun by the ghouls.

Police reinforcements began arriving on the scene to witness the carnage in the waiting lounge. The airport was now being fully evacuated. The second police unit took cover from some distance and looked initially to contain what they now presumed to be armed terrorists. In addition, the whole terminal was sealed in accordance with emergency airport procedures. This involved large metal grates coming down on key walkways. By this time, there were an estimated 30 zombies, 10 dormant corpses and seven armed officers still alive and operating as a unit.

The second police unit was composed of longer-serving officers with a well-known senior officer in charge. He approached the incident in a calculated way, balancing the facts and adapting his tactics accordingly. His first 'sit rep' confirmed this was not a terrorist incident, as there were now some 20 figures stumbling around, with others apparently feasting on fallen comrades. He calmly concluded that they had succumbed to some form of hysteria or drug-induced state. Officers were told to contain everyone within the terminal and to use lethal force as necessary. A perimeter of at least 10 metres was established. In effect, the site was contained.

Resulting Outbreak

The airport outbreak scenario is a 21st century nightmare scenario for zombie planners. Hundreds of passengers, long queues and easy transport links combine to make any outbreak in any major transport hub a significant risk. In fact, with the sheer volume of passengers and their increased propensity to onward travel to further destinations, our experts concluded that unless the virus could be contained on site, for example, in the terminal or better still on the plane, even a minor incident in any major airport could lead to the country being swamped by zombies within weeks.

It was concluded by the experts that two significant factors prevented a major zombie outbreak.

First, the decision was made, due to fear of a terrorist threat, to seal the terminal and the evacuation was well-organised and prompt. The ability to automatically seal off the area meant a sizeable chunk of the terminal was simply shut down, sealing in the zombies regardless of the action of the remaining police team on site.

Second, an experienced on site officer, even without specialist zombie training, managed to make some reasonable assessments regarding the threat and maintain his team's coherence. In almost every other scenario, his order to use lethal force so freely, would have led to fierce criticism and disciplinary action. In this case, he checked the ghouls within the lounge area and prevented a decent foothold.

Although our experts all agreed these actions would have limited the outbreak in this scenario, all remained very sceptical about the level of emergency preparedness at our major transport hubs. Timing would be crucial and more poorly defended and resourced areas such as container ports were thought to be highly likely points of entry for the zombie virus.

Scenario Building in Survival Planning

We use created scenarios because there is simply not the documented evidence to plot a major outbreak in the UK but what are the practical lessons for those of us planning to survive a Zed-Con 1 incident?

When debriefing after the workshops, the key lessons from the scenarios outlined were highlighted by our panel of experts:-

- Zombie incidents can have multiple start points – the vector of entry for the virus could be anywhere from a port to an airport, a lab to an unknown source. And, since you cannot defend everywhere, this has profound implications for zombie defence planning at local and central levels. As for personal defence, you will need your own fortifications and supplies ready to use at a moment's notice.

- There is a critical lack of knowledge around the zombie virus itself and the resulting Zombic Condition. The fledgling science of zombiology has not yet identified where the virus comes from or whether it lies dormant in specific humans. The failure to isolate the virus for any length of time has meant that as well as no concerted effort to develop a cure, we also have only guidelines about the speed of the conversion to zombie. So, you need to prepare to face the unknown. Experts simply do not know how rapidly the virus will spread so cannot accurately predict how quickly society will breakdown. It is safest to assume from day one, you are on your own.

- Critically, a lack of recognition of the problem by our local and central authorities means there is little and in most cases no preparation to deal with the living dead menace. For example, our normal disaster procedures for dealing with the causalities of any outbreak, such as mass mortuary facilities, would be a disaster when facing a zombie outbreak. We in the UK are perilously exposed to a major zombie outbreak and because our government is not prepared in anyway, if you are serious about surviving, you need to take control of your own destiny and plan to survive yourself.

Many of the broader themes in this summary will be of most relevance to our central planning authorities and it is recommended they should lead to the creation of a 'living dead' framework outlining the government's general approach to zombie outbreaks.

With this in mind, at the end of this chapter there is a template letter designed to be photocopied and sent to your local MP. It is your duty as a concerned citizen to raise this issue to your elected representative. However, it is hard to believe that even thousands of warnings will prompt our government to shift policy on this issue. As much of this chapter has shown, the authorities in the UK are poorly prepared to meet the living dead menace and in the final analysis, it will be your own personal level of planning and preparation which makes the difference between you and your family surviving or joining the ranks of the living dead.

MP –
House of Commons
London

Dear . . .

I, as a registered voter, am greatly concerned about the threat posed to our country by the ever-present menace of zombies. As my democratically-elected representative in parliament, I petition you to raise the issue of our nation's preparedness to face this threat at the earliest possible opportunity.

Specifically, I and many others call for:-

The creation of an overarching governmental framework outlining a general approach to policy for containing ghouls and monitoring any outbreaks, particularly recognising the need for prompt and decisive action.

The amalgamation of the various emergency preparedness bodies into a centralised and resourced Zombie Security Agency. The role of the ZSA would be to oversee our security preparations, plots outbreaks and advise on government policy. Crucially, this new organisation would report directly at Cabinet level.

The creation of a National Institute of Zombiology to address the crucial lack of scientific knowledge around zombies and the zombie virus. This institution should be fully funded and be an environment in which our science community can explore and research ghoul-related issues.

Finally, UK representatives of international organisations such as the United Nations should raise the question of zombies at the next possible forum. It is vital that the issue of battling ghouls be discussed at this level as it is truly an international problem. The living dead know no boundaries.

I would ask that you give this issue your prompt attention and look forward to your response.

Signed

Complete Zombie Defence

This section of the guide will examine the fortifications, supplies and skills you will need to drastically improve you and your family's chances of surviving a zombie apocalypse. If the facts and figures from previous chapters sounded grim and you are asking what can be done, then these following chapters will provide advice on everything from home fortification to food storage, weapon choice to defending against horde attacks. Think of it as the workbook you will need to ensure you survive whilst others around you are being overrun and eaten by the ghouls. Central to this survival strategy is the '90 Day Zombie Survival Plan' which provides a comprehensive framework to help you prepare and survive any major zombie incident. This will be our first topic.

Planning and Preparation: The 90 Day Zombie Survival Plan

Current analysis indicates a 90-day survival window is the most sensible option for most Britons in terms of planning, the resources they can maintain and the available space for storage. More importantly, experts agree that whilst the first two to four weeks of the apocalypse will be chaotic and dangerous, in the following four to eight week period, well-prepared survivors should be in a position to consider their next moves and plan accordingly. So, for example, this could mean improving their current location or seeking an alternative location for long term resettlement. Ninety days is not a scientific figure and those planning for the coming of the living dead may want to look further ahead and lay down stocks and supplies for years in advance. All of these options are considered in later sections but for now it is important to understand that just as you insure your car, home, even pet, the 90-day Zombie Survival Plan is your insurance policy to survive the ghouls providing you plan, prepare and follow the guidelines. The real importance is that this plan will hopefully buy you a 90-day window in which to not only keep you head down and survive but also consider your options for life in what will be a country dominated by millions of zombies.

A famous survival expert coined the phrase "preparation through information" and information gathering must be the first step in any emergency planning. One criticism of our central and local authorities outlined in previous chapters is precisely that they have no real information on the threat posed by zombies and therefore are in no way prepared to organise any effective defence.

By now, you should already be aware of what a zombie is and how to take them down. You will know something of their capabilities and restrictions. When it comes to their habits, it's pretty simple – they want to eat you. This knowledge will provide the foundation of your survival plans.

Anyone planning to survive the ravages of the zombies needs to consider the following questions as they research the various sources of information available (many of which are referenced at the end of this book).

- How can I defend myself and my family against the zombies?
- What supplies should I lay down and how do I decide what to store?
- Will my house be strong enough as a fortress?

- How can I fight any ghouls that make it past my defences?
- How long can we survive where we are and where would we go if we had to move?

As you begin to think about a country teeming with ghouls, the list may seem endless with numerous areas which all require urgent attention. Suddenly, that poorly-fitted patio door and collapsing garden fence take on a new perspective. Looking around the home, all you will see are areas where ghouls could break in. Your cupboards suddenly seem very bare, with nothing that will last past two months but an old tin of spam.

Preparation is very much the key and the good news is that with the right preparation you can greatly increase you and your family's chances of surviving a major zombie outbreak. You have already made the first step by picking up this book. You may have read others or started a small library. The old cliché 'knowledge is power' is as true in the fight against the living dead as it is anywhere else.

Once your information gathering is complete, get started, you never know when the zombies will come but remember you don't have to achieve everything at once. All of us, especially these days, have limited money and time so prioritise any action plan. For example, you could start by taking an inventory of what supplies you have in the house and then gradually build up a 90-day stock over time

Why do I need a 90-Day Survival Plan?

Our assessment in previous chapters has hopefully shown that our brave emergency and military services will be quickly overrun by the hungry ghouls so your plans need to consider that you will almost certainly face the zombie apocalypse by yourself. Your sound planning and preparation could be all that stands between you surviving and becoming a meat snack for wandering ghouls.

Whether the authorities regain control or not should have little impact on your emergency planning as you need to plan for the worst case scenario. This principle will underpin much of your planning. You cannot rely on a police response, an ongoing supply of electricity, Tesco's being open – all of these things will easily evaporate in the first few weeks of the crisis.

Be warned that in the early days of a zombie outbreak our brittle and lean supply chain society will quickly break down with resources such as food, fuel and even water becoming scarce and valuable commodities. The safest thing is to assume you will not be able to gather or even top your supplies from the first days of the crisis and even with this rule there may be exceptions. For example, in most living dead scenarios, the country will lurch towards the crisis - there won't be an official start date. Zombies don't do fixed dates and you are responsible for ensuring your stocks are always full and as important, maintained.

One only has to look at the panic caused by a few days without petrol to see the impact on consumers: massive queues, aggressive attendants and bumper to bumper traffic. Imagine the masses as reports of the crisis start to filter through. Supermarkets will be stripped and local shops emptied as people panic to build up stocks in the time they have. You may be friendly with your neighbours now but one can easily imagine the normally docile Browns or Smiths after a few days without food or electricity and with your local Tesco a burning shell from looters. Make no mistake, wherever you live, civil unrest will present as much of a danger in the opening weeks of the crisis as any ghoul. It will be important that you 'run silent' in your home. Help by all means if you can but you must not endanger you or your family by advertising your carefully prepared stores.

The first weeks of the zombie uprising may therefore be characterised by riots, civil unrest, looting and the collapse of the thin blue line as our police struggle to cope with the sheer weight of ghouls.

During this phase, there will be open battles in the streets with the living dead and roving bands of vigilantes fighting the zombies. Again, it is important to stay inside, stay low and away from windows. It may even be possible to make the location look abandoned to avoid the interest of any looters.

It is likely in this phase of shock and panic some form of curfew may be enforced by the authorities as they attempt to regain control of the streets. This will make any sourcing of supplies at this stage even more difficult and dangerous. As things go from bad to worse, new zombies will mix with crowds and police will struggle with any shoot-to-kill instructions which may have filtered down.

Significant journeys will be almost impossible for most parts of the country, with the possibility of roadblocks, accidents, fuel shortages and even bandits. Many prominent survival books have proposed innovative and inventive survival plans based on remote Scottish islands or isolated rural locations. The attraction of the wilderness is also emphasised as a way to allow us to sit out the worst of the crisis in comparative safety. However, for most urban Britons, this option is not a realistic option. Imagine the M25 around the M4 junction on a rainy Monday morning, then throw in a few hundred bloodthirsty ghouls running between the stationary cars and you will get the picture. The chances of you hitching up your well-stocked caravan and heading off to your prepared safe house on the Isle of Wight are slim.

If you are already in an isolated location then great and if you are serious about preparing to face the zombie horde then relocation may be an option but for most of us family and job commitments tie us to urban areas. You will need to plan to survive where you are!

The following outline suggests the most likely scenario for the zombie outbreak and your key priorities at each stage. Obviously, not being eaten is top of the agenda in each section:-.

Phase 1 – Fortify and Stay Put - Prepare your home, check your stores and just survive the opening phase. You will run silent, keep safe and stay alive.

Phase 2 – Assess Current Location and Monitor - Keep vigilant, guard your location and deal with any threats. You will need to get a grip on your supply situation and any potential foraging in your immediate area.

Phase 3 – Determine your long-term options - Is the crisis under-control or have the ghouls taken over? You will need to decide whether to move on or stay. Equally, you'll need to think through your long-term survival strategy in areas such as food and water.

There are so many factors which could affect your carefully-prepared plans that it is vital your planning is both robust and flexible. Some of these areas will be explored within this volume, such as for example, what to do if you caught at work when the ghouls emerge or if your secure location is overrun. But there are countless others which can and probably will upset your arrangements. Always keep top of mind that your objective is to prepare for these broad phases with self-sufficiency and above all security, high on the agenda. Sections of this book will help you in areas such as fortifying your home, preparing yourself mentally and even which weapon to select but it is not designed to take the place of the many detailed general survival books on the market, some of which are listed at the end of this volume. This book will cast the bluish-grey shadow of the zombie apocalypse over this wealth of survival information and hopefully enable you to adapt to a scenario few consider and even fewer prepare for.

Home Defence: Fortifying Your Home

A fortified and well-stocked home will be one of the safest places in the growing chaos of the zombie uprising. Once the dead begin to rise and more worryingly, wander around looking for fresh meat, you will be relying on the walls of your humble semi-detached, terraced house or flat to keep both yourself and your family safe. No matter how tempting it is to break out and search for the ideal location in a crisis, our clogged roads and the breakdown in social order will mean your chances of survival will be greatly increased if you just shut and lock the front door. However, whatever home you have, you need to prepare if you are planning to use your home as a refuge through the weeks and months of the zombie crisis.

The first step in home defence against the living dead is keeping your home in good repair. Often overlooked as survivalists rush out to buy large quantities of wood and bricks with which to block up any windows, maintaining areas such as the roof and drainage are vital prerequisites for your defence plans. Fitting steel security bars or rolling metal blinds will be pointless if the underlying structure of your home is not secure. Any property can be seriously weakened by unseen damage and decay and an effective routine should check off possible problems such as damp and subsistence.

Similarly, any covered rotting timber or framework could easily be overlooked only to collapse under the weight of a horde of hungry zombies. Conditions such as dry rot are by their nature sometimes difficult to spot, that is until the first ghouls smash through.

By following a careful maintenance routine, you will also acquire some invaluable DIY skills which will be useful as you will need to rely on your own skills once the dead are in charge. It may be obvious but even the best household insurance won't pay out once the ghouls take over. The key phrase here is preventative and it is important to remember your home is not just an asset; it is the refuge on which you will be depending.

There are certain proactive choices you can make in your home which will become a solid foundation for your home defence plans. For example, the routine changing or servicing of a front room gas fire is the ideal opportunity to convert to traditional solid fuel which will be invaluable once the mains are cut off as well as being a boon for romantic evenings. Along with your new open fire, you will need to acquire the necessary maintenance skills and understand the importance of ventilation. It is also worth noting that most open fires require the chimney to be swept at least annually.

The point is some home features such as an open fire, converting to double-glazing or even fitting solar panels, can greatly support your survival plans. Good and adequate loft insulation should also be added to this list. It is advisable to move any loft conversion plans forward as you prepare for home as these can create some valuable extra storage and a useful lookout position.

A good starting place is to make a balanced assessment of your home and the building's current defence capabilities. Many of the leaflets provided by the police or neighbourhood watch can come in very useful to support this assessment, for example, they often point out the vulnerable areas thieves target such as low windows, other ground floor access points, blind spots or inadequate patio doors. Many of these areas are exactly the same points you will need to inspect during a zombie defence exercise.

The main differences are of course that whilst a burglar alarm may warn you of an incursion it will not 'deter' these hungry attackers.

Equally, barbed wire may slow ghouls down but they tend to shuffle through these obstacles in no time, normally as the result of one unlucky zombie falling and acting as an inhuman bridge. Home security firms will often carry out a complete free assessment of your home and it is recommended that at least three such assessments should be completed to help you keep track of the latest developments in home security.

You should make a complete list of areas which require attention. Many of these will be discussed in the following sections of this volume but this is very much an ongoing process and should be constantly repeated. It is important that you look at your property with 'new eyes'. Do not underestimate or overlook anything. For instance, it is easy to discount a small ventilation window as too small for anyone or thing to access but you need to consider whether a desperate ghoul could reach through and grab a member of your party. Also, some ghouls will be in pieces, possibly lacking legs or even an arm. Could one of these draggers crawl through at this access point?

Prepare a list but do not panic if at first it seems like an endless amount of time-consuming and possibly expensive works. As with all areas of survival planning, you need to work your way through the plan, and prioritise where possible. There will be tough decisions to make and you will need to manage according to your own resources. Remember, every improvement you introduce whether it's a better front door or a two-metre concrete wall, will improve you and your family's chances of resisting the zombies.

Any list of adaptations and improvements which need to be made to your home should naturally focus on priority areas such as the ground floor, any doors, windows or other access points and these are a good place to start. As in most types of fortification, the ground floor needs to be well-protected from any assault. A key difference in a zombie assault or siege is that as opposed to a one-off and targeted action such as a burglary, the living dead will be a ceaseless pressure on your defences. Your front door for example, won't be kicked in, it will be subjected to a constant and growing pressure by the ghouls as they try to force their way in by pushing forward. Any windows will be subjected to the same attack with sharp fingernails clawing at the glass and possibly picking away at any window putty along the way.

Although it has never been proven that a zombie can climb any kind of ladder, it is worth adding that as ghouls collapse or trample on each other, they can create a growing mound of living dead which can enable them to access higher and even second floor access points so these windows should also be counted in. Don't underestimate the living dead!

With windows, double-glazing is essential. Indeed, the person who invented double glazing deserves the anti-zombie equivalent of a business award as many older or sash windows can be easily prised open by the grabbing claws of the living dead. The new sealed units are much tougher and most are supplied with robust internal locks. It is worth checking these locks and fairly cheap upgrades and additions are readily available. Interestingly, in most break-ins, lockable windows are in fact left unlocked. In other cases, keys are lost or misplaced. This is a mistake you cannot afford to make with the ghouls; they aren't breaking in to steal your DVD player or your priceless *Star Wars* figurine collection.

Double or triple glazing should be extended to include all windows both for the added security and the insulation qualities. If funds are limited, then the ground floor should be the priority. It is worth contacting your local council as many offer incentives to help homeowners carrying out energy saving projects such as converting to double-glazing or loft insulation. Any measure which insulates your home will pay dividends when the power fails and in any cold weather.

With all windows, curtains or blinds are recommended. The best option would be to reinforce or fortify your windows on the inside, ensuring the curtains are all that can be seen. You can even create burn marks around the window to make your home look abandoned.

The information around window defence is equally applicable to doors – modern double-glazed doors tend to be far stronger than some of the ones fitted in the last few decades. The solid wooden doors of the pre-war era can provide a very robust anti-ghoul defence providing they are in good condition. If possible, avoid glazed panels and where they are fitted they should be hardened well-fitted glass. Key areas for attention around doors include hinge areas, locks and how well fitted the door is. Weakness in any of these areas can see your solid looking barrier collapsing under the weight of the ghouls.

Any hinges or supporting metal work should be tightly screwed in. Do not rely on a door fitted by your builder. Check the points where the door is fitted to the frame and indeed where the frame is fitted to the wall. If you do have a weak front door, it must be changed no matter how costly.

Locks should be either a rim or a mortise lock and both if possible. Most security chains are a useful additional but will hold the living dead for no longer than a minute or so if the door is pushed open. This may however give you the chance to warn your party and get upstairs or to your agreed emergency point.

Doors which swing outwards may be the preference as they cannot be pressured in. The obvious drawback is you may become blocked in under the sheer weight of ghouls or piles of the living dead. Being able to get out of your fortress is just as important as being secure within it. Breakouts, routine patrols and urgent maintenance are all possible reasons you may need to make a foray into the outside world.

One area of danger to watch for particularly in 1960s and 1970s dwellings is the inadequate sliding patio door. In many cases, would-be thieves can lift these poorly fitted features off their runner to enter a home which may have a solid front door and secure windows. Even if it sits behind a good fence, your home is really only as strong as its weakest point and if you have one of these patio doors which was never really designed to be an external door, you need to rectify the situation immediately. Some householders have tried fitting wooden bars to jam shut their sliding patio doors. This is a poor stopgap and getting it changed as soon as possible is the only real option.

Much has been written in the anti-zombie community on the value of security shutters or bars across windows. Whilst it is true that rolling shutters are thoroughly recommended for any garage doors or even main doors, the cost can be prohibitive. In addition, bars may prevent entry although they will not stop a clammy hand reaching through. Where sufficient resources are available, the ideal situation would be to be able to lock all ground floor access points with rolling shutters. It should be remembered that for the best defence this should be on the inside, with the lock inwards so your window from the outside still looks normal with hanging flower curtains. There is no need to advertise the fact you are prepared. A well-fortified house may well attract roving bands of survivors desperate to find a new refuge for themselves, particularly in the opening weeks of the zombie apocalypse.

Bricking up windows to create a safe room and having reinforced and lockable interiors doors are all ways in which you can "compartmentalise" your home. This will allow you to seal off any incursions quickly giving you a chance to regroup and preventing the ghouls from overrunning your shocked party. The key principle to understand is that of a 'compartmentalised defence'– that is, having a series of internal strong points, fallback positions and a safe room to fall back to if or when the ghouls break through your perimeter.

The stairs are an obvious central choke point in most homes and whilst some zombie survival guides recommend hacking these to pieces the moment the dead rise, with careful planning a more sensible approach can ensure you maintain a robust defence but that you can also still easily access the key ground floor areas of your fortress. It is recommended that your stairs where possible be converted to a 'drawbridge' type arrangement where the whole stepped section can be easily pulled up and secured tightly to the ceiling. Having the stairs pulled up could for example be a default position during night time.

Special attention should be paid to ensure the design does not enable any ghouls to grab and pull the lifted stairs down. Whilst they may lack the dexterity to get a good grip, any of the rotting clothing may become caught and drag the stairs down. A good way to think about it is that if you can pull them down with your hands, then so could the ghouls, who have an uncanny knack of finding a way through.

Although this may require the services of a good carpenter and some adaptation as all homes are different, drawbridge stairs will represent a strong internal defence should your ground floor be overrun.

Establishing an External Perimeter

Your current external perimeter will in most cases be the humble garden fence which is normally wholly inadequate for defence against the living dead. Even the solid-looking six-foot wooden slated fences so common in this country are not in any way designed to hold against any kind of lateral pressure. More often than not, the sunken posts are not even bedded in concrete foundations and most can be pushed over with a single shove.

Any home fortification planning should give serious consideration to installing and maintaining a solid perimeter fence to enclose any garden area your property may benefit from. If you intend to use your outside space for storage or growing a small vegetable patch, it is vital this area is secured ideally with a tall and strong steel palisade fence. Robust steel fencing is widely available and is often used to secure commercial properties. Some options include useful top features such as an overhang to make scaling more difficult.

Many steel fence providers will also include the option of a secure gate option to replace the hopeless wooden latch version in most gardens. It is prudent to have at least two entrances which provide you with both an emergency exit route and a useful exit for any forays or culling missions amongst the ghouls.

There are two important points which should be noted with reference to secure fencing and ghouls.

First, with reference to doors, exposed padlocks or any area where you need to reach close to the bars will expose your hands to the grabbing ghouls. A single scratch from a rotting zombie can have serious consequences so any option which involves you reaching a hand over the top or through the bars is not feasible. It sounds like common sense but many perimeter gates will be rendered useless as the living dead pile up against them and those inside are unable to get close to the lock due to their hungry, grabbing hands.

Second, even the strongest steel fencing is see-through by design, and there is ample space between the upright pillars for ghouls to stare with drooling mouths at the humans under siege. Again, it seems like an obvious point but all your fencing will require an internal screen if it can be seen through. The dead-eyed stare of the zombies has a sapping effect on the morale of those using the outside space and confirmation that fresh meat is only a grab away will continue to attract the hordes.

It is possible to incorporate other security features into your garden defences such as barbed or razor wire. However, as has already been mentioned, this will only slow down ghouls as any pain deterrent of pushing through the sharp metal will be lost on the living dead. In addition, some survivalists believe a fortified home surrounded by excellent barbed wire defences is more likely to attract human gangs so ironically, it is less safe than a 'normal' looking home.

Any major changes to your home will most likely be regulated by a local or central planning authority. So if you are planning to build raised fire platforms behind a garden fence or a 13-ft anti-ghoul concrete wall, then ensure all necessary permission is obtained. Cosmetic changes which may affect the value of your property and any extension will certainly require specific permission. You do not want to waste resources on expensive anti-zombie preparations only to be told to take them down soon after. It pays in this area to build a good relationship with neighbours as local planning law often allows people who live close by to have a say on major developments. Perhaps you could form some form of zombie neighbourhood watch to help prepare for the coming of the ghouls.

Having neighbours and friends buying in to your plans is obviously the ideal situation but in most cases this will not be possible. You need to remember that for most of the general public zombies are still on a par with Frankenstein, pixies and unicorns. You may therefore need to manage your important preparations carefully. For example, many features can fit in with your lifestyle and become dual-purpose. For example, a swimming pool may double as an invaluable water or storage area as well as being a boon for summer barbecues and late night dips.

Outbuildings

All outbuildings should be secured in the same way your home is with particular attention to any sheds or garage doors, both of which are weak areas in the average home's defences. Luckily, most garden sheds will be safely within your perimeter fencing and can provide useful extra storage space. However, most garage doors open directly to the road or drive.

Up and over garage doors may look like strong metal barriers but they are very weak as anti-ghoul protection. The weight of a small band of zombies could easily collapse this thin metal sheet most likely overrunning whatever supplies you have stored there. It is a wise investment to upgrade to a robust metal roller garage door as soon as your finances allow.

Some outbuildings such as greenhouses and even tents can provide extra storage space but are non-events when it comes to defence. This does not mean they are useless only that they are restricted in what you can use them for.

You may wish to take advantage of any tall trees in your garden to construct useful lookout posts or a tree house. These locations may also serve as useful bolt holes should your outside space be overrun but are of course not a serious long-term survival option.

As with many other areas of emergency planning, you should have in place a 'disaster scenario' plan with reference to your secure outside space. For example, even with the most robust steel fencing, there are always ways in can be breached – by a falling tree or telegraph pole during a storm, by an out of control vehicle or by ghouls simply piling up outside creating an unsavoury mountain of bodies which the zombies simply stagger up and fall into your garden. The important thing to note is no garden is completely safe but you can make it safer.

Finally, the value of a secure outside space should not be underestimated in its impact on morale. The idea of being locked up for up to three months in a fortified house presents significant psychological challenges to the average person and the diversion of garden plants and at least getting outside in a safe area can have significant benefits. Tactics and techniques for surviving a siege will be considered in later sections but for now it is important to understand the vital role played by morale and as much room and outside space as possible.

Converting your current home, no matter how long or how much resource you spend, will ensure it is at least zombie-resistant but you can never make a home zombie proof.

The living dead have an uncanny habit of finding a way into places so constant vigilance will always be required. The important thing is that you will have given your party a fighting chance in your new fortress

Multi-tenanted Buildings and Flats

Many Britons, particularly in our large cities and towns, live in flats or in rented accommodation. Both of these scenarios make home defence more of a challenge, with it often being more difficult to make any structural changes to the property you live in. For example, it is unlikely your local housing association will respond positively to your request for an anti-ghoul cattle grate to be installed at the communal entrance to your flat.

First things first. Where you are either in a large multi-tenanted building or rented accommodation, the most obvious but not always the easiest option is to move. Of course this may not be a feasible option but there is always the possibility of finding a 'less worse' location. In rented accommodation, this is often the best alternative short of actually moving out of a central urban location.

It is also worth remembering most locations offer at least some benefits. For example, if you are lucky enough to live in a well-established block with known people, this may present an excellent opportunity for survival through co-operation and pooling your resources. With the right set-up, an organised and well-defended block would have a good chance of surviving the ghouls.

A first step in any multi-tenanted building would be to barricade the ground floor and possibly brick up any vulnerable windows. Working as a team, to pool resources, work out a rota for guards on the lower levels. It is also worth remembering that many flats have excellent access to large water tanks and storage areas. Equally, if a walled garden or communal area is available, it may be closed off and used for recreation and even fresh vegetables. Many developments now are surrounded by impressive gates which may serve as a perfect perimeter fence.

On a more negative note, the current trend towards easy access, plenty of glass and open plan arrangements could be a disaster in zombie defence. The solid doors and narrow corridors of many pre-modern blocks can greatly support your anti-ghoul measures.
Special attention should be paid to any underground space such parking areas which could become dangerous ghoul pits. They will probably be dark with the electricity down and it may not be worth the risk clearing them, so for now barricade them off.

Whatever building you are in, your defence against the living dead is only as good as its weakest point of access. You need to survey your fortress, for although zombies lack dexterity, they can easy fall through any open window or their dead hands can prise open a door. Also you need to be aware of constant pressure on the fire doors – always have a chain so if it is busted open, the doors will be held even if only temporary.

With a larger building, it is essential that plenty of zombie alarms are used so think of anything which makes a sound. For instance, empty cans piled up can alert you to any intruder if they are disturbed, either human or inhuman.

On the other side of the scale, you may find yourself in a small flat or bedsit or in a situation where you do not feel like you can trust your immediate neighbours as part of your survival plans. Poor preparation and shock may mean that normally friendly neighbours transform into desperate thieves, willing to fight hard to protect their own lives and possibly take advantage of your carefully laid stocks.

The most obvious issue in a small flat is storage space and you will need to be very creative in finding spaces as well as adjusting your list of survival goods to meet your restrictions. For example, areas such as under the bed or cupboards can provide much needed space but equally you need to plan ahead, so rather than purchasing sacks of oats or rice, the pre-packaged army-style meals in a tin may be preferable as they can stack neatly into a small space. You will need to be 'lean' with your supplies but in other areas such as window and door security, the same lessons on fortifying a house apply.

One special consideration in a small flat will be dealing with any human waste. A normal tendency in a siege scenario would be to simply throw any waste from the window, particularly if you are a few floors up. The main drawback here is it will clearly highlight to any wandering gangs that a flat is occupied. An alternative may be to dump any waste in a nearby empty flat. Any empty flats may present a good opportunity to expand your secure living space providing you have the resources.

The biggest threat in any multi-occupancy building is fire. Even with the best survival preparations in the world, you will be as vulnerable as everyone else if a fire starts in any part of your building. This is a difficult risk to mitigate and to some extent the threat is common to all fortified locations but the best insurance is to have several decent 'bug out' locations, i.e. a pre-scouted alternative location to which you can make a dash if your current location is compromised.

Laying Down Stores

As with defending your home from the living dead, feeding and supplying your family through the zombie crisis requires careful planning and preparation. Little can be achieved if on the eve of the crisis you join the throngs and panic of desperate shoppers at your local supermarket. You could end up facing the zombie apocalypse with a tin of beans, a pot noodle and what you have laying around the house. If you are serious about survival, you need to be serious about your preparation in areas such as consumables and in particular your food and water needs.

At first glance, it can be tough for a newcomer to survival thinking to nail down the key issues. After all, the UK has developed into a mature industrial economy since World War Two with most consumers now on the end of a vast and quite delicate delivery chain which may have seen their humble potato travel from Turkey, their grapes from Spain, even their apples from China.

To cut a long story short, we are now completely separated from our food production. Most of us have few agricultural skills beyond growing a few strawberries or herbs in the garden. This subject will be touched upon later but it is enough to note here that your preparation really begins with a sound knowledge of food and diet – what the body needs and how to keep it healthy.

So, some of the key factors you will need to consider will include:-

- Do I have a good supply of drinking water?
- What will I do if the mains are cut off?
- Which foods should I store?
- How much do I need?
- What's the best mix to keep?
- How many people will I be feeding?
- Where and how will I store it?
- How can I make sure we have everything we need to survive?

The advice which follows has been broken down into sections to help guide your preparation but be aware that this is a vast topic. These guidelines should be supplemented and adapted by your own research. For simplicity, the key areas are water, food and other essential supplies. Remember, the objective is to meet your basic requirements in these areas for a period of at least 90 days. It may be that things quieten down after the first few weeks of the zombie crisis and you can forage for further supplies but equally, you may be trapped in your fortified home or flat with only the stores you have built up and these need to be enough for you and your family to survive.

Water

None of us can survive long without clean drinking water and yet most of us rarely think about the water we drink. We turn on the tap and out pours clean, drinkable water. Despite the oft repeated claim that people don't drink enough water each day, the issue of supply is rarely if ever discussed. However, as the ravaging ghouls take over and the UK descends into chaos, it is going to be impossible for anyone to guarantee either the supply or quality of the water we all need to survive. Add to this that in the initial days of the crisis, all available bottled water will be quickly snapped up or looted and securing a supply of clean drinking water will be a key battleground in the war to survive the zombies.

As in any disaster planning, one must plan for the worst case scenario. After consultations with several industry experts, it is clear that no one knows how long the supply to clean drinking water to homes would last. It is likely some will last for weeks maybe even months. Others may quickly be disrupted as pipes are damaged in the chaos. Some supplies will become contaminated as bodies find their way into supplying reservoirs. The underlying fact is that to survive the zombie uprising, you need to be able to guarantee the water supply to your party for at least the 90-day period.

As a general rule of thumb, an adult will need 2 to 3 litres of water per day depending on factors such as climate and the amount of exercise undertaken. In reality, this estimate does not even consider water for activities such as washing. Taking this calculation forward, this means a family of four would be looking at a minimum supply of around 1,000 litres. For comfort and extra security, a figure nearer 1,300 would be more prudent.

The best way to think about your water needs is to consider that all the taps stop the moment the outbreak occurs. Whilst there is unlikely to be an official start date to the crisis, your clean water supply could be cut off at anytime as the risen dead overrun parts of the country. You need to be prepared.

Your first action must be to take all practical steps to build up a reserve whilst the water is still on. This means filling every suitable container, one of the best ones being any baths, which can be used to store water for washing if it is not suitable drinking water. You will need to plan well for this phase of the operation to ensure that you maximise the water you can squeeze and store from the network. Be aware, you can never be certain when this water will become contaminated. What you can be sure of is that you won't be receiving a letter from your water company. A note of caution: many containers such as plastic milk jugs will become brittle over time and offer a poor storage option. Specially designed PETE or PET, plastic containers are the best solution.

A key action will be to turn off your own supply of water at various points as soon as you can, to ensure that what 'hidden' water you have in your own system stays there. A good knowledge of your plumbing is essential here to know which valve will need to be closed to ensure you don't start losing precious liquid. Often overlooked areas include cold water tanks in the loft as well as the sometimes substantial volumes in heating and other piping around the home.

It is clear that with the appropriate action and knowledge, you and your family can quickly create a useful water reserve but this supply should be looked upon as an addition to your drinking water supply. Experience has shown that activities such as washing are important not just to hygiene but also maintaining good morale.

The quickest and most obvious way to build up your water supply is to buy and store bottled water. In most cases, good bottled water will last 12 months and with an ample supply, you could be in a good situation water wise provided you maintained good water discipline. Other more expensive options include having your own static water tank installed in your garden. These above or below ground strong plastic tanks can store anything from 1,000 to 10,000 litres and beyond with options to either rent or buy outright.

Both forms of water storage require discipline in maintenance and quality, regularly checking what you have in stock. Contaminated water could have fatal consequences. Equally, maintaining strict water discipline will be essential as the crisis progresses as will securing an additional source as your 90-day period moves on. As you explore other sources of drinking water, the danger will be that many of our rivers and reservoirs will be contaminated by rotting bodies and ghouls. Any additional water you secure should be boiled and filtered. You may also use purifying tablets but these tend to leave an antiseptic taste to the water so ensure you have some fruit cordial if you have children.

Considering your water needs is a vital part of any survival plan and last minute planning in this area will be disastrous. It is best to view planning for a 90-day water supply as a key pillar of your strategy. Once you have it sorted out, even if these means laying down your minimum requirements, you will be freed up to concentrate on the many other pressing challenges you will face.

Food

Many of the points around drinking water apply equally to food. In the first few days of the crisis, any remaining stocks will quickly disappear and not be replaced. As is the case with thirst, hunger will drive the most determined defenders out of their well-prepared strongholds in search of supplies.

Your plan should be to establish and maintain a 90-day stock of food. If you are solo, it may be that with some basic stores, you may be able to survive on what you have in a well-stocked house but with a larger party or family some serious and considered planning will be required.

Building a store of food may seem like a daunting prospect in terms of cost but it should be remembered that with prudent planning and measures such as buying extra items on a weekly basis, a reasonable store can be built up overtime for those without the budget to create one overnight.

What you supply can be flexible depending on your own preferences. For example, it is pointless storing cans of spam if the entire family hates it. There are plenty of options and these factors can have a disproportionate impact on morale. What is certain is that all the food you plan to store needs to have a shelf-life sufficient for your needs. It is prudent to have a mix of canned, commercially packaged and other foods which with the right choices will give your supplies anything from one month to three-plus years if stored correctly. Longer term storage items will typically have a low moisture content and include staples such as white rice, rolled oats and even dried apples if stored correctly. As a general rule, the lower the temperature, the better for storing most foods. The table below offers some shelf-life guidelines for dehydrated foods stored in airtight containers. Of course, to make the most of this food, you need a good water supply so an alternative may be army-type C-rations which come in easily stored cans. Many of the items below can be bought in any supermarket and whilst much of the food we buy on a weekly basis will spoil within a few days, with the right items, your food stocks can easily be designed to last anything up to 20 years if required.

Shelf-life Guidelines for Dehydrated Food Stored in Airtight Containers			
Item	**Approximate Shelf-Life**	**Item**	**Approximate Shelf-Life**
Boxed Cereals	9 mths	Garden Seeds	4 years
Cereal Bars	1 year	White Flour	5 years
Canned Fruit	1 year	Brown Rice	6 years
Dry Soup Mix	1 year	Small Red Beans	8-10 years
Ketchup	1-2 years	Broccoli	8-10 years
Peanut Butter	1-2 years	Soya Beans	8-10 years
Ramen Noodles	1-2 years	Noodles	8-10 years
Baked Beans	2 years	Cocoa Powder	15 years
Canned Meats	2-3 years	Spaghetti	15-20 years
Canned Vegetables	2-3 years	Potatoes	20-30 years

More detailed survival guides provide endless lists of food which may be stored including some of those mentioned above. Survival stores even offer complete 90 day emergency food ration kits for around £400 per person which will enable you to reach your target quickly and ensure you have a good balance in your diet.

Most people are used to a wide range of food and tastes, so it is still worth ensuring that your stocks of chilli and spices are kept up. It is amazing what a good curry can do in any situation to improve the morale of the average Briton. As the weeks of survival press on, humble powdered milk will come into its own not only because it can be used to keep supplies of drinkable builder's tea but also when added to many improvised survival dishes such as wheat cereal or oatmeal, it has the almost miraculous quality of turning bland dishes into 'creamed' versions. Store plenty of powdered milk as it will pay dividends and don't forget the luxury items such as chocolate and fruit cordials which will also wonders for morale. You will also need to adapt to your food storage plans to take into account any special food requirements or if you have babies or young children within the group.

One way to boost your food supply is to grow your own fruit and vegetables in any space you have within your secure compound. If your garden for example is safely screened from the ghouls, you could set up some greenhouses which will greatly increase the variety of food you can produce. Even with limited space, you can begin to produce at least some of your food requirements and provide invaluable fresh items to an otherwise prepared food diet. Carrots, potatoes and tomatoes are all relatively easy for beginners to grow and can provide a decent yield even in their first season. Herbs will also be a useful addition to liven up your survival rations. Key considerations when deciding to grow your own will include soil type, what to grow, having the right tools and learning how to deal with any pests or plant diseases but the rewards can be significant. Many people find gardening a most relaxing hobby and there is no doubt that it could provide a diverting pastime to keep members of the family occupied, particularly if you are besieged by zombies.

Storing any large volume of dried or fresh food will need a management plan to ensure items are correctly rotated, labelled and that stocks are maintained. Storage, which can be a problem in most homes, should be carefully considered as most of these foods require dry and cool locations. With this in mind, places such as under the stairs or cupboards may be good options whilst lofts which tend to get very warm are less suitable. Any management plan must include a regular review of your stocks. Spoilt food, either by poor storage conditions or even rodents, could spell disaster for your survival plans.

It is also worth noting that a serious shock to the body system of a radical change in diet can produce uncomfortable and debilitating side effects. Although it is not going to be a popular activity, it is recommended you and your survival team go through a 'practice' weekend at least annually and preferably every quarter. This could with some effort and imagination be turned into an adventure weekend and would involve surviving on minimum rations, not using electricity and not washing. The objective is to help the whole group familiarise itself, even if only for a while, and the significant challenges you will presented with once under the siege of the grey and hungry ghouls.

Other Items

This broad category includes everything from survival favourites such as soap and matches to invaluable aids such as a wind up radio and 'luxuries' such as toilet paper and shampoo. The principle is that you should plan to survive as you want to live. Whilst it is true there will be far less time for luxury and factors such as a the loss of any central heating may hit your party particularly hard, the little extras you plan for now could make a challenging situation bearable.

Any "other" items list could become endless but key areas to consider include:-

- Tools and supplies (spare tools, DIY supplies, plenty of matches)
- Sanitation (toilet paper, towelettes - a life saver if water for washing is scarce, bars of soap, garbage bags)
- Clothing and bedding (extra blankets, a decent sleeping bag, plenty of hats and gloves)
- Children's items (formula, nappies, any medication, etc)
- Entertainment (a supply of games, books, playing cards, etc)

Some areas such as medical prescriptions deserve particular attention and will almost certainly require a visit to your local GP. Your supply of any life-saving drugs will be uncertain in zombie Britain and where possible a good supply must be stored well before the crisis. Although often not as urgent, the same rule could apply to prescription glasses, artificial limbs, wheelchairs, walking aids. All of these items will be challenging to obtain so you need to think through carefully your parties needs and plan accordingly. Survival shops can offer a range of 'emergency' first aid kits. Remember, it doesn't need to be in a fancy box or fit neatly into a tin, make a list and collect what you need. Also, remember basic first aid skills are as important as having the supplies or drugs themselves. Take advantage of any medical training you can and work to keep your skills updated. Standard work-related health and safety courses will not be sufficient. You may well find yourself dealing with all different ailments even broken limbs. You should at least have a rudimentary knowledge to deal with these kinds of situations. A priority in any healthcare situation should be to ensure no one drinks contaminated water as this is the most likely source of disease. This should be clear to all survivors as you will have limited medications to deal with any serious infections. Completing an analysis of your party's medical needs is always an invaluable exercise and should be used to build a list of essential items.

An important lesson from previous disasters such as hurricanes or storms has been how important it is to deal with any waste or sewage produced. The zombie crisis could see basic services quickly disrupted and poor preparation in this area can not only be uncomfortable but also a health risk. This is particularly the case if you are besieged by ghouls and unable to dump any waste off your fortified site. The first point survival experts make in this area is to ensure you have enough bleach as it is not only excellent at killing any germs and dealing with odours, the bottles can also be used to store any liquid waste if things get really desperate. There are plenty of guidelines about how to create an emergency toilet for example in a covered pail, chemical toilet or even a wild west style sawdust potty, all the way up to getting a specialised company in to fit a permanent emergency toilet in part of your garden. The important point is to ensure none of your food, water or garden is contaminated with sewage so you need to think about this challenge sooner rather than later.

If you take seriously the lessons around preparing your home as a fortress against the living dead, then it is likely you will have already built up a decent selection of tools and supplies. However, it is also worth checking that you have sufficient and spare tools as they will be frequently used as you maintain your home during the zombie crisis. There will always be DIY jobs to do around the fortifications such as strengthening defences as well as the routine tasks of maintaining a home which you now have to do yourself. So, keep a good stock and look to build and add to this as you work through your preparations.

As part of your survival plan, it is important you make a thorough list of items which may in pre-uprising days seem like “extras” but will after the event became vital pieces of kit to support your ongoing battle. Obviously, a small library of essential survival books will be invaluable and will be just as useful once the dead have risen. Choices such as ample supplies of batteries and torch bulbs also scream out as clear choices but less obvious may be items such as good fire extinguishers or spare tin openers, the lack of either could have an out of proportion impact on your survival plans. It is a good idea to create an ‘entertainment box’ where you can store any leisure items such as board games, books or toys to keep any children occupied but also for the rest of the party to use during any downtime. It is also worth keeping additional blankets in the house. As a rule of thumb, take what you currently have and double it to ensure once the heating goes off, you are fully covered.

With limited storage space and finite financial resources, every survival planner must make their own decision on what to stock and in what quantity. Some such as a first aid kit are essential basics, others such as extra weapons depend very much on how ‘active’ you intend to be supporting your fellow living humans against the ghouls. What is certain, time now planning is time well spent and will enable you to concentrate your resources on what will be most important to you and your party. Remember the essentials but also the value of having even just a few luxury items which can make all the difference as you face a sea of besieging ghouls.

Power

For most of us, it is impossible to imagine our homes without being able to rely on constant electricity; indeed, in most of today’s homes electricity or gas power everything from heating and hot water to air conditioning and even can openers. Opinions on how long our power will stay on when the zombies take over has been the subject of great debate amongst survivalists for many years. It is possible that it will go down within days or could last longer – we simply do not know. Whilst some power stations, particularly nuclear ones can work until for weeks unmanned until they automatically shutdown, other parts of the network such as power lines, substations and storage facilities are extremely vulnerable to civil unrest

The safest assumption is our power will fail from day one. It may drag on but plan to be power self-sufficient from the first days of the crisis. The phrase "power self-sufficiency" is becoming far more common as we all become more aware of the impact on the planet and our carbon footprint in general. In this context, it refers to energy you can generate within your compound for a reasonable length of time. However, before getting carried away with alternative energy sources such as wind or solar power, the most important component of the power self-sufficiency equation in a survival scenario is on the demand side. Even in the most optimistic forecasts with your home having its own generators, the roof covered in solar panels and a wind turbine, you and your team will not be able to meet what may be considered your "normal" requirements for energy. We have simply been spoilt for too long with energy. With survival in mind, you should consider the essentials first.

Whilst it is possible and even good practice to at least explore renewable energy sources, the most practical option is probably to purchase your own simple gasoline generator which is a basic engine which produces usable electricity. Portable versions are available and they can be easily set up in a garage or outbuilding with the correct ventilation.

A typical portable generator will produce around three to five kilowatts which should normally be sufficient to keep your party warm in at least one room if combined with a safe open fire. As for fuel, a small diesel generator will take around a gallon of fuel per day but obviously very much depends on what you are using. Best practice is to use any power very sparingly, the priorities being cooking, lighting and heating in that order. Do not assume because you have a generator that your home should be lit up and heated every night; you simply won't have the power. All items in your home will draw on your limited power – some like electric heaters or hotplates are very thirsty taking 1,500 watts or more whilst others such as an energy-efficient light bulb can draw less than 40 watts. The most sensible plan is to get a professional in to install a wiring system and reader panel so you can manage the power usage from your generator. You can then try powering up different utilities to get the right configuration of heat, light and any extras.

If you are organised enough to plan and prepare a decent generator, advertising the fact you are still up and running power wise will attract every roving band of humans as well as the hungry zombies, but cautious usage, particularly around key areas such as controlled lighting, cooking and moderate heating, can greatly improve the quality of life within your home base.

Communication

Within your fortified location communication will not be such a problem but any activity outside your perimeter will require your team to be in regular contact. Most military training places maintaining effective lines of communication as one of the most important factors in a combat situation. At a tactical level, communication will help you to stay ahead of the ghouls and negate their massive numbers.

Establishing a set of agreed hand signals is a good starting point for use when out on patrol or even when you are running silent in the home, you will only need four or five main hand signals to cover most situations. These should include an "All Stop – All Silent" signal to indicate to all members of the party that you have spotted or suspect something. This should be something basic and clear such as a raised clenched fist. This signal should not start a panic – there may be no ghouls or other humans around. It is something members of the party can use quickly to create a silent environment for further observation or listening.

The evidence we currently have is that zombies have a level of hearing less acute than the average human but enough to make any conversation or shouting dangerous in unsecured locations. It is not yet fully understood exactly how zombies hear as many of the delicate parts of the ear lobe do not seem to function in the living dead. The scientific consensus at the moment is that zombies sense noise vibrations rather than hearing any sounds. Of course, they would be unable to process any verbal communication anyway and spoken words most likely sound like a prolonged dirge to them, useful only to highlight the presence of potential food.

Another well-recognised hand signal will be the two fingers held up pointing to the eyes – which generally means 'seen something' – in this case ghouls. The signal may be supplemented by a pointing action to indicate direction. You will need to agree a set of signals with your team but as a rule of thumb; any more than five and people will get confused. Find out what works for you, but keep it simple. There are plenty of guidelines available in military training books.

There will be occasions where something more than hand signals is required. For example, if you send a couple of team members to check on a bug out location or on a mission to forage, then being in long-range communication can be invaluable. It is also possible that team members may become lost, isolated or cut off. In this case, effective communication could save lives.

For functionality and cost, investing in a basic walkie-talkie set-up will be a sound planning decision and one that will deliver significant benefits when the mobile phone and landline telephone network fails. Various disasters from around the developed world have clearly shown in times of crisis, our mobile phone network becomes quickly swamped and overrun with traffic. Do not rely on your mobile phone to keep in contact. As for the landline network, our system simply has too many dependencies to be relied on. More obviously, most phones now need to be plugged into the mains. It's always worth keeping one that doesn't.

Although the walkie-talkie market has some restrictions in the UK in order to protect the bandwidths used by our emergency services, it is still possible to buy a decent set-up including four walkie-talkies for under £300. As with most markets, you get what you pay for and there are options available for less but be sure to select the set-up which meets your anticipated needs. For example, most models can be powered by standard triple A batteries but you will have to ensure this is the case and then stock up on any spares. You should keep a good store of batteries – not forgetting to rotate batteries as you use them to ensure they stay in best condition. Walkie-talkies are graded against standards around areas such as their robustness, resistance to moisture and receiver range. The best solution is to ask for a set-up which compares to the standards required by the military. Most good stockists will understand this.

As with any kit, having the set-up is one thing - a thorough training programme is quite another. Each of your team should know how to maintain and operate a walkie-talkie before the crisis hits. Test your walkie-talkies in the field. Whilst most units will provide you with a maximum operating range of up to two miles, remember, this will be greatly reduced in urban areas. Have a careful look at accessories such as carrying cases or even headsets if you have the funds.

The good news is that advances in technology mean models are now lighter and more robust than ever before and prices are reasonable but do your own research to decide which set-up suits best. For example, there are often discounts available if you are looking to buy additional units.

Communication is one of those areas of survival where the sky is the limit for the set-up you can get, providing you have the money. Although not as fashionable these days, amateur radio and 'CB' is still a popular hobby, particularly in the USA. Whilst the kit can be expensive, this may enable you to search for and stay in touch with survivors miles away, providing they have an equally powerful set-up. If you are not a radio enthusiast, then the best advice is to get a system of walkie-talkies set up then move on to other pressing issues.

Preparing for the Zombie Apocalypse with Disabilities

A country dominated by hordes of ravenous zombies presents some additional challenges to those with disabilities which need to be carefully considered. Whilst there are several excellent reference sites offering guidelines on survival for the disabled during emergency situations, there is scant information around about surviving the ghouls. This section collects some of these guidelines which should be supported by other sources of information on emergency preparedness for those with disabilities.

First things first. Preparation is vital for everyone looking to survive the zombies and whilst everyone will need to consider their specific requirements or preferences, it is recommended that if you have any with disabilities you complete a personalised audit of your own requirements against some of the scenarios presented in this volume. If there are additional members of your party with disabilities, each should complete an individual assessment. The starting point for this exercise is to think about how the emerging chaos of the zombie apocalypse would affect your everyday life in key areas such as any ongoing medical requirements or any personal care equipment which needs either maintenance or power. Whatever your level of disability, assume the lowest level of functionality to guide your planning.

A bespoke audit of your requirements then needs to be added to some of the proposed lists in this book, such as your household supplies or bug out bag where relevant. It is also worth adding some very clear notes to any bug out supplies so if you are dependent on, for example, an oxygen cylinder or insulin, well meaning helpers do not overlook this.

As a rule of thumb, if you have serious mobility problems it is recommended you store at least 180 days of supplies. This may sound excessive and is certainly more costly but this is the best case scenario and builds in more time for you to either develop your own long-term strategy or link up with other survivors.

When reading general survival advice for the disabled, be aware that for some this may be inappropriate in the immediate aftermath of the zombie crisis. For example, one international guide recommends the use of "visual signals" such as white blankets out of the window to attract the attention of potential rescuers. As has been established, attracting the attention of desperate gangs of the living can be just as dangerous as the zombies and may not be the best policy. If you are well-stocked and well-fortified, think very carefully before you advertise yourself to the world.

For weapons, you will need to consider which is most effective to your personal situation. For instance, a good cricket bat stores quite nicely in a wheelchair pocket whilst a longer weapon may be preferable for the blind or partly-sighted as this will enable you to 'sweep' a larger area. One good tip is to consider the special preparations which are needed if you or any member of your party has any verbal impairment. There will be a real danger that panicky people will attack on sight and it is likely the absence of any verbal response will be adequate for them to assume you are one of the recently turned living dead. Best practice here is to either use a clear sign or more practically a whistle to alert other living humans. Remember, people will not necessarily be acting rationally so it may seem excessive now but prove a lifesaver further down the road.

Most disabled people are very familiar with overcoming challenges in daily life which other people take for granted. For example, most disabled drivers will be familiar with the quest to find a service station with 'Service-Call' whilst any wheelchair user will confirm that using the underground network in London requires some serious and careful planning. This means that in some ways people who manage with disabilities, be they blindness, deafness or mobility problems, are used to the level of planning and overcoming obstacles needed to build a really robust survival plan.

The best defensive strategy for anyone looking to survive the ghouls is to establish a trusted network of family, friends or neighbours who can support you through the crisis. This is particularly relevant if you have serious disabilities. There is no doubt the zombies will pose a very real danger in some specific cases, for example, those with poor hearing will be vulnerable as they will be unable hear the low mumble of an approaching ghoul or may not hear the crash as a door is forced open. There will also be the practical challenges such as how to recharge an electric wheelchair and the danger of reduced mobility in general. However, to some degree the threat of the zombie hordes will be a great leveller in our society. Everyone will need to prepare; everyone will need to plan; everyone will have their own requirements. The only difference will be that those with disabilities will need to very carefully consider their own requirements in their planning. As has been mentioned, the skill and patience many disabled people need to function in areas such as transport or holidays abroad, will equip them with these skills already.

The Bug Out System

Whether you are safely behind the fences and walls of your fortified home compound or holed up in another strong point, there is always a chance something will go wrong. The ghouls are tireless and a front door left open, a poorly fitted window or even a looting attack by other humans could leave you stunned as the hungry living dead press on into your fortress. The Bug Out System is an emergency set of procedures designed for this occasion and should be drilled into all members of your team so when or if the ghouls break in or your current location is in real danger, this is the plan B to fall back on.

The three key elements of an effective bug out system are a bug out bag, bug out location and bug out plan. This section will review these elements and it is strongly recommended you incorporate this system into your survival plans as soon as possible.

Bug Out Bag

Most good survival guides will outline the necessity of having an emergency or bug out bag and offer a brief overview of its suggested contents. With the motto of being prepared, this is your one source of essentials should the worst happen during any crisis. So, for example, if your home is overrun quickly in the opening salvoes of the zombie uprising, this is what you would grab as you dash outside to make your escape. If you work a distance from your home, you can keep a version of this bag at your place of work. Equally, there should be an alternative version in the car.

Remember, the prime purpose of this kit is in an emergency. It must be designed to be light, comfortable and unobtrusive. In most cases, a hard-wearing smaller rucksack is ideal. The kit you have in your emergency bag needs to provide for your basic needs for a period of say 24-48 hours. The real objective of this bag is to help you survive until you can make your way back to your home base or another secure location. A frequent mistake is to overfill a bug out bag. Remember, you will not be thankful for those extra woollen socks as the ghouls drag you down under the weight of your over-sized backpack.

There are many lists of contents so here is one suggestion for a standard sized emergency bag but feel free to shop around and mix and match contents. If it is for the car, maybe you have more room, if it is at work or in the office, you may only have a small drawer.

Bug Out Bag – Suggested Contents:

- A small airline blanket
- Protein/geobars/chocolate
- Bottle of water
- Matches
- Mini-first aid kit
- Compass/map
- Good flashlight
- Local town plan or map
- Climber's axe
- Packed waterproofs
- Spare teabags

Any kit must have some form of personal defence element and you need to select what you feel confident and comfortable with. In this case, a small climber's axe has been included as experience has shown that this is the item which is most easily explained away and can be easily stored. The outline includes a few snacks and drinks to help keep your strength up. If you prefer a different food, then as long as it keeps, put in what you want. Some foods such as chocolate and mint cake are well known by climbers and others for the instant energy boost they give you. Overall, remember the objective of this whole pack is to give you the time you need to get back to your home base and the rest of your supplies.

If you are travelling more than say 24 hours from home, it may be worth considering expanding this pack to facilitate the longer journey you may face.

A version may be stored at your workplace and maybe a more significant one in the boot of your car. If you spend a lot of time at any other location, then it may be worth considering leaving an emergency pack there. The principle is that these bags should look very much like a 'change of clothes' rather than a huge army-style pack with knives and water bottles dangling. It is important you generate as little attention as possible with the storage of your packs or come the day of the zombies, you may arrive just in time to see a panicky work colleague disappearing out of the door with your kit.

Consideration should also be given to any maintenance of your emergency packs. A simple schedule of rotating food and water or testing equipment should keep things up to standard. Remember, it is pointless have a system of emergency packs if they are not maintained or tracked.

Whilst it is certainly impossible to cover 100% of the places you may go with emergency pack availability, as with much survival training, by establishing a robust network of emergency bags you are significantly shifting the odds of survival in your favour.

Your emergency bag should equip you with what you need for what could be a long and dangerous journey back to your home. On this journey, even if you are reasonably close to home, you need to consider the scenarios you are likely to face and plan accordingly.

Motorways in the UK are clogged with traffic most of the time and the early days of the zombie apocalypse are likely to write off much of Britain's network. Whilst obviously not getting anywhere will be a frustration, thousands of panicky people and hungry zombies could easily become a nightmare scenario. With breakdowns, fuel problems and the advance of the ghouls, the motorways will not be a place to be.

Equally, many of our other roads will be blocked in the first hours of the chaos as people try to flee the area or get out of the city. Any public transport will quickly fail in this country. If damp leaves on the line can stop our trains, then imagine the impact of a horde of zombies -- the network will be paralysed.

A good assumption is therefore that you will have to rely on foot to get back to your home, with the possible option of cycle or motorbike if you have access. The most likely scenario is that if you are caught at work, grab your emergency bag then start to make your own way back to your base.

Now, this will be no easy journey and you will need certain skills to enable you to navigate your way safely through zombie-infested territory to your home. The SAS in their training focus on the ability to move silently even disappear, in either a street or crowd. Awareness is a big factor, with the need to develop an excellent sense of what is around and a good level of perception of what is going on. Factors such as how you blend in or dress will also play a part. For example, a massive emergency backpack may well draw the interest of an unruly mob, particularly as the unprepared become more desperate for supplies.

Remember, in your encounters with either the living or the dead, your objective is avoidance not combat. You are not equipped to start a one-person war. Helping others is second nature to most of us but in this case you will need to determine quickly whether you are in a position to help. Your party back home may well be relying on you so there may be some tough decisions to make as you make your way to your home base.

With this in mind, you should prepare extensive route maps for your dangerous journey home. You should know your primary route and practise it until you know it like the back of your hand. Then, create alternative routes to try to take into account that some roads may be closed, or to avoid a hospital or church. You may even want to scout out 'bolt-holes' along the route, locations where you know you may be able to hold up for a few hours in necessary. Patience will be as important part of your survival as any piece of kit in your bag.

Bug Out Location

The term 'bug out' location refers to a secondary site which is known by the team and can be used if your current location is overrun. A good bug out location is a vital part of your home defence plans but can also be useful when on the move. If your camp is overrun, just a simple meeting location can save hours of searching and attracting the attention of other ghouls.

It is important to be both practical and realistic when selecting a bug out location. In some cases, it may just be an easy to remember location where you can meet if your party is scattered or overrun. A typical example may be in a small copse of trees familiar to your party. Here, it will be possible to at least lay low until any survivors have been collected. You may want to hide some emergency supplies here and even a few weapons, food and some water if possible. It is a good idea to avoid popular places or well-known locations.

If you are on the move, then bug out locations will need to be agreed at regular intervals and will simply be a practical location to meet if separated. In this scenario, it is important the agreed location is known by all members of your group.

In other cases, a bug out location may be a fully secured alternative to your current location. A good example would be a secure lock up with strong rolling steel doors. A combination lock may be a good option to enable all party members to access the location as required. Within, there could be spare sets of supplies and everything you need to either stay at the site or re-group whilst you search for a more permanent location. This option will obviously take most planning and resources.

As a note of caution on a well-prepared but empty bug out location, the living dead will, as has been pointed out, create chaos on our streets and unoccupied locations will be prone to looting as order breaks down and people become desperate. The more discreet and secure it is, the better the chance you will find it intact when you need it.

Whatever the standard of your main bug out location which may be called the 'alpha site' or something similar, it is vital that possible routes to this site are reviewed and a second and possibly third site identified. The locations should be close enough to be within easy reach of your current site by all party members but at a safe enough distance to enable your party to regroup in safety. Remember, not all of your party will be as mobile so plan for this.

All of your party should be familiar with bug out location information and scouting missions are advisable to ensure they are still viable. Avoid regular patterns such as daily checks as this may lead other survivors and even the ghouls themselves to your carefully prepared spot.

Where your time and resources are limited as you rush to prepare your home to defend against the living dead, simply agreeing a couple of locations is a positive step forward and one which could prevent much heartache if your family or party becomes separated. Remember, the most important point is that you agree at least one location with your team and that everybody understands it.

Your Bug Out Plan

However elaborate your Bug Out Plan, it is essential all your team are well briefed in its details. For example, if you have children, it is vital they clearly understand any bug out locations where you plan to meet. Equally, you will all need to know where bug bags are kept and ensure they are maintained. It is a good policy to rotate any consumables within your pack. Check regularly on torches or any other equipment.

Some zombie survivalists document their bug out plans and then laminate them so they can be given out or fixed around the home. Every member of the team must be able to recall the main parts of the plan and importantly, have a good working knowledge of any agreed bug out locations and routes. Ideally a bug out plan should be completed well before the zombies rise. Keep it simple but it will mean a lot of repetition so you may need to think of innovative ways particularly to keep younger team members interested such as quizzes or games based on the plan.

The essential point is that if your fortress is breached, people's first reaction will be panic. This is when you as leader should clearly take the lead if you feel your location is under real threat. Remember, if you are in doubt, then bug out is the best move – you can always return to your location later on and retake it. Your priority should be to keep yourself and your team alive. Thus, a clear bug out plan is as important to your survival as a good weapon. Do not let it be overlooked.

Bug Out Locations to Avoid

Whilst there will be no truly safe locations, only safer locations once the dead rise, certain places deserve a special mention as sites to be avoided as bug out locations in the opening month of the crisis and possibly longer. If you are caught at one of these sites then your only tactic is to get out quickly and put as many miles as possible between yourself and the developing chaos.

Airports, Docks and Transport Hubs

UK airports and docks handle literally millions of passengers daily. If you have ever witnessed the chaos at Heathrow airport on a bank holiday or with even minor delays, you will understand why these and other transport hubs should be last on your list of possible refuges. It is not hard to picture the desperate crowds trying to reach the last flight out of zombie Britain or the last ferry to safety. It would only take one of the living dead to create a dangerous riot or free-for-all. Indeed, projections have shown the mere fear of the living dead will generate dangerous crowd behaviour and a breakdown in order.

Although there are armed police at all important UK transport sites, these teams are not designed to cope with hundreds, possibly thousands of rioting civilians. It is possible with hysteria at very high levels, riots and unrest could be as easily created by frustrated queues of people as by the living dead. Coach stations, train stations and underground networks will all suffer from the same panic and paralysis as what staff and facilities are available become quickly overrun.

Put your passport away, you are not going anywhere once the chaos breaks and you should consider moving if your house is near one of our major transport hubs.

Hospital and Health Facilities

It is likely in the early stages of a zombie outbreak any "infected" victims will be rushed into our already overcrowded hospitals. Where there is any incident which causes mass fatalities in our major cities, emergency plans are already in place to create extra capacity in these and other centralised locations for dealing with either casualties or the deceased. With no preparation or effective quarantines in place to deal with a zombie outbreak, the living dead will run amok in many of these facilities, helping themselves to the veritable buffet of human meat which used to be the patients and health workers. The thin line of unarmed security will be overrun in the first few hours of the crisis leaving our hard-working hospitals as deadly areas of ghoul concentration rather than sanctuaries in a crisis.

Whilst our central resources will be swamped initially by those infected, then by casualties of the chaos and finally by the unstoppable waves of ghouls, local facilities such as clinics and surgeries will be deserted and most likely looted. Both doctors and nurses will struggle to get into work and will be more concerned with the health and safety of their own families and those around them. In the chaos, it is safe to assume little in the way of emergency or medical help will be available.

Modern medicine is powerless against the Zombic Condition and so you should stay well clear of any healthcare sites which will rapidly become 'no go' zones for any survivors. The living dead will quickly dominate these locations with buildings literally packed with trapped ghouls.

Places of Worship

Just as with airports and hospitals, crowds will flock to places of worship for the support and comfort of their religion in this dire time of need. Those poorly prepared may look to their local church for support and other community groups may meet to face the crisis together in locations such temples, mosques or synagogues. Unfortunately, all of these places will be a virtual death sentence as the infected mix freely with others to create a chaotic and deadly cocktail of the desperate, the hopeless and the very hungry living dead. With the noise and activity, hordes of zombies will be attracted and few will escape alive from these buildings, many of which are old and have limited access.

To make matters worse, many of our religious communities will, with the best intentions, reach out to support those in need including the infected. They will not however be prepared for the violent attacks which will surely follow as the dead rise and start to cause havoc. Some communities with a strong 'pro-life' and human dignity stance may 'encourage' the spread of the zombies by failing to appreciate that those they are helping are no longer human but the living dead. You should also be wary of any 'end of the world' cults who may see the zombies as some sort of punishment on mankind and may even attack any remaining humans to complete a divine plan.

If you have any religious beliefs, your faith will undoubtedly be important in the opening months of the crisis but stock up on any items you need beforehand as once things start turning grey, it will be too late to pop into your local church or temple. There will be testing times ahead.

Farms and Rural Retreats

The rural life with visions of farm animals, plentiful crops and cosy isolated cottages may be a tempting proposition as the rest of the UK falls to the zombie onslaught. However, even presuming you could make it to your rural bug out location, most farms in the UK are hardly isolated and as survivors flock out of the city, these locations will be quickly overrun by the desperate. Following the exodus of the living, will come the living dead, in the shape of hordes of zombies driven out of urban areas by a lack of food.

The biggest danger of a farm or rural retreat as a temporary refuge is that any growing comfort factor of being 'isolated' in this country is purely an illusion as you will frequently be much closer to a population centre than you realise. In most locations, it is only a matter of time before either the living or the dead find you and as a defensible location, most working farms score very low with wide open spaces and spread out buildings. It may be that some geographical locations are preferable to others and the Highlands, south west and north Wales would obviously score better as they are more isolated. But travelling to these sites once the crisis really kicks in will be an almost impossible challenge.

The Zombie Apocalypse Abroad

Some of the guidelines of being caught away from home may also be relevant to anyone travelling abroad such as ensuring you always have access at least to a basic bug out bag. However, finding yourself in a foreign country during a zombie outbreak presents some additional hazards which need to be very carefully assessed. First, whilst seeing the world and travelling abroad is undoubtedly a worthwhile venture to expand your horizons, you must accept that it puts you and your family at serious risk. No matter the country, you will be away from your home base, your stores, weapons and your support network of friends, relatives and neighbours. In the worst case scenario, you could find yourself alone and in a strange place.

As with our other scenarios, research and preparation are again the keys to survival. For example, if you are visiting a city abroad you should at a minimum be familiar with the general layout, have access to a good road plan and be aware of key sites. Preferably a good knowledge of the language is important but where this is not possible, at least knowing the basics in addition to key living dead crisis phrases such as "I'm not a ghoul" or "Don't' shoot, I'm not one of them!".

You should look to extend your preparation into areas such as any additional vaccination requirements for the countries you are visiting. So, if malaria tablets or inoculations are required, ensure you have cover for at least two to three months as you may not be able to resupply. Similarly, water treatment tablets are easy to carry and may be a lifesaver if bottled water is not available.

Before you travel you should be fully briefed on any specific information or particular travel warnings. In a low-level crisis of any sort, it is advisable in many parts of the world to carry a supply of small denomination dollar bills. This may prove useful in procuring any supplies which are around. Of particular relevance to a zombie outbreak are any societal sensibilities about the treatment of the dead. For example, some cultures have strict religious guidelines on the treatment of bodies which may still apply even when the aforementioned corpses are walking around feasting on the living. A cautious and prudent approach is advised. Even though your natural instinct may be to lay into a downed ghoul with the chair leg you found in the café, be aware of what the locals are doing. How they are reacting or behaving is usually a good guide.

Some travel guides advise a dash for the embassy or consulate as soon as the crisis develops and if you are close by this may be something worth exploring. But, be prepared for the crowds; it may be that these guarded sites quickly become swamped. Most embassies have become veritable fortresses in recent years due to the threat of terrorism so are normally strong defensive locations. They will also be the focus of any evacuation plan so may be worth the risk. Be aware you will need your passport to be sure of entry; it won't be enough to claim the nationality so keep it safe and keep a copy.

When caught in a zombie crisis abroad and where you are unable to make it the embassy or another secure location, you should avoid the natural temptation to want to flee the country as soon as possible. In most countries including our own, the transport network and hubs such as airports or docks will be in meltdown as people try to flee the region. This will make these locations tough to reach in the best case and in the worst case some of the most dangerous places as panicky crowds combine with growing numbers of ghouls.

The key strategy for surviving if caught abroad is about finding a location where you can defend yourself for the first few days to give yourself some time to plan your next move. If may be possible to link up with zombie survivalists in the city or to prearrange a safe house but in most cases you are more likely to find yourself in a hotel room or guest house. It's far from ideal and with a limited bug out bag you will probably only have supplies for a day or so. As a piece of general advice, it is a good policy to try to work closely with any survivor groups. For example, if your hotel management starts to pull together and works to fortify their location, join them. Even if you can't speak the language, use your knowledge and skills to add to the group. Being a trusted and valued member of any local network will greatly increase your chances of survival. It means taking some risk but it also means you will be able to tap into local knowledge. It is important you do not become an irrelevant mouth to feed by just barricading yourself in your hotel room. In some cases, you will need to venture out to link up with others.

Under Siege

Whether you are barricading in your new Barratt home or have taken up refuge in a former castle residence behind 15-foot thick walls, bearing in mind the number of zombies, there will undoubtedly be a time when you become besieged by the living dead. Realistically speaking, this is likely to be a few weeks into the crisis, when the ghouls are in the ascendancy and have run rampant across the country devouring any humans unfortunate enough to the caught. Once the easy prey is consumed, the hungry living dead will turn their attention to the remaining living in their fortified dwellings. For some, this struggle will be worse than the initial chaos of the zombie uprising. The long hours and days of waiting, the constant threat of a breach and the unnerving moan of the living dead will defeat more humans than being physically overrun.

A working definition for being "under siege" is that you cannot easily clear away the ghouls from your immediate area – their numbers are just too great. In the worst case scenario, you and your team of survivors may be facing hundreds, even thousands of hungry zombies, relentlessly moving against your outer perimeter. The impact on your little community will be significant and if unchecked, feelings of hopelessness and an atmosphere of despair will become as dangerous as the shuffling, grey masses outside.

Opinion is divided on the crucial issue of how quickly ghouls will 'realise' that a home is occupied, how easily one dribbling ghoul will attract others and how long they will maintain their 'siege'. What is known is zombies have a keen sense of smell and an overwhelming urge to find fresh meat. They are also remorseless and patient, often giving off a desperate and sometimes sad vibe. But do not be misled, they are meat-eaters without morale and are driven by an overriding objective to feed on you and your family.

It is therefore unlikely they will be distracted away from a potential meal unless by a more attractive human alternative. This may be an opportunity to use a member of your party to lure away any surrounding zombies, a dangerous but sometimes necessary tactic which will be discussed later.

So, if your fortress has caught the attention of wandering ghouls, which in turn attracts other ghouls and you find your home fortress under siege, there are some key practical steps you need to take but also some important decisions to be made with your group.

First, you should of course check your perimeter defences regularly, assess any weak points and set up a thorough and routine system of checks. When under siege, you will also have the time to work on and strengthen your defences. This is an ongoing process. Fences may be fortified; fall back positions agreed and even additional building work on defences if you have the resources. Your fortress should be a hive of activity and there should always be work to do.

Next on your list should be to take an updated inventory of your supplies with water being the main priority. Getting a clear picture of your supplies will be crucial in deciding your next move and in managing morale within the team. Rationing will already be in place but may need to be more draconian. It very much depends on how easily you can access other buildings or sources of water and food. Remember, under siege may mean you are cut off from any external sources of supply, and any foraging will be significantly reduced. Whilst many of the older generation may remember the strict rationing of the 1950s, for most of us not being able to eat what we want, when we want will be a new thing. The secret is to start managing the food and water from day one. Plan ahead, stick to the agreed plan and always have a picture of where you are with regard to supplies.

Regular briefings with your team should become part of your day. Tasks should be allocated to team members to keep everyone occupied during the long hours of waiting. Idleness will be one of your worst enemies and as a leader you should keep a close eye on your party to watch out for any warning signs. It is important that a strict routine is set and agreed. This will call for military-like discipline with a rota for guard duty through both day and night. No matter how strong your perimeter is, there is always a chance some external factor such as a falling tree or telegraph pole will create an opening for the ghouls. A ground floor guard therefore is recommended providing you have sufficient numbers. If you are restricted then guard duties in four hours stints may be used. Be prepared for the irregular and disrupted sleeping patterns which are such a prominent feature of army basic training. Other important tasks to rota could include monitoring any radio you may have, maintaining a high look out and cataloguing your supplies. Where possible, try to keep to regular meal times and no matter how humble the meal may be, try to turn dinner times into a regular social event.

As a leader, your goal in the short-term should be to "normalise" the feelings of the party as soon as possible. This is where training and preparation pay off. Whilst members of the team may have got over the initial panic of the zombie uprising, keep a careful eye out for the longer term impact of post-zombie stress disorder which can see survivors becoming insular, angry and depressed. Sometimes this is just a delayed response from the realisation that the old world has very much passed and that the new world looks bleaker, harder and with more menacing ghouls. In situations of considerable stress such as a zombie siege, it is vital you display your leadership qualities at all times. The tireless ghouls at the window and their incessant moaning will have a sapping effect on your team's morale and you need to counter it with a Churchillian style of leadership, based on a 100% belief you can and will survive. Many sieges will break through morale collapse rather than zombies overrunning the defences.

Effective communication with team members will be important and do not be afraid to arrange diverting activities such as a quiz evening. What better way to face the zombie apocalypse than with a challenging game of Scrabble or a fiendish pub quiz. You can always go to a high point, looking out over the sea of grey zombies and play who can spot the funniest ghoul competition. If you have the power and a DVD player, then a regular movie night can provide a priceless escape from the suffocating effects of a zombie siege.

There are various scenarios you should consider as to how the siege will progress. One is that you and your team maintain quiet discipline; the ghouls either lose interest or more likely are drawn to something else and slowly drift away from your refuge. There is little research available to help assess the persistence of zombies or how quickly they could move off in their search for fresh meat. As a relentless opponent they are likely to maintain their siege but it is always possible some other unlucky humans will lure them away.

Therefore, you must also face the possibility that the ghouls will maintain their vigil and their teeming numbers will simply multiply as their moans attract other zombies. Special attention should be paid to any fencing in this scenario as their pushing weight of numbers will greatly increase the pressure on any external fencing and it is these areas that are most likely to give away and allow the living dead to come flooding in.

On the face of it, there would seem to be two main options when under siege by the living dead.

(1) Sweat it out and wait for the zombies to either move on, collapse or for help to come (providing your supplies last)
(2) Break out of the siege, bashing your way to clear the living dead – in history this would be called a 'sally'

However, the situation in reality is far more complex involving a careful and pragmatic assessment of your resources and offers a broad range of options which will help you to create a more 'proactive defence'. In medieval times, armies under siege would rarely sit back allowing their attackers to plan and develop their attacks in peace. There would be constant sallies, spoiling attacks and raids not always with the objective of a break out but often just to disrupt and reduce the attacking force.

Of course, any proactive action will not affect the morale of your enemy and they have no 'organised' plans other than to have you and your party as their next meat snack. But, carefully planned 'culling missions' over a period of time may well start to reduce the numbers of living dead to a manageable volume. Ideally, these raids should come from an unexpected direction, with your 'fighters' coming from a second exit where possible.

A typical culling raid would involve a team of at least three bursting out with their weapons and bashing as many zombies as possible. Obviously much will depend on your situation and besieging numbers but a good cull is quick and hard hitting. Before the ghouls get a chance to respond, your team should be safely back behind the perimeter wall.

Culling raids may on certain occasions be possible from a safe distance if you have a good ranged weapon. An alternative solution if you have the supplies is a game of zombie brick toss which involves swinging a brick high into the air by either hand or a sling and allowing it to plunge to earth hopefully taking out a zombie head en route. Providing you are not taking down an important wall, the zombie brick toss game can be an amusing and diverting pastime whilst under siege. Various formats of the game can be developed including a 'snooker' version where zombies wearing particular colours are worth different points, or maybe to select a target ghoul and all go for that. Do not underestimate the de-stressing impact of this amusing and diverting form of cull.

The value of any culling raid is closely related to the numbers you have surrounding your fortresses. Where we are talking about thousands, a simple cull of 20 or so ghouls will hardly affect the siege, although it may improve morale. But where we are talking about zombies in the hundreds, in stable numbers, a set of culling raids over time can greatly reduce the overall numbers and make a full-scale breakout easier.

As a final word on culling missions, it is worth remembering that these are dangerous missions, and an experienced culler will take as few risks as possible. The primary objective is survival so careful planning is a prerequisite and be prepared if conditions are inappropriate to drop any plans if it is deemed too dangerous. Weapons will be considered later on but those doing the culling will need excellent bashing or slashing weapons. Teamwork is also a vital component. Lone fighters, no matter how good they are, are often overwhelmed by sheer numbers of ghouls. Watch each other's backs and always keep an eye on your escape route. If the team is cut off from your home base do not be afraid to find a short-term location to rest and recover your strength. Zombies kill mostly when their prey tires so stay sharp and alert at all times. It is important to remember that whilst a sweep around your fortified home may help make you feel less besieged, equally it may just attract more zombies. What it won't do is 'teach the ghouls a lesson' or damage their morale but it is one sure way to get yourself on the menu if you slip up.

The logical progression from a culling raid is a full-scale breakout by your party. This is a major operation which should not be undertaken lightly. In some circumstances, however, such as supplies running low or even a perimeter which you know will not hold, a breakout may be your only option. This area will be explored in greater detail further on but for now it is worth considering the significant level of organisation and planning to move a party safely through a zombie-infested area before you even burst through the ghouls circling your home. Culls may have reduced their numbers but equally, your party may consist of elderly members and small children.

Defending Against Horde Attacks

There will be a time in your ongoing battle for survival against the ghouls when you and your party will be caught outside of your fortified base and face a so-called 'horde attack'. This is a documented phenomena when a trigger event such as a noise from your group, provokes a reaction from formerly sedate or dormant ghouls. It may start with a single zombie but then spirals rapidly as ghouls teem from every doorway. There is no numerical measure of a zombie horde; it is typically when ghouls 'attack' in greatly superior numbers, almost giving an impression of coordinated strategy. If you are solo, then four or five attackers can seem like a horde.

So, at some point most likely whilst you are foraging for supplies or moving as a group, you will face this frightening experience and need to be prepared.

First, you should do as much as possible to avoid entering 'horde friendly' locations. For example, narrow corridors with few exits and poorly scouted surroundings are a recipe for disaster as zombies may easily surround your group and even in relatively small numbers overwhelm you. Effective scouting and developing a 'sixth sense' for dangerous locations are two key areas to prevent this kind of attack. Where you are unsure of a building or get a 'feeling' a location is not right, listen to it and move on. Rather than something mystical, this feeling is probably just your subconscious telling you it has picked up far too many blind corners or simply doesn't know enough about the location to have any confidence. This is where real life differs from the movies. To be a long-term survivor, caution and knowing when to step away are as important as when to escape from a location just in time with some invaluable supplies. Always remember the vital word is survival.

A second key to defending against a horde attack is team organisation. Whilst it may be possible for a single human defender to skulk away from an attack or move quickly to escape it, for a group, this will be more complex. For example, if one or two break away, the remaining may just cave in under the weight of ghouls. You and your team must have some agreed protocols for dealing with this situation which should form flexible operating guidelines enabling the team to respond to different challenges. Some guidelines are common sense such as always carrying a hand weapon and never overloading yourself. Others such as always listening to the orders of a team leader require training and practice to avoid parties scattering under the first wave of zombies. It should also now be clear that any group will need good leadership to issue clear directives when attacked.

Third, you should have a sound tactical understanding of horde behaviour and team strategies for defending an attack. For example, zombie hordes will generally head directly towards live humans and not attempt flanking manoeuvres. However, it could be that additional ghouls, new to the horde, join from different directions and thus your first key leadership decision will be securing a line of retreat. It is important to grasp that whilst your group may be able to defend any one particular attack, in some dangerous cases, hordes will simply continue to grow as noise attracts new ghouls to the desperate struggle. Do not underestimate the overwhelming desire that zombies have to eat you. This will drive them to any potential meat feast with the strength and ferocity of the desperate. Logically, you will not be able to win by bashing down every zombie. Their numbers will be too great and after time you will be weakened by fatigue swamped by sheer numbers.

Your first impulse when faced with a zombie horde should therefore be to identify a line of retreat and fall back in good order but as any military textbook will inform you, a fighting retreat is considered to be one of the most difficult manoeuvres to complete. The good news is that this is not the army and you will not be pulling any large artillery pieces. Any foraged supplies should be quickly dropped and items such as filing cabinets, desks or trolleys can be easily used to block the horde's advance. With no great level of intelligence, a horde will keep on going and may even wedge itself against an obstacle as the first line of ghouls falls and the second batch trips over the first. One tip may be to carry a pocketful of marbles or steel balls which can be quickly dropped in the path of any oncoming ghouls causing them to slip and trip all over the place, again causing chaos for the zombies behind and buying you crucial time to escape.

One strategy to defend against a horde is to use a line of retreat to find any kind of secure location. In an ideal scenario, you and your team should put as much distance as it can between it and any zombie concentration but this may not always be possible. For example, where you are battling in a larger building, you may be faced with by a warren of poorly-lit corridors so unless you know the layout very well, you could easily run your team into a dead end, literally. Getting you and your team to a safe location will give you all time to recover, regroup and most importantly, plan your next move. A typical 'safe location' would be one you can seal off, possibly with a solid door or blocked stairs. Even dashing into an office and wedging the door shut will hold the ghouls off for a time. As was noted previously, zombies are extremely persistent and patient and if not clawing at the door, will most likely wait indefinitely outside your refuge so sitting them out is not going to be an option. Also, there is always the risk that you run your team into a room with no exits or windows – moving at such speed it is unlikely you will have had time to assess your temporary bug out location. However, on balance, getting this crucial breathing space away from the horde's relentless attack will give you the time you need to take that crucial next step and there are few rooms which cannot provide a second escape route, even if you need to go through the roof and break into an adjacent room. Dropping down a floor is a tried and tested method for escaping ghouls as you can first make a small survey hole, check the floor below, then facilitate your team's escape.

Where you and your team are forced to fight a horde or are in combat as you retreat, you should decide your best team set-up to cope with this pressure. Typically, this will involve putting your 'biggest hitters' as the rearguard, with longer weapons such as halberds and swinging actions to keep the ghouls back. These members need to be strong, confident and disciplined to prevent panic which will see the whole group overrun. In general, the team should stick together with you roughly in the centre to maintain discipline and direct the group. A scout may detach from the team to seek potential exits or safe locations.

No book can ever prepare you to face the terror of a horde attack by ghouls but the guidelines in this section will hopefully provide an insight into how hordes behave and some of the tried and tested ways of defending against them. In general, you should try to get away as soon as possible and avoid a slugging match in which zombies will use their sheer numbers to overrun you and your team. If are alone, you can move quickly and silently to avoid the horde. In a team, you will need to work together to escape.

Flying Solo

Whilst many of the recommendations discussed assume a group of survivors, typically family members or friends, it is equally possible you may find yourself alone during the zombie uprising either by misfortune or design. Whatever your motivation or story, the challenge of surviving or being besieged as a solitary defender are substantial. Physically, the basic challenge of maintaining your defences and keeping yourself fed and watered will be tiring. Furthermore, countless studies of those in isolation frequently highlight how quickly solitary individuals can lose their sense of perspective and become despondent and even depressed when cut off from human contact. There is a danger that during long periods of isolation, survivors can start to see or perceive things that are not there. For instance, the solitary defender may start to see the same zombie waiting or start to imagine ambushes and plans. Remember, the ghouls do not have a strategy or plan but the mind can easily play tricks on those left alone.

The real danger of being on your own is what will happen if you are injured or become ill during the zombie crisis. With no one else to shoulder the burden of checking the perimeter or supporting you with food and water, you could find yourself in real trouble. Any foraging missions will also be more dangerous when alone and you will be unable to defend your home fortifications whilst you are away. However, there are also some advantages to facing the ghouls by yourself. You alone can manage your supplies and monitor what is left so it will be easier to ration what you have and stick to it.

Science fiction and survival films across the decades have explored the theme of surviving alone and some of the best of these are recommended in the further reading section of this book but for now the old adage of 'keeping busy' is not a bad place to start and a solid work rota is even more important when surviving alone. As the electricity fails and without others to guide you, it will be very easy to lose track of more normal life patterns without a rigid routine and relaxing pastimes are strongly recommended even if it just something like growing and keeping a small herb garden. Any distraction is essential to keep the moans and groans of the living dead from driving you into their hungry arms.

Ghoul Shock and the Moan Effect

One factor which is virtually impossible to prepare for but can have a massive impact on those who come face to face with the living dead for the first time is a phenomenon known as "Ghoul Shock".

Horror films depicting pale blue human-like ghouls or hours of reading undead fiction novels cannot prepare you for the real horrors you will face in the zombie apocalypse. This could include badly decomposed zombies, ghouls with missing body parts even disconcerting but equally dangerous 'kiddy ghouls'. The sights, sounds and smells of the living dead are both terrifying and shocking.

Ghoul Shock is a mental phenomenon with physical effects which can be disastrous. Sufferers, when faced with their first ghoul or a particularly harrowing specimen, simply freeze on the spot, failing to respond to either the cries of their team or the inherent danger of being near a zombie. Essentially a kind of short-term shock, the primary cause is the sheer horror or even ghoulish fascination with a particular zombie. Think how passers-by often just stare blankly at a car crash, knowing it is disgusting but unable to look away. Nothing can prepare you for this – maybe only knowing it will happen can enable you to make some plans for it.

In contrast to the suddenness of Ghoul Shock, your team's morale may be affected by the constant low decibel moan of the living dead which can have a disastrous impact on a besieged team's morale, particularly at night when sound travels further or much of the team is sleeping or inactive. This phenomenon is known as the Moan Effect and begins to affect people after days or weeks of exposure. If you have the batteries, low-level music may be an option, depending on your tastes. For example, endless hours of Phil Collins's greatest hits may lead you or your team mates to voluntarily walk into the hungry hordes of the living dead. The zombie apocalypse is no excuse for poor taste so ensure you have a good selection of music. Ear plugs are a more cost-effective and efficient alternative and could end being the best £1 you spend for your survival kit.

Awareness of the kind of stress you and your group of survivors will be under will help you prepare where possible and you should always be alert to the potential impact of ghoul shock or the Moan Effect on other members of your team. As with many areas of survival, knowledge and awareness are the best tools you have.

Getting the Survivor Mentality

As countless survival guides will tell you, the most important weapon in the struggle to survive is the mind. One only has to refer to some of the true survival stories listed at the end of this volume to appreciate the sheer determination to survive and even prosper is at the heart of the struggle. This may be battling disease, climbing a mountain, surviving in a hostile location or battling the living dead; the mental challenge is the same.

The menace of the groaning dead and the pressure of living through the zombie apocalypse will be one of the greatest mental and physical challenges you will ever face. The SAS instil what they call the "attitude to survive" in much of their training. This is the mental fortitude and approach to drive for life no matter how many moaning ghouls face you.

Studies of survivors from various natural and manmade disasters have pointed to a common strength in that most people who do survive seem to have a fierce internal drive to see the crisis through, regardless of discomfort. This inner strength is often linked to a clear objective which is almost programmed into the individual, such as a strong desire to be reunited with family or be proven innocent. In this case, your objective is for you and your family or party to survive the hungry ghouls and not become easy meat snacks for the zombie hordes.

The shock of witnessing this breakdown of civilised society will have a massive impact on you if you are not prepared sufficiently to face it. Whilst you can never insulate yourself 100% against this, knowledge, training and awareness can help you and your family to survive what will be a turbulent and dangerous time.

It is also important you consider the reaction of others to the crisis. One only has to look at the understandable but sometimes hysterical reaction to catastrophic world events to understand that extreme circumstances lead to extreme reactions. In some cases, power blackouts for short periods have led to wide scale rioting and looting.

The masses of the living dead turning up will make recent manmade or natural disasters look like a picnic in Hyde Park. Hysteria will quickly take hold of our local communities as the hungry zombies plough into panicky masses of unprepared and confused people.

It is important to develop mental and physical skills you will need as soon as possible and there are varied options to achieve this. The Territorial Army, for example, provide a wealth of training across key areas such as field craft, survival skills and basic infantry tactics. It also supports fitness training.

Skills such as camping, hiking and sailing could all make a difference so any adventure holidays are also an excellent place to start. Equally, one zombie survivalist planner regularly has 'no electricity' weeks within his household in an attempt to familiarise himself and his family with living in a modern home without many modern comforts. In fact, any survival training will greatly support your efforts and reduce the culture shock of living in Zombie Britain.

The foundation to personal survival and therefore your ability to protect your family from the hungry dead is your level of physical fitness. This includes your health in general as well as any strength or endurance training you are doing. It is vital you start to develop a disciplined regime as soon as possible and that you continue to develop this plan to ensure things are kept both fresh and challenging. Walking is an excellent starter to any programme and a regular and sustainable regime of fitness is recommended for all of your family. Many a survivor's battle against the living dead will begin with an introductory session at their local gym or fitness club.

The grim assessment of the previous chapter on the UK authorities' response to the living dead uprising could easily lead Britons into pits of despair. One may almost feel like giving up, settling down with endless takeaways and whiling away the time with US chat shows until the ghouls show up. However, as discussed, with the right attitude and prompt action, you can drastically increase the chances of you and your family surviving the zombie challenge. You have already made your first step by picking up this book. Maybe you have reviewed some of the excellent sources of information on the internet. The important thing is you have now taken some action towards preparing yourself for the challenges ahead.

As with your current reading, your first set of actions will be around information gathering and soaking up knowledge about the threat you are facing. There are some excellent survival and emergency preparedness guides on the market, some of which are referenced in the summary to this volume. You will find less reputable published material on the zombie angle into survival. An unwillingness to face a sceptical media has undoubtedly put off many skilled and knowledgeable individuals from submitting their ideas for survival over the blueprint of a zombie uprising. However, the positive news is much of the information in the disaster survival books which are available is of value to those planning for the zombie apocalypse. Important lessons on food storage, water provision and surviving without electricity are all invaluable.

The skill of the zombie survivalist is to soak up these ideas from various sources but always to have in mind the unique challenges of battling the living dead. No regular survival book will prepare you for this.

The survivor mentality is therefore a combination of your underlying objectives, your mental and physical fitness and your preparations. You will need to consider carefully each of these before facing the challenge of the moaning ghouls.

Personal Defence

The traditional guidance is that in personal defence against the living dead, you can't go far wrong when taking on a zombie by delivering an effective blow to the head. And, to some extent this is the case. Essentially, serious damage to the brain is the only way to stop the living dead but it should be remembered that even with a partly-caved in head, tests shown that the living dead can continue to function with half a brain smashed in.

Living in a zombie world requires you to apply the principle of 'personal space' to new extremes. Zombies may be slow and lumbering but this concept can help you manage risks. Always think about maintaining distance from any zombie even if you are moving at some speed. The distance a ghoul can reach out is known as the 'bite zone' or 'snack radius'. Never give the living dead the chance to get close enough for a lunge or grab. Complacency will be your biggest enemy and zombies are quite capable of surprising the unsuspecting with a relatively quickly lunge. Be aware that any scratch or wound could transfer if not the virus itself, then certainly bacteria which could lead to serious blood poisoning.

The important principle in any combat is to understand your enemy and their strengths and weaknesses. Your opponent may be a shuffling and uncoordinated shambler but equally they will not suffer any loss of morale. They are single minded and focused on making you their next snack. Remember zombies do not have supernatural powers and they are not immortal. They do not have a grand plan other than to feast on you and your family.

Hand to Hand Combat with the Living Dead

Weapons will be considered later and few things will be as important as a good hand weapon but there may be times when you face a ghoul without a weapon and are forced to resort to unarmed combat. Most zombie experts warn strongly against unarmed combat with ghouls and it is to be avoided if at all possible but in some desperate cases you may have no other option,

Whilst several experts have hinted at a secret Chinese martial arts designed for combat against the living dead, there is no 'formal' method of combat against zombies. Many martial arts and other forms of combat rely on pressure points or disabling your enemy, both of which are useless against ghouls. It is just as likely that whilst you are delivering your carefully planned Jackie Chan move, any ghoul only has to reach and make a single bite to do you fatal damage. Any lock or close combat is therefore fraught with danger and risk.

When faced with the unarmed combat with the living dead, your guiding principle should be to look for the first opportunity to make a break for it. Your aim should be to create an opening for you and your party to exit from the situation. This will most likely include a well placed kick to unbalance your living dead opponent or a quick blow to knock them down.

It goes without saying that any object to hand may help you achieve this knock down, be it a lamp stand, piece of wood or even a frying pan. Knock or push the ghoul down and then run.

Martial arts training on how to place kicks or throws can be useful but most grappling and self-defence training which often relies on close combat or hitting key pressure points will be less useful. For example, kneeing a zombie in the groin will do nothing to stop it lunging in to take out a chunk of your flesh. Your best tactic is to knock down or unbalance any zombie quickly then make your escape. Don't stick around to finish them off.

Unarmed combat is always the last resort and any training, along with your fitness programme will certainly improve your personal confidence. Whichever form of combat training you choose, it is vital to consider the unique challenges you will face when battling ghouls, factors such as your enemies' lack of human weak spots and their propensity to reach out and either claw or bite down on any piece of flesh available. The melee weapons discussed later will become your priceless accessory in zombie Britain but you need to prepare for the chance you may face a ghoul or ghouls without your trusty cricket bat or crowbar.

Clothing

This issue may be long down your 'to do' list but as the crisis kicks in, once again some basic preparation will pay big dividends to survivors. You don't need to be a brain surgeon to realise loose and floppy clothing isn't going to be in vogue in a Britain overrun with zombies. Ghouls are grabbers by nature and although they lack any dexterity with their hands, they will always reach out trying to grab an easy human meat snack. With any loose clothing, they could easily entangle their rotting limbs or broken nails on a sleeve. This delay could be fatal as you tug to break free and are set upon by more hungry ghouls. Killed by a baggy M&S jumper you got for Christmas is never a nice way to end it all.

Clothing should therefore be tight fitting, hardy and reasonably tough. Some fabrics such as denim, although unlikely to prevent the penetration of jagged ghoul teeth, will provide some protection.

It is important clothing does not in any way restrict movement which along with higher intelligence, is your main advantage over the ghouls. For example, motorcycle leathers, provided they allow for good movement, may be a striking and fashionable option for the zombie apocalypse. The well-protected gloves worn by bikers may be an excellent choice provided you can still hold your weapon firmly.

Sensible footwear such as walking boots with steel toecaps are a good idea. These should be comfortable and broken in well in advance. Do not under-estimate the pain and suffering blisters can cause when you are on the move. You will have enough other problems to worry about. As any experienced soldier will tell you, looking after your feet is time well spent in a survival scenario. This not only means the right boots, well broken in, it also means keeping your feet clean, dry and healthy. You should treat any problems as you discover them and get any professional help as soon as it is needed during training.

It would be logical to consider the merits of different kinds of armour as part of your personal anti-ghoul defence and one can easily imagine walking through a crowd of zombies safely encased in the rare 15th century armour you liberated from Norwich Castle. However, extensive field tests of full metal armour have shown the weight of the plates and the energy required to maintain any degree of movement considerably outweighs any defensive benefits.

It requires a massive effort just to walk a short distance even without the need to raise any sort of weapon in combat. In addition, most metal armour is far from complete with many soft joints between the plates. One quickly conjures up the impression of the ghouls pulling you to the ground in your heavy armour and their hungry hands clawing at the various leather seams found in all suits. You would in effect become a canned snack for the zombies.

In addition, at today's prices a quality suit of body armour could run into tens of thousands of pounds and would take months to produce provided you can find a metal worker to complete it. Hardly an effective use of scarce resources which may be better spent on converting the stairs or reinforcing your front door.

Chain mail is a lighter alternative and is made up of small rings of joined metal which form a mesh from which various forms of garments can be produced. Now most popular for historical recreations and made using new materials such as fibre glass, real chain mail clothing is certainly a more viable option than full metal plate.

Any detailed historical research will reveal most 'soldiers' during medieval times were in fact various forms of militia men who could not afford plated or chain mail armour. But they did develop some very practical forms of padded and leather armour known as a Gambeson which is the direct ancestor of modern equivalents such as body armour used by the armed forces and the light anti-stab vests used by most police authorities.

These garments are designed to protect your core and vital organs but will not prevent ghouls from biting or clawing at either arms or legs which are often most exposed to their attacks.

To reiterate, when considering any form of body armour it is important to appreciate the impact any additional weight will have on your speed and agility. These are two of your key advantages over zombies so think very carefully before you compromise them for what you may see as extra protection.

You need to think wider to stock your survival wardrobe so as to include 'safety' wear such as gloves, face masks and goggles. Whilst direct combat with ghouls should always be avoided where possible, those experienced in combat against the living dead have strongly warned about the amount of 'splatter' involved as you hack your way through the zombies.

Although there have been no documented cases of transmission by splatter, no-one wants to be the first and in addition, some debris is filled with bacteria your body could better live without.

Your principles should be protection first – so certainly safety goggles, good gloves and a mask to cover your nose and mouth should now be considered essential wear.

Some ideas have been floating around the zombie community about the option of completely masking the human scent through some form of body suit and whether this would put off the ghouls. No firm conclusions have yet been reached on whether this is a viable option or not.

The Fernandez Experiments

In December 1979, the controversial Brazilian scientist Dr Juan Fernandez conducted a series of studies at a Brazilian Army training site deep within the Amazon basin. Based on documents later leaked to the press, it would appear Dr Fernandez was experimenting with personal defences against the living dead. Some sources have suggested this work was either directed or funded by the CIA but this has never been confirmed. From his work, Dr Fernandez produced a lengthy study, of which only several pages have made their way into the public domain. The Brazilian Army apparently supplied up to 10 ghouls on which Dr Fernandez carried out a set of experiments primarily to determine whether it was human 'scent' which drove zombies to attack and if an experimental anti-zombie suit would be effective. Observers have since noted that the science to manufacture this full body suit could only have been produced in the US as it was made of a particular advanced manmade fibre called Micranax.

From the results which were leaked, it seems volunteers from the army were put near ghouls to determine whether their drive to feast on the living is by observing a live human or whether there is some other form of chemical stimuli or scent. Without the suit and separated by a mesh fence, the ghouls displayed their natural response to the human presence lumbering towards the barrier, salivating and in a frenzy to get at the meat. Dr Fernandez noticed the ghouls in the control group seemed to 'smell' the human. Interestingly, in other trials, the zombies demonstrated they possessed a sense of hearing but at a reduced level in comparison to a live human.

When a volunteer repeated the process but this time encased in the Micranax suit, the set of ghouls repeated exactly the same behaviour. From their starting position in a huddled mass and staring blankly in the same direction, one ghoul seemed to notice or 'clock' the movement and the same feeding frenzy behaviour occurred

These trials were repeated over a couple of weeks with similar results. Other interesting experiments were also completed, testing zombie reactions to other meat sources such as cow and pig. Unfortunately for the zombie survivor community, no details of these experiments and their results have surfaced or been released.

So little scientific research has been completed in zombiology and the results we have are far from conclusive but seem to indicate ghouls hunt by both sight and smell. Dr Fernandez concluded that whilst there were variations in the abilities of the living dead which were reflected in some cases by the state of the corpse, in general zombies have human-level visual abilities, an inferior auditory capacity and a slightly superior sense of smell. Beyond this the study is inconclusive.

In terms of personal defence against the living dead, Dr Fernandez highlights the fact you must take nothing for granted when combating the living dead. It is feasible they could catch the 'scent' of live humans. Equally, if they see movement and the 'pattern' indicates live meat in their limited brains, they will come.

Weapons

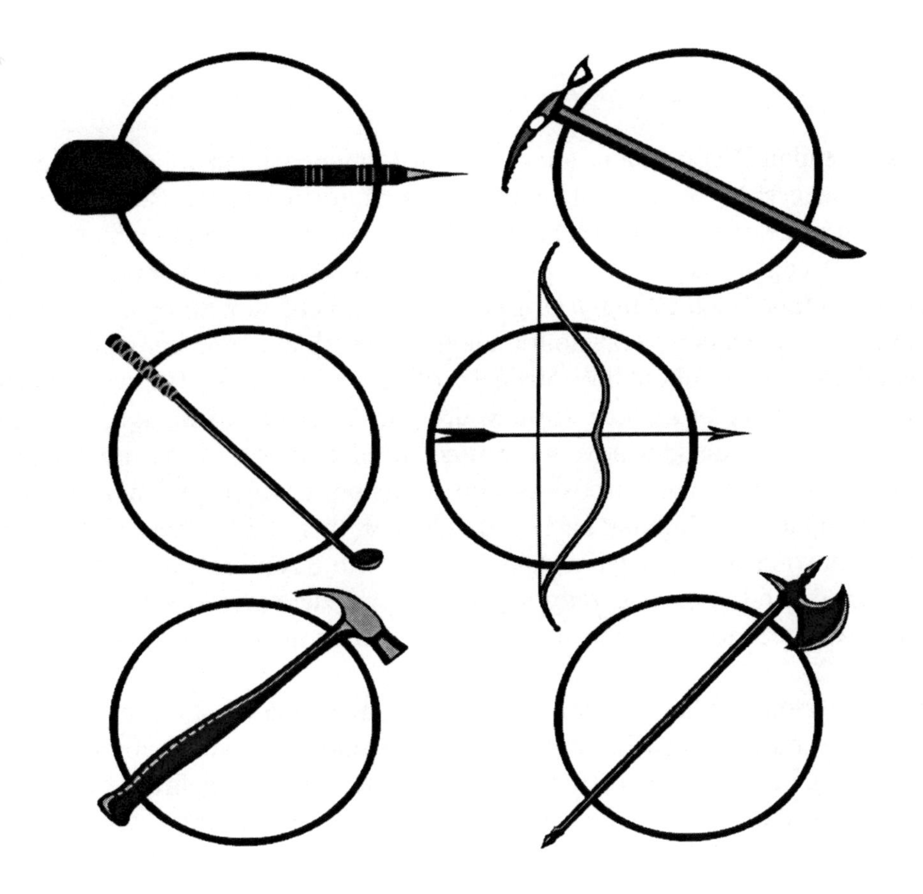

This section will examine the various choices you can use to defend yourself against the living dead. The focus is on weapons which are available in the broad sense of the word, so, some may need to be ordered on the internet but all are available and legal within the UK. The weapon types examined are divided into personal defence or melee weapons for close combat and ranged weapons for taking out ghouls from a distance. It is not an either or choice and something to think about as you review this information is that every member of your team must be armed with at least one melee weapon so you will need to consider carefully which best suits them. It is good practice to have some ranged weapons within your party but a melee weapon is essential for everyone. You may find additional items which you can use which are not covered here. There are literally thousands of things which could make an effective weapon. This guide should be your starting point, but don't be afraid to innovate and experiment.

Whatever set-up you decide on, it is important you prepare your 'arms' before the ghouls arrive, if you decide on a combination of baseball bats and clubs, then collect what you need and store them safely in a shed or garage. It is a good policy to keep at least one weapon within your home for immediate use.

Melee Weapons

A good melee weapon is your main line of personal defence against the living dead and will become an accessory you should never be without in zombie Britain. A useful definition is that a melee weapon is a handheld non-projectile weapon which can either be sharp or blunt-edged. This should be the everyday handheld weapon you keep on your person at all times, something you may hang on a belt, something close by as you sleep. It should be big enough to take out a ghoul but small and convenient enough to be carried around as you go about the business of surviving. A melee weapon can be anything from a chair leg or kitchen knife to designer sword or battle axe. The range is endless and many have distinct advantages and disadvantages. Some are found lying round most homes, others are purpose-designed weapons which are more difficult to source. Even with the best planning and solid defences, there will come a time when you need to depend on your trusty melee weapon to deal with a zombie attack. As previously discussed, hand to hand combat is only advised to provide a window of opportunity to escape, so you will need to be able to slash, bash or bludgeon your way out of trouble.

Your choice of personal melee weapon is therefore one of the most important decisions you have to make and one that will undoubtedly save your life at some point during your combat with the ghouls. To support your research, the guidance below examines some melee weapons available with a focus on how effective these items will be in battle against the ghouls. Each will be overviewed and assessed against the following criteria on a scale of one to five to help you make a better decision on which weapon is best for you :-

Durability: How robust is the weapon against the living dead, Will it break on first contact? What kind of maintenance is required?
Ease of Use: How practical it is. This weapon will need to be with you at all times, can you easily carry it?
Availability: Is it to be found lying around the house? Can it be easily bought or is it a special order item?

Damage: How effective is this weapon at doing what it needs to do-that is, crushing zombie heads? Will it knock them down in a single blow or will it leave their brains intact enabling them to lurch forward and do you some serious damage?

This will enable us to give each melee weapon a DEAD rating to assist in your decision making. It is worth remembering good preparation and an effective training regime will improve your personal rating on these weapons. For example, whilst the classic sword may not be lying around the house and does require some careful maintenance, it can be ordered by mail and with the right training, you can maintain it in excellent condition. As with many other areas, this information is designed to empower. Remember, there are few bad weapons, they are different and need to be carefully assessed against your own skill level, proficiency, strength and size. It should be noted this list is not exhaustive but has tried to include melee weapons from the most common categories such as things lying around the house ranging from chair legs to cricket bats and the Irish shillelagh or medieval halberd.

Melee Weapons Assessment

Do It Yourself Clubbing Weapon

If the you are unlucky enough to find yourself facing the zombies without a weapon, then you will need to fall back on whatever you can find to serve as a 'make do' clubbing weapon. If you are in a home, table legs are a good choice. If you are outside, any steel or iron bar will have to do. This category also includes spades and other garden implements.

Durability 2: Maybe it will last, maybe it won't – with a makeshift weapon you just never know. The best policy is to plan to use it only as long as you have to until you can fall back on your own prepared melee weapons.
Ease of Use 2: Most people can wield a clubbing weapon but as they are not purpose built, you won't have a proper handle, the weighting may be awkward and you won't have practised with it. Sure it will club a zombie but it won't be the weapon of choice.
Availability 3: If you look around, you can normally find something to use. Tables are a good starting point but are not always easy to take to pieces in a hurry. You might be surprised at how sparse the average office is of potential anti-ghoul clubbing weapons.
Damage 2: You may find something that can do some serious damage but equally may end up facing the ghouls with a small office chair. A good club will always send a ghoul down but the extent of the damage will depend on what you are using.

Any do-it-yourself clubbing weapon is hardly the best way to face the ghouls but it will at least provide you with some protection scoring an emergency **9/20** DEAD rating. Some options such as spades or crowbars will deliver better figures so it does depend on the weapon.

Household Cutlery
As crazy as it sounds, for the unprepared, the kitchen drawer is the first place they will look for weapons with which to fend off the living dead. The typical kitchen will yield a range of options such as forks, kitchen knives, even potato peelers.

Durability 0: Some kitchen cutlery is designed to last but on the dinner table not the battlefield. Most will easily bend and warp. Even kitchen knives will quickly blunt.
Ease of Use 3: No extensive training is needed to handle this weak collection of weapons and they're easy to keep in pockets.
Availability 5: Every home has a kitchen which could yield defensive treasures. There are also usually plenty of options available.
Damage 0: At best a kitchen knife will go straight through the living dead, leaving them free to advance on you. Forks, other knives and spoons are worse than useless.

These will end up being the weapons of the desperate as they battle the zombies and they collectively score a very poor **8/20** DEAD rating.

Walking Stick
A good stout walking or hiking stick can provide a practical and stylish weapon against the living dead. They are very much clubbing weapons, easily knocking ghouls out of the way and buying you valuable time to make your escape.

Durability 4: A well-made wooden walking stick should see you through the apocalypse. It is made to be used and has excellent weathering capabilities.
Ease of Use 4: Excellent as a traditional club, and also invaluable as an aid on long walks. It may give you a gentlemanly demeanour heading towards old crony – could be the classic look you are after.
Availability 4: Good. Most outside pursuit shops stock walking sticks, there are also some excellent specialist shops in city centres. It's harder to get hold of a hidden sword stick.
Damage 1 (+2): A standard stick will do little long-term damage to a ghoul other than knocking it down. Its value is that it buys you time to escape. The hidden sword option offers good potential to cause more damage to your living dead opponent.

The walking stick scores **13/20** on the DEAD rating unless it is one with a hidden sword in which case it comes in at a much improved **15/20**.

The Snooker Cue

Many Britons play snooker on a regular basis and come to trust their sturdy cue at the local club so it may be natural to turn to these as an anti-ghoul device. Whilst it is easy to admire a smooth cueing action on the green table, against zombies, the snooker cue is seriously lacking as a decent weapon. This will be discovered the first time you try to take out a zombie and your prized cue cracks in two as the living dead plough in to munch on you.

Durability 1: Very poor and likely to snap in two over the first zombie head. Made for indoor use only.
Ease of Use 3: Easy to handle and breaks into two sections for easy storage. Often comes with a snazzy case.
Availability 3: Good, available at any sports shop or club.
Damage 0: Minimal impact and may be more useful for poking than whacking. You would be better off grabbing a decent tree branch.

The humble snooker or pool cue therefore scores a low break of **7/20** on the DEAD rating.

The Cricket Bat (or Baseball bat)

More common in the UK than a baseball bat and many would argue a classier option for dealing with the living dead. You can emulate cricket heroes such as Botham as you swing the mighty willow to clear a path through the zombie horde. Built to be easy to handle, the size and weight of the bat may be an issue for daily use but nonetheless a stylish and very English way to face the apocalypse.

Durability 4: A good solid weapon, best kept dry and provided you remember the linseed oil, should give seasons of anti-ghoul operations.
Ease of Use 4: Easy to handle, time in the bowling nets will only improve this sturdy weapon. Downside is it may be cumbersome.
Availability 4: Excellent and a superb willow range with many reasonably priced bats from India. Children may have a useful smaller version.
Damage 4: Very much a smashing weapon, good damage potential with a good swing and built for the clean hit. You need to watch for glancing blows which will do less damage.

The cricket ball may even be useful for throwing so the classic cricket bat scores a boundary-reaching **16/20** DEAD rating.

The Axe

Used for as long as man has made tools, this simple weapon combines a haft (handle) and metal-shaped head. The two main types are functional axes, for chopping wood and DIY jobs, and the battle axe, designed specifically with the warrior in mind.

Durability 4: Fairly robust, particularly the modern types. A good battle axe will however need maintenance to keep the metal in best condition.
Ease of Use 3: Varying greatly in size, the smaller axes can fit comfortably on the belt; larger battle axes may need a special sheath. It has the option of throwing as a Native American tomahawk but this requires a high level of skill and accuracy.
Availability 3: Not as common as presumed to be. Few in the UK now have the need to cut wood. It can easily be bought and there are some excellent battle axes available over the internet.
Damage 4: The real power of a good axe is in the cleaving, in effect splitting zombie heads. Good technique can make this an impressive weapon in the right hands as long as it does not become lodged anywhere.

Either as a functional tool or as a dedicated battle weapon, a good axe is a very useful addition to your defence and chops in at a **14/20** DEAD rating.

The Ice Climbing Axe

Not a common item around the house unless you are a seasoned climber but well worth a look as a personal defence weapon. Built for the most extreme conditions and designed to hand from a climber's belt, this presents an interesting alternative to a larger axe or sword. This specialised axe is included on the recommendation of a seasoned zombie hunter so comes highly recommended.

Durability 5: Robust and built to last in the most challenging of conditions.
Ease of Use 5: Normally comes with a good handle and size which means a small angle of swing so also effective in cramped conditions. Easy to store with a belt clip.
Availability 2: You need to shop around to get one so preparation is required. Easy to purchase on line.
Damage 4: A tough one to score. Against a solitary zombie, it can be very effective as it will go straight through a zombie skull. Also a strong chopping weapon. The downside is, it may get lodged in a ghoul, leaving you open to attack if there is a pack.

The hard core ice axe scores an Everest-climbing **16/20** DEAD rating – basically, get online and order yourself one of these invaluable aids.

Golf Clubs

Because it is a growing sport in the UK, many homes will have easy access to a golf club. In addition, they have the benefit of being part of a set, possibly enabling you to equip the whole family but remember, golf club construction may be a complex science but it is one focused on the job in hand, i.e. hitting a golf ball not taking out the living dead.

Durability 2: A good quality club will have a strong shaft of either steel or graphite. It will however suffer stress after a few whacks, particularly on hard surfaces. It is not a purpose-built weapon so will easily bend on contact.
Ease of Use 3: Stylish and easy to carry, although the golfing caddy could be very cumbersome. It's hard to keep on your person at all times due to its length.
Availability 4: Very good. If there's a set in the house, you have access to a whole range of weapons.
Damage 1: A wood will have an advantage over an iron here and whilst both are clubbing weapons they both lack the power of a decent weapon. Less effective against zombies and a strong chance of a glancing shot which will not stop a ghoul. New lighter clubs pack a very weak punch.

A typical wood gets a very average **10/20** DEAD rating, other clubs score lower than this, although a good putting wedge can do some damage.

The Hammer
Thousands of years old with hundreds of different variants, the hammer is a common and respected weapon in the anti-ghoul arsenal. There are some very complex equations involving kinetic energy transference but the shorter version is that few handheld weapons offer such good bang for your buck as a sturdy household or 'claw' hammer. Sexy variants include the shattering and geological mallet.

Durability 5: Excellent. A good hammer can be left in the rain, dropped, etc. They are typically of very robust construction.
Ease of Use 5: Most people are familiar with this tool and there is normally a rubber cover for easy, non-slip handling. Also, looks good on a tool belt and has the added benefit of being multi-purpose.
Availability 5: Perfect, every household has at least one.
Damage 3: A common 'claw' mallet can deliver a knockout blow to the living dead but is a weapon which often needs more than one strike to get a 'kill'.

Found almost everywhere, the hammer delivers a solid **18/20** DEAD rating and should be an essential part of your personal zombie defence plans.

The Shillelagh
A traditional wooden club weapon from Ireland with a wicked looking knob on the end. Normally a rich black colour, the best ones have had this wooden knob filled with lead,

producing a powerful swing and smash effect. This is a purpose-built clubbing weapon with a long illustrious history.

Durability 4: Traditionally made from blackthorn wood, the shillelagh is a robust weapon but the wood needs to be taken care of and prepared carefully before use.
Ease of Use 5: The weight of a good shillelagh feels good in the hands. The smooth wood and design makes it a weapon which is a joy to handle. Ideal for wearing around the waist and a perfect way to fight ghouls whilst honouring any Irish ancestry.
Availability 1: If your grandfather does not have one, then you will need to work hard to find a real one. There are plenty of imitations for tourists so beware of these. Hard to find in the UK, you may end up getting an expert to make one for you. More common in Eire.
Damage 5: A good swing combined with the wooden knob on the end of a shillelagh will deal with most ghouls. Because of the angle of the knob, glancing blows also do considerable damage.

A superb weapon for the practically minded and any lovers of Celtic culture. They come in at a Blarney-shattering **15/20** on the DEAD rating with availability being the main challenge.

The Halberd

A new term to all those not well-versed in medieval history, this is a two-handed pole weapon with a long shaft which has a special kind of axe fixed to the end. A powerful multi-purpose weapon with a type of hook on the back of the axe-head for gouging. Anyone who has been to the Tower of London will have seen the famous Beefeaters carrying this tall, imposing weapon.

Durability 5: Robust and built to last. Be wary of replica weapons; it needs to be the real thing.
Ease of Use 3: Like any 'pole arm' weapon, some training is required but it was originally designed for use by unskilled peasants and is easy to handle. Too cumbersome to carry all the time.
Availability 1: Rare and hard to find. More so the real thing rather than a replica. Some sources online.
Damage 5: Capable of a knockout blow to any zombie, with the right level of skill can quickly be swung as a slicing weapon.

This rare but effective piece of medieval hardware scores a Beefeater-defying **14/20** on the DEAD rating with only availability and its size letting it down.

The Dagger and Knife

There is a difference between the two: a dagger is primarily designed for stabbing, the knife for cutting but there is also a lot of crossover as in combat against the living dead both are incapable of doing the necessary. For example, both daggers and knives depend on a precision stab, cut or injury to halt a human opponent but these rules simply do not apply when battling zombies. Unless the head is severely damaged, the ghoul will march on regardless.

Durability 4: A good well kept dagger or knife will last you through the zombie uprising but blades must be kept clean and dry after use.
Ease of Use 4: Easy to handle and keep on your person. Various sizes and types available. It has the same danger of cutting yourself as with any other small-bladed weapon.
Availability 2: Harder than you think. Good kitchen knives are common but proper daggers will need to be ordered mostly online or in specialist shops.
Damage 0: For ghoul-stopping power, the dagger lacks any punch. A precision stab won't stop these attackers, neither with slashing a wound into the torso. Zombies will simply lurch forward and take a bite out of you.

The widely respected dagger or knife scores a limp **10/20** DEAD rating. It may be useful to have around the house for practical purposes but against the living dead it is extremely limited.

The Sword

Probably the most well-known handheld weapon in history, it is available in a wide range of types, from heavy claymores designed for cleaving to delicate fencing weapons for precision in the sporting arena. When battling ghouls, cutting and slashing is what is required so generally the large sword types such as the cutlass or scimitar are the best. The slim or short stabbing types are not particularly effective.

Durability 3: A quality good sword will last but needs some specialised care. Swords vary greatly in quality. Again, you are looking for a real sword not a replica.
Ease of Use 4: Depending on size, it is much heavier than people expect and requires some training to master safely. Not rocket science but more difficult to get accurate slashes than you would expect. Looks good on a belt or special sheath.
Availability 2: Reasonable, mainly from the internet but again you will need to ensure it is a combat-ready sword and not a replica. There are a lot of pretend samurai swords out there which will break on the first ghoul head.
Damage 4: In the right hands, it is capable of taking a zombie down, and also of slashing effectively to get the job done. It can also take off a zombie head or limb with the right stroke.

The sword scores a respectable **14/20** on the DEAD rating provided you can get hold of a real one. Learn how to use it and ensure you comply with any legal guidelines.

Ranged Weapons

Whilst melee combat with zombies will always be a dangerous business and should be avoided where possible, a ranged weapon may enable you to avoid close contact with any grabbing ghouls and take them out from a safe distance. A ranged weapon is one which will launch a projectile such as an arrow or bullet towards your target from a distance at a sufficient speed to take your objective down. The most important handheld ranged weapon in the last 300 years is certainly the gun but the obvious issue in the UK is that firearms of all sorts are extremely rare. Indeed, virtually every zombie survival film or game involves endless firearms, limitless ammunition and a blistering range of shotgun, machine gun and classic two-handgun action. But in reality, at least in the UK, all forms of firearms are difficult to obtain for most of the population, being pretty much restricted to those engaging in country pursuits and professional criminal gangs. No one knows the true number of firearms in the UK but it safe to assume the majority of us will not be able to get our hands on any sort of gun in the lead up or immediate aftermath of the zombie uprising.

Availability is one reason why firearms cannot be considered a viable option for home defence in the UK. Another is the often overlooked fact that you actually need to be a very good shot to take down a zombie with a firearm. Remember, the stopping power of most guns is often in the injuries they can cause, but glancing an arm or a 'cap' in the stomach will not stop a ghoul. As the saying in the zombie community goes, you can't miss fast enough with a gun.

One consideration for any serious zombie survivalist is to emigrate to a country where firearms are legally available, the US being the most obvious destination. It would be a big move and one which would have to consider other factors such as possibly the better availability of rural locations. When you review the information in this volume, you may decide we are simply too exposed to the threat of the ghouls in this country and move on.

Without firearms, anxious Britons are left with a range of options when considering ranged weapons. Some of these are reviewed below using the same DEAD rating as was allocated to melee weapons. Again, these are just a sample of what you may be able to use.

Each will be overviewed and assessed against the following criteria on a scale of 1-5 to help you make a better decision on which weapon is best for you :-

Durability: How robust is the weapon against the living dead, Will it break at your first 'shooting party'? What kind of maintenance is required?
Ease of Use: How practical is it? This weapon will need to be with you at all times, so can you carry it easily?
Availability: Is it to be found lying around the house? Can it be bought easily or it is a special order item?
Damage: How effective is it at doing what it needs to do-that is, crushing zombie heads from a distance? Will your projectile knock them down in a single blow or will it leave their brains intact enabling them to lurch forward and do you some serious damage?

The Bow
This humble weapon may conjure up images of a Robin Hood-style of warfare with carefully placed shots taking out two zombies at a time and it is true that the bow can be a deadly and very accurate weapon in trained hands. Archery is a very popular pastime with clubs across the UK and is even included in the Olympics.

Durability 3: Fairly good but some bows are susceptible to the rain and you need to ensure you go for good quality.
Ease of Use 2: Whilst easy to fire off one arrow, the training process to achieve any kind of accuracy requires months, if not years. It is a classic easy-to-try activity but one very challenging to master. Wearing your bow however across your body with your arrows in a quill around the belt may give you a decidedly elfish appeal.
Availability 3: Good online availability and from clubs. A bargain bow can cost around £150 but the top of the range ones head towards £1,000 and beyond. A good supply of arrows is also required plus you may want to purchase a small green hat with a feather.
Damage 2: This weapon cannot be scored highly. Of course a direct head shot would do the job but for most this is an unrealistic pipe dream making the bow a tempting but ultimately an ineffective option.

The bow scores a surprisingly weak **10/20** on the DEAD rating making it an unreliable choice at best. The real issue is few people nowadays have really mastered a bow and it is a skill which needs to be developed over years not days once the zombies turn up.

The Crossbow
Less well known than the bow and arrow combination, the crossbow is a bow- mounted weapon which can fire a 'bolt' at considerable speed towards your living dead opponent. It was widely regarded in the medieval era as a weapon for the unskilled as it is generally easier to master than the bow and can inflict considerable damage.

Durability 4: Good with modern versions made of robust plastic and manmade fibre. Some care required.
Ease of Use 4: The crossbow is a weapon which can very quickly be picked up and the basic principles learnt. As with all ranged weapons, practice will improve performance but the return for hours trained is very good on this weapon. Options are also available for some excellent sighting scopes even on cheaper models.
Availability 3: Good online availability and from clubs. Prices similar to the bow and you also get what you pay for. Some excellent variations available such as repeating crossbows.
Damage 3: Although a powerful option, the crossbow still requires considerable skill and nerve to get a ghoul headshot. However, the good sight does make this easier.

The crossbow and its variants score a peasant-empowering 14/20 on the DEAD rating making it an interesting option for zombie defence if you can get hold of a good one.

Shuriken
Better known to most comic readers as 'throwing stars', the Japanese term shuriken has come to cover a range of deadly-thrown blades or small metallic stars. Made famous in countless ninja movies, the easily stored weapons may be an attractive and impressive option in your anti-ghoul arsenal.

Durability 4: The best feature of this range of weapons is they are robust and easily kept in top condition.
Ease of Use 2: Although easy to store on your person and easy to throw, the chances of an accurate hit are miniscule without years of ninja training.
Availability 2: Not great, with some supplier's online but product varies greatly in quality with many 'display' options which are not always clearly labelled.
Damage 1: Naff. Even a direct hit to the head will not penetrate deeply enough to stop a hungry ghoul; you may as well be firing a pea shooter at a lumbering zombie. It has the same stopping power.

The shuriken and its variants score a poor **9/20** on the DEAD rating making it an unusual and ineffective option for zombie defence.

Darts
A common part of British pub culture and there is no doubting the accuracy of some players. However, in the stressful conditions of a zombie attack, it is unlikely your mate from the Five Bells will be able to get his pack of darts out, check their flights and then stand still to throw them at the ghouls. In addition, with at most an inch of penetration, they are unlikely to stop even the weakest ghouls.

Durability 2: Not built for outside use and with delicate flights needs plenty of care.

Ease of Use 2: Easy to throw but takes years to master. Also, they have very short range. They come in a neat pack for storage.
Availability 3: Good availability and wide range of colours and flight types. The Union Jack flights will look particularly striking in combat.
Damage 0: Even with a '180' score of hits to the head, three darts will not stop a ghoul. Their penetration capability and velocity is simply too low to do any real damage.

Due to their weak stopping power, darts miss the board with a puny **7/20** on the DEAD rating.

Nail Gun
The fact that nail guns manage to cause some 40,000 injuries worldwide per year says something about how dangerous they can be. Designed for both commercial use and the DIY enthusiast, it can launch up to six inch long "nails" at amazing speeds. They come in handheld versions or can be powered by a compressor. Some designs can reach 1,400 feet per second or 427m per second and easily have the force to deal with the living dead. Fast moving nails and an automatic fire capability make a good nail gun sound like the perfect zombie defence weapon.

Durability 3: Fairly good. Most models are built to last but you tend to get what you pay for. Industrial nail guns have more demands as regards support and maintenance.
Ease of Use 3: As with so many projectile weapons, easy to fire off nails are harder to master for accuracy. The rapid fire capability must be used with caution.
Availability 2: Smaller versions are easy to pick up; the more serious models will need a specialist supplier. Power is a consideration whether it is a compressor or gas-powered. It may be obvious but no power, no nail gun for the big hitters.
Damage 5: A commercial nail gun can fire a long timber nail up to five inches into the living dead. As for power, most guns will have no problems penetrating zombie skulls. Ghouls may take a couple of hits to take down but equally they may be pinned to walls or fences by the nail.

Some practical restrictions may leave it as a home-based heavy support weapon rather than an everyday hand weapon so it scores a balanced **13/20** on the DEAD rating.

Air Gun
An airgun or pistol can look like a real gun and can certainly give you the Jet Li look you may be after. But as anti-ghoul weapon, it has some serious restrictions. Typically, these weapons fire a pellet or BB using compressed air or another compressed gas.

Durability 2: Most good quality guns are well-built and robust with their own carrying case. Delicate sights and scopes need care as will any moving parts.

Ease of Use 2: Fairly good with some training. Accuracy rather than being able to fire the gun will be the main challenge. As a worldwide sport, it is possible to compete and join clubs to improve your accuracy. Match grade ammunition will also help in this area.
Availability 3: Widely available and legal within the UK. Joining a good airgun club is the best route to take to learn about the weapon and ensure you have the right piece. A good quality air gun with telescopic sight will cost you around £100. The ammunition is very cheap.
Damage 1: Even an Olympic level shooter will struggle with this weapon to stop a determined ghoul. These guns lack the power, even with a good head shot, to drop a zombie. They would be best as a deterrent against human looters or gangs.

Anyone who has ever tried to reload an air rifle will realise how long that can take and a good network of club support cannot make up for a crippling lack of real stopping power which means they get a very average **12/20** DEAD Rating.

Catapult
Forget the troublesome schoolboys of yesteryear; a modern handheld catapult can be a powerful and dangerous weapon, firing projectiles such as steel balls at blistering speeds and over considerable distances.

Durability 4: New catapults are particularly robust with both the plastic and metal versions being tough and durable.
Ease of Use 3: Fairly good. Easy to fire, light to handle and easy to carry. Any degree of accuracy will take some serious practice sessions.
Availability 3: You will need to shop around for a good catapult with the best being available online. Avoid cheaper versions as they lack power and are not 'combat' catapults.
Damage 1: The weapon's big drawback. Even a high-powered steel ball will not be powerful enough to stop a determined ghoul. At any range at all, the effectiveness becomes even weaker.

The catapult offers an accessible if limited weapon to any ranged weapon arsenal only scoring **11/20** on the DEAD rating.

Javelin
A raid on any local school will produce a bounty of potential weapons, the most promising of which is the javelin. It is easy to see why with its good range, wicked looking edge and seemingly ghoul-busting stopping power.

Durability 3: Modern javelins are made of strong fibreglass construction and built to withstand the ravages of a British school term so the apocalypse should be no problem.

Ease of Use 2: Probably last thrown during your school days, the weapon is easy to throw but difficult to master for accuracy. A stylish but cumbersome accessory, it will give you a trendy Spartan or Amazon look.
Availability 2: Obviously not something you find around the average home but good availability at sports supply shops, schools and sports clubs.
Damage 1: The chances of a hit are slim but any direct hit will impale or may pin the ghoul to the ground even if it does not 'kill' it. Overall however, the stopping power is low due to the accuracy challenge.

The modern javelin is cumbersome and inaccurate and scores a very limited **8/20** on the DEAD rating.

The Whip
No questions will be asked if you do have a decent whip around the house when the dead rise but any female members of your team who fancy themselves as a budding *Catwoman* should think twice before grabbing any form of whip as a weapon.

Durability 3: A good leather whip will last, but needs to be treated and kept dry.
Ease of Use 2: Far more difficult to master than it appears. It also requires metres of space to crack. May be worn as a stylish accessory.
Availability 3: Good on the internet and there are various types. Riding crops are widely available but are more clubbing weapons.
Damage 0: As feeble as the *Catwoman* movie. Against humans the weapon relies on its stinging and slashing effect but against the living dead it has no such stopping power.

Difficult to master and requiring significant amounts of space to use, the whip scores a weak **8/20** on the DEAD rating.

A Note of Caution on Weapons

In the hands of the untrained, any weapon is dangerous and many of the options considered are specialised tools which require thorough training and the same respect given to firearms. Always obey the laws of your country and be sure to take advantage of formal training where available to hone your skills. Always ensure any weapons are obtained legally and a licence obtained where required. Equally, store all weapons safely and out of reach of the untrained. As with most areas of emergency preparedness, knowledge and awareness are the key phrases.

Surviving in Zombie Britain

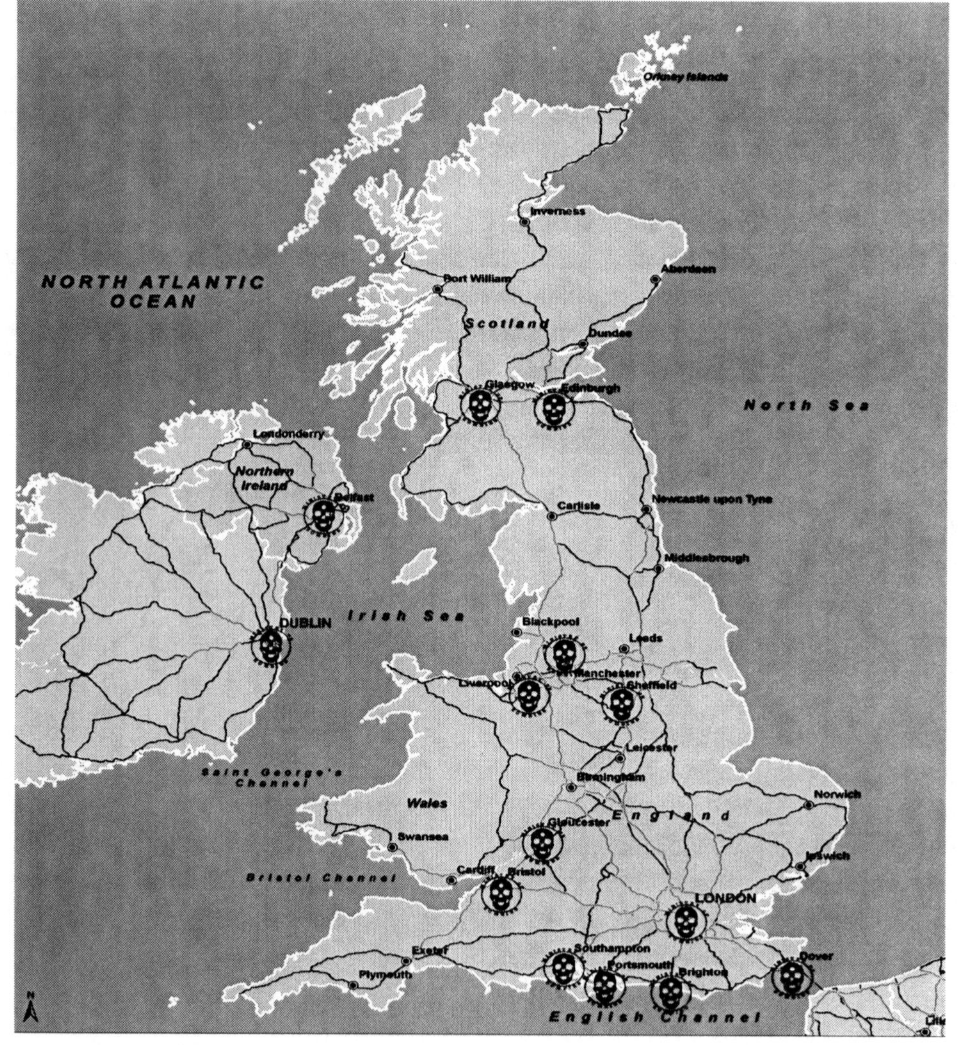

Our assessment in previous chapters has painted a bleak picture of the UK in the immediate aftermath of a significant national-level zombie outbreak. With just a thin blue line of mostly unarmed police and an even thinner green line of troops, our society will soon be swamped by a hungry greyish line of bloodthirsty ghouls. You heard the numbers before, those still alive could be facing anything up to 40 million ghouls and it won't be pretty. As was shown in the case studies, small incidents may be contained but in a similar way to earthquakes, the UK is ill-prepared in almost every way for 'the big one' – in other words, the day the zombies break through our paper-thin defences.

This section will explore some of the key issues human survivors will face in zombie Britain after the opening chaotic month of the crisis which will have those well-prepared safely squirreled away in their fortified homes. For the unprepared, it will have meant weeks of running from place to place, trying to dodge the ever-present menace of the ghouls. As ever, this is very much a practical guide so the real question will be what should you be doing if, after 30-50 days sheltering in your fortified home, you begin to realise there isn't going to be any return to normality, the cavalry aren't going to arrive and the shuffling grey masses are here to stay. Your thoughts will logically turn to your next steps, vital issues such as whether to stay where you are or move on to a more viable long-term location.

Zombie Britain – Day 50

So, what exactly will brave survivors be facing say 30-50 days into a major zombie incident? For starters, the country will be teeming with ghouls, with most urban areas dangerous and depending on the season, things may begin to get particularly smelly as the stench of death permeates the air. Rotting corpses will litter most streets with stray pets running wild and uncontrolled fires raging through some areas.

From safely inside your fortified home, you will probably see very few if any other live humans. Whoever is left will be held up much like yourself. Depending on your location, zombies will be numerous, wandering the streets, leaning in doorways and even lying dormant. But, make no mistake, these streets are no place for the living and ghouls will spring into action at the sight or scent of a living human.

Most zombie experts agree that by around day 50, any visage of central or local authority will have collapsed. The police will be little more than maybe a burnt-out station or abandoned police car. Emergency broadcasts may still be active but be prepared to feel like yours is the last fortress holding out. You should always keep in mind there will be other survivor communities, lying low, just as yours is. There may still be human bandits, possibly armed and preying on those better prepared than themselves. It is your job to survive, so for the time being, stay quiet, keep a low profile and stay alive. There will be time later to link up with other survivors; for the moment, keep on your 90-day survival plan.

By all means send out scouts if you can but ensure they are discreet and stay well hidden as they may provide invaluable feedback on survivor sightings or zombie movements. Listen to your wind up radio for any emergency broadcasts - work out a rota to manage this process. Don't get despondent if you do not hear any transmissions or see any survivors during scouting. Don't assume you are alone. There will be survivors out there but for the moment they will be well hidden. It is possible society will not be completely overcome; there may even be pockets of resistance or forces struggling to establish 'zombie-free' zones. Military planners suggest the most likely location would be the south west corner of the UK which, through natural barriers, may be easier to seal off. The various remnants of our armed forces may, under good leadership, concentrate on securing an area or region for the thousands of refugees displaced by the living dead. One can only begin to imagine the constant threat of infection as streams of the living merge into these safe camps and it is probable they will soon become as dangerous as the zombie-infested areas themselves.

More likely, however, is the grim truth that society as we know it will have collapsed completely by Day 50 with little or no central organisation or government. In this case, isolated and embattled communities of survivors will exist across the country in isolation, cut off and fighting a doomed battle against the growing hordes of the living dead.

Zombie Behaviour Day 50

You will become very familiar with zombie behaviour in the first weeks of the crisis. There will be the normal cumbersome movement followed by the quick grab or lunge normally accompanied by the screams of humans as they try to escape. Food will be plentiful for the ghouls as they tear their way through our busy towns and cities. But, how will the living dead behave as the weeks turn into months? Will they start to hoard and 'hunt' in packs? How, if at all, will they adapt as food becomes scarcer? Will they simply rot away in our damp climate?

The true answer to these challenging questions is we simply do not have enough research to determine how zombies will behave as live humans become more difficult to find. Some zombie experts have projected the zombie masses will strip the country of any living matter including all animals and insects. Others have suggested they will behave more like classic predators and become inert and dormant for much of the time, surging into action when driven by their dominant urge to feed. If we assume natural law applies to the ghouls, whatever their physiology, they will become like other predators and spend much of their time resting to preserve energy when faced with a shortage of food. In this scenario, any survivors could be easily surprised by packs of ghouls as they enter an apparently deserted area only suddenly to be surrounded by formerly dormant zombies tumbling from every corner and alley.

The most widely accepted zombie research sees a complex mixture of all of this behaviour with the exception of ghouls showing any degree of deliberate organisation such as pack behaviour. Some ghouls will no doubt wander Oxford Street or gather at Tube stations, loitering aimlessly, their brains driven by some retained memory of their former life. Others will lay siege to any last survivors with the patience of Job, their moaning masses surrounding buildings where it is known live humans are present. Some will certainly do themselves in, either falling into the sea, rotting or simply falling into places they are unable to escape. Be prepared for some horrific sights as you come across the living dead crawling around with missing limbs still desperately reaching for you. Some will be scarcely recognisable as human. Remember, zombies can still function with major body parts missing.

The scene across much of the country will be pitiful and sad but for the survivor, the weeks approaching the 50-60 day mark will be a crucial time to review your long-term plans and start to make some important decisions for rebuilding a permanent human settlement.

The following sections will outline the challenges facing long-term survivors based on the key decision all survivors will need to make: should we stay where we are or move to a different location? In some cases, you may have no choice but in most a careful consideration of your current set-up and your future needs together with some good preparation and scouting should guide your decision.

Whatever the motivation, relocating in a country dominated by the living dead will be a significant challenge particularly if you have a family party. There are a number of considerations to explore when deciding whether you should stay put and expand what you have, or move on to either a scouted long-term location or unknown destination.

- Security: how robust is your perimeter and other fortifications for the long-term? Will those outer fences hold, and are they a long-term solution?
- Resources: how accessible are extra resources? Is there any scope for growing your own food, is water easily accessible and what is the potential for foraging?
- Morale: is the location suitable for long-term settlement? Is there space to develop; room to create better accommodation?
- Environmental factors: are there any other external risks such as fire or roving bandits to consider?

This important assessment needs to made about your current location and its viability assessed against your capability to move which will in turn be dependent on factors such as your numbers, the condition of the party, the distance to your destination and the density of zombies en route.

Staying Put

The 90-day survival plan outlined is very much a minimum standard to aim for. It is possible a well-stocked and organised party will be able to survive for a far longer period in their fortified home. Staying where you are and developing your current location is the first option you should consider. Most likely you are in your home with many familiar items around you. Equally, you should have your supplies and a clear idea of your inventory and as important, your local area. Even developing into buildings in your immediate area may be a viable option and one which does not involve you facing the zombie hordes out on the streets. For all the talk of the perfect long-term zombie hideout, many survivors will find staying put in their own home is in fact the safest option.

An obvious route to improve your fortified home is to look at expanding into your immediate neighbouring buildings. Ensure you check your surroundings regularly from either a top window or better still a rooftop lookout post. Confirm how many zombies are in your street and how many are wandering close by. If all is quiet, it may be possible to dash from one building to another but always take into account most doors will be locked so plan the time needed to either pick the lock or break open the door. Any movement or sound will attract the living dead so don't take any unnecessary risks.

Where it is not possible to leave your home fortress then you need to adopt a different strategy and here, lessons must be learnt from the many manuals available on military tactics. Soldiers experienced in urban warfare are rarely out in the open for any length of time; the risks are simply too great. So, they frequently knock through the walls to neighbouring houses thus avoiding the need to go outside and face enemy fire.

The zombie-holocaust survivor will require a variant of this tactic to expand his or her living space. Where you have an adjoining house and you suspect it is empty, there is no need to leave your fortress. It is probable you have an adjoining loft and this is the best route to take when looking to expand. Using a sledgehammer, take down part of the wall so you can crawl through into your neighbour's loft. Once there, carefully open the loft hatch and survey the location. Ironically, making some noise is the best way to draw out any waiting ghouls who may have been trapped within the house. Allow some time to observe before dropping members of your party down to the landing. Clearing a location will be reviewed in more detail further on but for the moment, it is important to understand this can be a time-consuming and dangerous exercise. However, once the main perimeter is secured, then you can begin to fortify as your own home. With further doors being created, this technique can double your living space and be repeated on other buildings.

Where the road and building layout allows, you may be able to use lorries or other large vehicles to block off road access and try a more ambitious tactic but one which could leave you with a secure set of buildings and protected courtyard area. Whilst any blocking vehicles will not be ghoul-tight at first, they will at least give you and your party the chance to close the remaining entrances manually with further obstacles. It may also restrict the flow of ghouls into your immediate area as you take care of any of the living dead trapped within. If you are lucky enough to live in a small close or cul-de-sac, closing off one end of the road and then sealing it off will enable you to create a protected 'green zone' which can then be cleared and used. For example, front gardens can be converted into shared vegetable gardens, stores can be foraged and you can link up with any other neighbours trapped within their homes.

If you live in an apartment or flat and opt for the stay put option, then you need to adopt a different process but the principles are the same. Working with neighbours will almost certainly be necessary in a block of any size and you need to consider carefully whether you know and trust those around you with your supplies and your life. If you decide to team up or if you have enough in your own party, clearing a building of zombies is one of the hardest anti-ghoul manoeuvres and one which needs to be slow, methodical and always in a team. With the power out, every darkened corridor or stairwell will become a potential death trap for survivors.

Your first priority in clearing an apartment block is to block off your immediate corridor, for example with a large sofa, table or more easily a locked door if you can. Listen carefully for any close by ghoul activity within the flats, knock on their doors and check for survivors. Securing access to a stairway will be vital for your clearing operation. Use the stairs to head to the ground floor where you will face your next major project – sealing off all of the main doors and entrances. This will be a very dangerous operation and any schematics or plans of the building will be invaluable in helping you to plan your operation. Remember, lighting may be down, and corridors and rooms may be dark. You always need to know where you are.

For the moment, leave any basements or parking areas as you will have your hands full with securing the other communal areas. Underground areas always seem to attract zombies and ensuring any entrance is well-blocked may secure this vector for the short term.

Most apartment blocks have a front reception area. Start here and be cautious of any fire exits which may have been used during a hasty exit. Secure any doors or windows, close down any areas which cannot be secured, for example, windows may be completely smashed, etc. Your objective here is to prevent any further zombie infiltration – in effect to contain the problem.

The sealing-off operation is just the first stage of a very dangerous ghoul-clearing campaign ahead. Over the next few days you will need to systematically clear every single room, corridor and cupboard in the block. You will need to make the grim but realistic assumption that hungry ghouls lurk behind every door so you will certainly need a strategy to clear the block, particularly if you are few in numbers. In fact, your most dangerous enemy at this point is the mistaken idea that you are in your new sealed-off and safe zone – in the short term at least, the opposite is true; you have trapped yourself in possibly with hundreds of hungry ghouls.

There is no standard best practice for clearing a block of zombies; opinion is divided on whether to start at the top, bottom, etc. What is certain is you will need to work in teams, preferably of three and never alone. Do not split up, go slowly and be thorough. You must learn how to open doors safely to clear a room. Ghouls are not bright and any slight noise, movement or human smell will often cause them to give themselves away at their excitement in anticipating a good feed. Use this to your advantage by slowly opening doors, checking, then maybe tapping or creating noise to attract any ghouls. Be particularly careful of any en-suite facilities where zombies may have become trapped during their 'illness'.

Where an area or floor is very dense with ghouls, do not overlook the option of sealing it off and clearly marking it. Strong masking tape placed diagonally across a blocked door is standard procedure. Perhaps the most useful piece of anti-zombie advice ever given is the often quoted phrase that zombies are like water: if there is a way into somewhere, they will find it, eventually. They are tireless and single-minded and have often burst open fire doors or poorly secured entrances by sheer weight of numbers. So, take regular breaks and clear the building over days, don't try to do too much once the front doors are blocked. Tired people make mistakes.

When selecting a living area within your block, it may be prudent to create an inner line of defence around the floor you have decided to occupy. The secured ground floor will be your must first perimeter but you must also have second and even third lines of defence. As well as the uncoordinated activities of the living dead, there is just as big a threat that any stray human looters may see a sealed building and break in just to look around. A 'derelict' look to your front reception area and garden may encourage such groups to move on so any 'distressing' would be a good idea. Extra lines of defence and even false walls will help to make your living environment more secure.

Remember, there is no such thing as a safe place in a country dominated by the living dead, just ways to make a place safer. You should always be vigilant and prepare a multi-layer defence with agreed fall back options.

Once you have successfully expanded your fortified home into either neighbouring houses or flats and decided on any changes in living location, you can move on to the foraging phase. This will involve systematically trawling the entire sealed-off area for any resources which may be of use to your community of survivors. This list could include clothing, any food supplies, tools, weapons as well as any books, games or other luxuries which may make life more bearable for your group.

Again, it is vital you work as a team. Because an area has been swept, it does not mean dangers do not still lurk in the darkness. Sweeping always misses ghouls so always be on your guard, be armed and be cautious.

Once you start collecting booty it may be a good idea to start allocating storage areas to different groups of supplies. Do not underestimate the need for resources, you may not need clothes or shoes now but remember that when you do, you will not be able to nip to your local shops. Bringing all of your supplies together will enable you to take a clear inventory of what you have and help identify any gaps you need to fill.

Finally, you need to agree a new set of operating procedures with your party which may now include additional new members. This could include a rota of patrols, a guard rota or simply guidelines on the different defence zones. It is easy to become complacent in a fortified base but as sections further on in this book will explain, active patrolling must always be a part of your zombie defence plan and this may mean inside your base but it will also mean venturing out into the world of the living dead.

Moving On

So, expanding your homestead is an excellent option providing your current location meets your long-term requirements but what if it turns out your fortified house or apartment is not viable for long-term settlement? It may have provided an ideal refuge during the opening months of the crisis but cramped conditions or a lack of supplies may be making life difficult at best and even dangerous. It may be something determined by external factors such as out of control fires close by or a move to a longer-term location may have always been on the cards. As the leader of your survivor community, you should be thinking this decision through as soon your party is safely within your home fortress and ideally, you should have a plan, if only in outline, by Day 50. You can use the risk assessment advice and guidelines provided earlier in this chapter.

The challenge of moving is formidable but in some cases, where for example food and water are becoming a serious problem, you will simply have no choice. Obviously being able to stagger any move over a period of time may alleviate some of the issues. However, this may not be possible in all cases. For example, if your outer perimeter is in danger of imminent collapse, you are approaching your limit for supplies or even if you have welcomed in one too many stray humans – the need to move may be more pressing.

Any travel through 'bandit country' is dangerous but imagine leading a band of survivors including screaming toddlers and Auntie Vi with her dodgy leg. In addition, you will all be weighed down with any supplies you require for the journey. As with any convoy, you will move at the pace of your slowest member and whilst the ghouls are not long-distance runners they are fully capable of overrunning your limited party by sheer numbers. Any members of the party who fall behind will be at the mercy of the following pack of blood-thirsty ghouls.

As with most areas of survival, planning is key but even preparing a basic movement plan can make for daunting reading. For example, it will need to include any scouting plans, potential obstacles, your main routes and several alternative routes as they will doubtless be required. You will need to assess your destination, agree any movement plan as well as planning for the unexpected. Tough choices will need to be made on which supplies to take and what to leave behind. The danger, risk and difficulty of travelling through zombie-infested country increases exponentially with the distance you travel. It is a grim calculation but if you push your party too far or beyond its capabilities, someone will end up getting eaten. Also, in zombie Britain, with roads mostly blocked, even key bridges and tunnels down, your party will probably only average 10-15 miles a day depending on factors such as fitness and ghoul activity. These figures will make long-trek hikes to remote locations such as national parks or our mountain areas an unrealistic objective for most parties.

It is good practice to identify at least three potential long-term locations before the zombies rise. You can then research these locations in the peace before the crisis and make the best assessment as to their long-term viability. Where this is not the case, you should do as much research as possible with the information you have. This will involve plotting alternative routes and noting any sites of potential interest en route. Specific locations will be reviewed in later sections but a good mix of types is important. Above all, do not leave with a general objective to say 'reach Scotland' or 'get to an island'. Your groups should always have a reachable destination and route mapped out. Travel plans will need to change as you encounter the ghouls but your end goal should be clear or people will start to lose faith. Aimless wandering is also a quick way to get members of your party killed. If your current location is overrun and you need to leave in a hurry, head for your nearest bug out location and regroup before attempting the long-term move. There are many possible scenarios but good planning around emergency bags, escape routes and bug out locations, will at least give you a fighting chance to reach your long-term destination if you need to leave earlier than expected or due to an emergency.

Your choice of long-term locations needs to reflect your party's ability to move so if you know you will be travelling with children or people with limited mobility, you need to factor this in. Do not count on any motor vehicles, if you have them then brilliant but projections are that most carriageways will be blocked. Foot or bicycle are the best planning options.

One zombie survival specialist who asked to remain anonymous detailed how his plans revolved around a robust home defence in the first month or so followed by a planned relocation to one of our off-shore islands. His current home is some 30 miles from the coast where he has a small motorboat hidden with bug out supplies already on board. He has allowed four to five days for his family to make the journey to a secure boathouse and from there plans to leave for his 'bug out' island. Reviewing this one individual plan, which he has asked are not presented here, demonstrates just how much thought and planning needs to go into an organised long-term survival plan including multiple routes, different bug out locations and temporary locations along the way.

Movement in Zombie Britain

Whether you are packing up and moving on to a new location, foraging for supplies or even overrun and end up leaving your current site in real hurry, there will be times when you need to move through zombie-infested areas. Even with your stocks of food, supplies, and your home fortress as outlined in the 90-day plan - you will eventually need to leave the relative safety of your base eventually. That's a fact.

This section examines the broad topic of movement within an environment overrun with the living dead, ranging from short foraging patrols to gather extra supplies to longer distance moves involving your whole party to a more sustainable long-term location. Finally, we take a look at the different modes of transport available and some intriguing alternatives such as taking to the seas for safety.

Patrols and Foraging

The sections on home defence emphasised the need for constant vigilance and of a regular routine to patrol the outer perimeter of your complex. Whether it's a garden fence, window or just your front door, checking your defences will be an ongoing task, constantly assessing threats to your security as the ghouls 'probe' your defences. It is easy to fall into the trap of thinking this is sufficient to ensure your security, after all, why leave the safety of your carefully prepared fortress and risk yourself in a world of the living dead? Well, there are actually some very good reasons for extending your operations to the outside world, even if this means facing the ghouls.

First, patrolling a wider area than your immediate neighbourhood will enable you to monitor any potential threats or opportunities such as other survivor groups, particular concentrations of ghouls or a close-by and secure unoccupied building which may enable you to extend your own living space.

Second, the average town in the UK has literally thousands of opportunities to forage for supplies offering you a priceless opportunity to restock or build up your stores.

In fact, well-organised survivor groups will merge patrolling and foraging, with small teams regularly leaving the complex to review the local situation as well as moving further out as conditions allow to investigate possible locations and collect up items which may be needed. There are a few key pointers which should be followed in any movement outside your perimeter. It should never be done alone; you should have teams of at least three. Each team member should be armed and fully fit to battle ghouls. Where possible they should have some form of communication such as walkie-talkie but in reality should rarely leave each other's sight. However, active patrolling is never without risk even when done with care.

The essence of good patrolling is observation and assessment. A keen eye and calculating mind will enable you to see potential threats as well as opportunities and take the defence of your home on to a more proactive level. For example, you might discover that due to a fallen building you could effectively block off a cul-de-sac or find a working lorry you could use as a large street barrier, offering the potential for a safe, open space. A good awareness of your surroundings is crucial to putting you on the front foot in your battle to survive the ghouls.

Finally, the most important rule to remember when foraging and one which if broken will get people eaten, is to not overload yourself with booty. If you find a cache of real value, say food, cans or even weapons, only take what your team can carry -- don't slow yourself down. If necessary, mark where the supplies are and make several trips. Never hurry or overload in ghoul-town – it will get you killed.

There are of course some implications and considerations around foraging such as the potentially thin line between foraging and looting. As a rule of thumb, zombie survivalists see any quest for survival supplies in the aftermath of the zombie apocalypse when order has broken down and the police ceased to function as foraging. Anything before this time is deemed looting, as it is taking supplies from another survivor community. It is strongly recommended that where you come into contact with a rival group, back away and live to fight another day. The projected numbers suggest very few human survivors so in theory there should be plenty of resources to go around. Don't risk any member of your team in a pointless turf war with other humans.

Regular patrol and foraging missions will help keep you informed on the world outside your fortress and can offer excellent opportunities to supplement your stores and supplies. As general guidance, you should avoid leaving your complex at all in the first two weeks of the crisis when things will be at their most volatile. This is the time you should be running silent. Monitor the situation with the radio and keep an eye on the streets from your window. Common sense will tell you if the area is thick with zombies, just stay in and wait. Your 90-day survival plan will mean you have all the supplies you need for the moment so be patient. When you decide the time is right, maybe start with a quick area check then straight back in. A next step could be foraging into other homes or buildings close by. Whatever you decide, keep your early operations outside the perimeter discreet and quiet. Don't go for the big supply run straight off. For example, if you do have a major store close by it will probably have already attracted some serious looting. Bide your time and wait for things to quieten down if you can.

Long-Distance Travel and Moving through Zombie-infested Areas in Groups

Patrolling and foraging over short distances and in small teams is one thing, moving larger groups, possibly laden with supplies, is quite another. The most common reason to complete this dangerous exercise will be that you are looking to relocate to a better long-term location. Your party in this case may therefore include small children, elderly relatives, members of the team with mobility problems and people heavily laden with the essentials for your new location. Any long distance travel in a country dominated by zombies will be a complex operation requiring the most detailed planning. You will need, for example, to ensure your route and any alternative routes are clear to all party members, that you have understood bug out locations along the way and that any daily objectives are achievable given the capability of your group.

You will need to organise your people in a convoy system with the most vulnerable in the centre and the best fighters upfront and on the flank. Because ghouls tend to be slow and lumbering, you should always have a strong fighter covering the rear which is ironically where most zombie attacks take place on humans. Regardless of how discreetly you move, the journey of any party of live humans will attract the attention of hungry ghouls before too long so ongoing defence will be required. But it is important to remember you are not on a crusade against the living dead. Your operating guideline is to travel as quietly as possible avoiding hordes where you can and minimising any encounters. You may need to lengthen your journey for example to go around urban areas or zombie crowds. You may also encounter bands of remaining humans who will have become increasingly desperate as their struggle to survive gets harder and harder. Again, avoid encounters if you can by staying clear of the most obvious foraging locations such as shopping complexes or town centres.

If you should directly encounter any other bands of humans, exercise extreme caution. Be friendly where possible and help those in need but be firm. Desperate times will create desperate people and be sceptical of outsiders; your party will depend on your judgement. If there is any element of confrontation back down if you can and retreat with your supplies and party intact. You should be prepared to fight if rivals attack either.

Be particularly wary of any lone humans you come across as they may have been thrown out or escaped their own party after becoming infected. These dangerous individuals will be keen to try to integrate into your party and an enemy within is most dangerous as they will already be within your security perimeter. They may disguise the fact they are infected by either blotting it out of their own mind or hoping in vain for some kind of recovery. If they turn at night, then they will cause serious problems for your party. Treat any newcomer with caution but also remember they may genuinely be alone and could bring valuable new skills into your party. Just keep a close eye on them at first.

The following guidelines should become second nature as your party transits through 'bandit country', if you like, these are the basics of taking a group through zombie-infested areas.

First, all of your party should have some form of defence such as an effective melee weapon and have the skills to use it. There may be exceptions to this such as very small children or the sick but you must maximise your anti-ghoul arsenal and discourage roving bands of humans from taking advantage. Remember to distribute your best warriors in line with the convoy system.

Second, do not be tempted to overload your party with supplies. In most scenarios, speed will be your principal advantage over the shuffling the dead so do not negate this advantage. If necessary, transport supplies on separate runs or if this is not possible simply be ruthless with your supplies. Overburdening key members of your team who need to serve on defensive duties could be fatal to your party.

Be aware that appearances can be very deceptive in zombie activity. It is possible you and your party will enter an apparently empty area only to be confronted by ghouls teeming from every building. Do not assume this is some kind of ambush or the zombies have developed some way to coordinate an attack. It is far more likely that no matter how quiet your party is, their noise or scent of live humans has just taken time to reach the dormant ghouls.

Ironically, a good way to avoid this is to use a forward scout to make a significant noise to check out a route as long as he or she can safely exit if numerous ghouls emerge. Remember, the living dead are not sophisticated operators and will be drawn out by using simple tactics such as banging a dustbin lid. The decision about whether to travel silently or to use this noise strategy is a tough one and must take into account the speed and capabilities of your party. If you have a lean and fast group, then go for the silent approach.

Opinion about whether to avoid urban areas is a subject of hot debate in the global anti-zombie community but is to some extent a mute point in the UK with so much of the country covered in dense housing or office buildings. Most routes will have to travel through urban areas but as our countryside lacks the vast open space and remoteness of North America, rural areas in the UK will present just as challenging an environment for movement.

Finally, you and your party must develop and agree a 'contact strategy' for when you encounter any of the living dead. For example, the military make good use of pre-agreed hand signals to communicate information from the soldier on point. It is vital the whole party understands when to stay silent and when to scatter. Whilst it is impossible to agree procedures for every situation, a simple set of agreed guidelines in areas such as dealing an unexpected encounter, will greatly increase your chances of coming through an encounter unscathed.

Scouting Methods

A good technique when heading out on any long distance travel is to use a forward scout to try out potential routes and highlight risks and obstacles before the main party arrives. Travelling up to a day in front, this pathfinder will check routes and propose changes to avoid blockages. A useful technique is where the guide leaves prominent marks in spray-painting along the route to guide the following party.

Using a lone scout breaks most of the rules laid out in the book regarding working in pairs or small teams; however, depending on the size and capability of your party, it may be the only tactically viable option. Your scout should be fit and be a strong fighter. They should be lightly provisioned and armed as their main objective is stealth and research, not engagement. This role demands as much patience as it does strength so discount any gung-ho Rambo types out to cull some 'zombie ass'.

With a realistic target location, a good scout may be able to review an entire route to your new location and transport small quantities of supplies. Other activities could include doing a quick sweep of your target location or preparing a strong point to provide a safe base in your new area. If your party is large enough, then using a scout is strongly recommended, particularly if you have effective radio communications. In this case, the scout will be able to confirm the viability of any long-term location and even start to block off a safe zone for your arrival. If, however, you are a smaller party, say just immediate family, then it is a better strategy to stick together as using a scout will only diminish your already limited forces.

Safe Locations in Transit

Many long-term settlement objectives will not be within a day's reach of your current location so you will need to consider how to rest and defend your group when on the move. Now, the idea of setting up then sleeping in a thin canvas tent in an unfamiliar location will fill you and other members of your party with dread in the current conditions. Weeks of surviving either under siege or avoiding the ghouls will have made everyone light sleepers even in the most secure parts of your refuge but where you plan any move greater than about 10 miles, resting in a temporary location will be a risk you just have to take.

It will be impossible to build strong points on every part of your route so where possible go for the safest locations you can find in the timeframe available. The best options are often high, either on top floors or even on top of buildings where the weather allows. Emergency locations could include tall, strong trees but don't overlook the possibilities below such as drains.

Scout out a basic perimeter and where possible jam any doors with locks or furniture. Be realistic with what you can achieve. Remember, your objective is to provide your party with some protection and at least a good early warning system of any ghouls. In most locations, a fire will be out of the question as it will attract unwelcome bands of both the living and the dead. In a building location, it is easy to set up a simple anti-ghoul system such as nine empty cans set-up in a pyramid blocking a main route. No zombie is skilful enough to avoid knocking over an obstacle like this and anything which makes a loud sound when walked into, will give you precious minutes of warning.

Be aware you will never sleep well when you are the move. Get what rest you can and this is likely to be at irregular times. Be prepared to be tired all the time. This is why strength and endurance training are so important in your pre-crisis training.

All sleep in the same room where possible and always post a guard; a member of your party should be wide awake and vigilant at all times. Any building can conceal ghouls and they will not always make themselves known at your initial point of entry. This is not by any cunning on their behalf, it may simply be because they had become trapped in closed-off areas or had been dormant until the scent of fresh meat spurred them into action.

The Mass Culling of Zombies

There may be circumstances which call for a serious culling of ghouls to clear your route or a viable long-term location. It could be that a horde of zombies is blocking a key route you need to take or you find your carefully planned long-term option is packed with ghouls. Obviously, if you can possibly avoid it then do, either go around or choose another location. However, there will be times when the best option is to attempt a mass cull of zombies. This section explores some of the methods available to cleanse a location of the living dead. Although far beyond what you would normally need, these various techniques may also be adapted to clear smaller locations to allow the safe transit of parties.

The easiest technique with zombies is to "lead" them into a pre-arranged area, trap them and then deal with them en masse. One technique is to lure as many zombies as possible into a predetermined 'kill zone' such as a stadium or other large enclosed space. Once trapped, a mass culling can be implemented through fire or other means to clear a significant number of the living dead. Any gates can be blocked and flammable liquid, most often petrol, laid around the location or sprayed on to the ghouls. The key points are a location which can hold the living dead and a delivery system to take them down. The main drawback to any 'leading' plan is something or someone would need to be the bait drawing the ghouls in. In other words, we are talking about a living person running ahead of the pack of living dead, making as much noise as possible and pulling them into a pre-agreed area. This role takes real courage for if you become trapped with the ghouls, escape will be impossible.

The manpower and resources required to pull off a cull of this size would be significant and beyond most small groups but where you have the numbers and the organisation, it is a useful technique for clearing larger areas such as a village or small town. It will never deliver 100% of the zombies but it can take out enough to tip the scales in your favour in any follow-up street battle.

Other options for mass culling include using mines or artillery where you have access to them but you need to be aware that just blowing the living dead to pieces will not necessarily stop them. Indeed this may leave you with an outbreak of notoriously difficult "snappers" to deal with as ghouls can continue to function without limbs.

More realistically, targeted culling may be used to support and in preparation for your travel plans. For example, a thorough cull around your fortified home will greatly facilitate the assembly and exit of your party as well as giving you some breathing space after being confined so many weeks. Even this kind of localised cull will require a good team of fighters and nerves of steel but will decrease the chances of your more vulnerable and heavily-laden travel party being swamped by ghouls. You may also decide to send a party ahead to clear out part of your long-term location.

One interesting alternative to any cull is to wait until winter before moving. Research has shown that exposed ghouls will either freeze or become semi-frozen in the cold months and their inability to move may present an ideal window of opportunity to make your escape. Some ghouls will certainly survive and be mobile where they have been sheltered or trapped in buildings but any sub zero temperature will reduce the overall volume of the living dead. Any benefit however must be tempered against the very real challenges of moving in winter such as frostbite.

Modes of Transportation

No matter how tempting it may be to imagine yourself cutting a *Mad Max* style figure in your specially adapted 4x4 with added decapitating blades on the wheels, transport in zombie Britain will be a challenging and dangerous business, particular over longer distances. In fact, you are more likely to be scurrying from doorway to doorway as you dash in streets teeming with ghouls. As has already been outlined, roads will be blocked, bridges may be down and any travel outside your fortress fraught with danger. By Day 50, there is no telling what state our country's transport network will be in. The early days of the crisis will have seen a panic to get out of town and cities and it is likely most main roads will be littered with abandoned vehicles. Accidents will have been left uncleared and key choke points such as tunnels impassable and dark with few if any working lights. Fuel stations will have been looted. So, your transport options need to be considered and against this chaotic backdrop, Britain will be a very different place.

This section considers some key modes of transport which will be available to you once the zombies take over. When considering your options, you will need to think about your circumstances, resources and the time you have available to plan. For example, if you in a rural setting, it may be possible and practical to use a decent car with off-road capability whereas if your fortress is in a built-up urban area, a fully kitted out Hummer will be less useful than a skateboard as you may well not be able to get it out of the garage.

The advice for the survivalist is to think carefully about your situation, your plans and your transport options. If you have already decided not to move to a long-term location but stay in your home fortress or local area then maybe a decent motorcycle would be ideal just for short-range foraging missions. However, if you have a larger party and are planning a longer distance move of people and supplies then you seriously need to plan how you will achieve this. This section will provide the raw material and data for this analysis.

On Foot

The most common form of transport in a Britain dominated by zombies will be on foot and it is wise to take this into account in any survival plans. Your first step should be to introduce a comprehensive fitness schedule for all family or team members before the dead rise. This must include regular walks of at least four hours and some longer days of up to eight hours. Weekends away in well-known hiking locations such as the Peak District can be a very pleasant way to combine training with a few days away and make it seem less of a chore. Walks of more than eight hours will give even the fittest survivalist a chance to test their stamina and their walking kit in more extreme conditions.

The main walking item, as any hiker or climber will tell you, is a well-fitted and well-worn in pair of walking boots. Don't underestimate the value of this item and ensure you take as much advice as possible and buy well in advance. Walking sticks are widely available these days and there are hundreds of types of backpack, so you will need to shop around to ensure you select the right piece of equipment. For example, you will need a robust sack of good quality and with the possible addition of a built-in water bottle.

One option to increase your mobility and speed may be the use of inline skates or rollerblades. On the feet of the untrained, these modern-day roller skates will get you eaten but if you are a skilful and agile skater, they will give you a significant speed advantage over the ghouls. To some, simply the idea of roller-skating through a heaving mass of zombies will be off-putting enough but it is one option to explore if you have the relevant skills.

Any journey on foot in Zombie Britain will be dangerous but if you are planning a longer journey to say a new long-term location, things certainly become more complicated. A mixed party on foot should not expect to cover more than 10-15 miles per day depending on the conditions and terrain so you will need to take this into account in any planned relocation. Still, a reasonable level of fitness, stout walking boots and well-worn in kit will be invaluable to you as a survivor even if you just plan to forage or raid in your local area.

Horses

Working horses have been used by humans for thousands of years, only being replaced completely in the developed world late in the last century and so may provide a traditional and invaluable aid to any transport plans once the petrol-driven wheels grind to a halt. However, it is important to put away any romantic visions of roaming through depopulated towns and cities or even following blocked motorway routes to your new long-term location as the reality does not measure up to this fantasy.

First, there are now estimated to be less than one million horses in the UK with concentrations in rural areas. So, the chance of actually finding a fit beast once things start getting crazy, is very small. There are even fewer horses in urban areas and as food becomes scarce, they may prove increasingly attractive as a source of fresh meat for any hungry survivors.

Second, for the majority of Britons, their experience with horses extends only to a donkey ride on the beach or the occasional assisted ride whilst on holiday. To an untrained rider, a horse can be a confusing and temperamental animal which comes with a bewildering variety of saddlery and other associated riding equipment before you even take into account the actual riding and care aspect. Basically, if you are not a fully trained and experienced rider before the zombies arrive, you will have an extremely steep learning curve to climb for a horse to become a practical method of personal transport.

One major factor which people rarely consider if just how much 'support' is involved in keeping horses. For example, you may cut motor vehicles out of your survival plans due to fears over the availability of petrol but you must also bear in mind an average horse can get through anything up to 14 kilograms of food per day. Equally, depending on factors such as size and climate, most horses consume a minimum of around 18 litres of water per day and for their health, this needs to be relatively clean water.

However, if you are an experienced rider and have good access to horses, then the payback could be that as other remaining humans struggle along without their beloved cars, you would confidently be able to clock up around 50 miles a day with your trusty steed. This could well take you away from any urban centres and open up the possibility of making it to an isolated country bug out location. Of course, every member of your party would need a horse and any thoughts of a cart should be dismissed as blocked roads will make these as useless as most cars.

So, the real benefits for transport and mobility must be weighed against the significant costs of keeping your ride fed and watered even without factoring in the services such as routine hoof and dental care. We know little about how zombies will react to horses but we can be sure they will still move to grab any rider so a horse will not protect you from the living dead. In rural areas and with the right set-up, the arguments are stronger for the use of horses whereas if you live in an urban area, it is hard to see the time and investment of keeping horses being worthwhile.

Cycling

Moving on two wheels will certainly increase your effective range and enable patrols or foraging missions to venture further afield than would be practical on foot. However, again, you need to prepare. It is no use facing the zombie world on a Halfords Twinkle – you need to consider something tough, durable, easy to maintain and is capable of carrying as much kit as you need.

For starters, with roads blocked and debris littering the street, you will need something hardy and be able to cope with the less-than-perfect road conditions. Add to this that your bicycle will certainly need a bit of weight, so if you do need to barge through or resist any grabbing ghouls, you are not instantly upended and turned into a spandex-covered snack for the zombies as your high-tech racing cycle shoots on into the trees without you.

The logical cycle choice is a decent mountain or all-terrain bike which is specifically designed for uneven surfaces and has the gears, brakes and suspension to deal with them. There are plenty of choices out there and you do not need to spend thousands to get a robust machine. You can get a decent mountain bike for around £200 while the professionals use machines costing anything up to £8,000 and more. The important points are to get expert advice and to buy something which fits. Of course, you may choose to adapt your cycle, turning it into the ultimate anti-ghoul machine with blades coming from the spindles and the optional five-metre whip aerial just for impact. Equally, you may prefer your cycle to be street legal so you, for example, ride it to work daily, enabling you to get used to it and as part of your overall fitness programme.

You will need to invest in the standard protective gear such as helmet and gloves as any accident or fall will be even more dangerous without the back up of any medical services; even the slightest fall could be fatal if there are zombies around.

There are other very practical accessories available including so-called "camelbacks" which are specially designed pouches of water to keep you hydrated on longer journeys. Specialised backpacks and panniers will be essential if you are planning to carry any supplies. In fact, there is no end to the accessories available if you have the budget. Again, get expert advice to ensure that what you buy can fit on your cycle.

It is vital that you understand the new environment in which you will be operating – this won't be the regular road cycle to work or a quiet cycle in the countryside. One important lesson is to not overload your bike. Take what you need but beware that an excessively weighty machine will greatly restrict your mobility. Speed is not much of a problem, after all on a bicycle, you will be able to outrun the quickest ghouls easily. Be wary of clattering into stray or fallen zombies or anything which will bring you down such as obstacles in the road.

The real challenge will come if you take a wrong turn and become trapped. A mountain bike fully loaded up with panniers and accessories can actually be very difficult to manoeuvre and you may become trapped by trailing zombies. So, the rule is to keep it lean and light – take a look at the cycle dispatch riders in any busy city centre and you will see them on stripped-down machines, carrying only the minimum and with no loose clothing flapping about. Many have also, through experience, developed a 'hyper-awareness' of what is going on around them which is much easier on a cycle than any motorised transport as you are open to the elements, there is no engine noise and you will not normally be wearing a full safety helmet.

Any guidelines must apply to all members of your party if you are planning on your cycles as a mode of transportation to another location. If it just for foraging, then you will get by with two or three machines. With a reasonable fit team and well-maintained bikes, there is no reason why you and your party cannot cover significant distances in zombie Britain providing you adhere to the general advice and plan your journey carefully.

Motorbikes

The motorbike will offer one of the best ways to get around and dodge the ghouls. Many of the advantages of a good mountain bike apply equally to a motorcycle in that they also have the ability to cover most sorts of terrain and can be picked up at a reasonable price. What a motorbike adds of course is the significant advantage of greater speed and distance. The possibility of using a sidecar adds the potential to carry more people and supplies.

One of the best choices of motorbike would be so-called “dual purpose” classes of bikes which are road-legal machines combining comfort and durability with a reasonable level of off-road ability. With these bikes, you can expect features such as good ground clearance and responsive suspension but also a more of a comfortable riding experience than you would have on say an off-road motocross or dirt bike. If you are just planning to use your machine for local patrols and grabbing supplies, then either of these options will be suitable. If longer trips are on the agenda then you will need to select a machine which can do the job – including simple things such as taking pillion passengers and supplies.

Pricewise, you can pick up a working dirt bike for a few hundred pounds but for a decent second hand dual purpose machine, you would be looking at anything around £1,000 and above. Whilst it may be tempting to spend more and purchase the latest sports machine, it is worth remembering that you will also need to maintain your vehicle, maybe indefinitely, and whilst some newer bikes require a fully equipped garage with skilled technicians, a knowledgeable amateur mechanic can complete most tasks on some of the older bikes provided you have the relevant Haynes model manual. Although not a dual-purpose bike, the Honda CB range has proved to be a particularly robust range with plenty of old machines around and a dependable and simple engine you can work on. For example, with basic tools and the right information, it is relatively easy not just to carry out routine maintenance such as the changing of spark plugs but also more advanced tasks such as changing piston rings on these older models. So, choose your motorcycle carefully and newest is not always best. Whichever you choose, get to know the machine and learn as much about the engine and workings as you can.

There is an endless range of accessories for motorbikes, particularly around carrying items such as panniers but again you need to watch the weight and manoeuvrability of the machine. You will need to keep a good stock of spare parts and fuel to keep your motorbike running smoothly. Most motorcycles have excellent figures for fuel consumption but again new owners of large-engined power bikes are often surprised at the higher than expected fuel consumption. It may be more sensible to go for a smaller engine capacity for which three or four jerry cans of fuel will keep you well supplied. Don't forget to keep a good stock of other consumables such as spark plugs.

As a general guideline applicable to all forms of transport, increased speed means increased danger and this is particularly so on a motorcycle. Most of today's machines are capable of doing well over 100 mph but it must be remembered the road conditions will be far from ideal and high-speed riding will be fraught with the danger of hitting an unseen obstacle in the road or even stray ghouls. The message is therefore to use your speed only when you have to and to ride cautiously at all times.

With this in mind, it is thoroughly recommended you and any relevant members of your team go through the motorcycle training and tests to enable you to practise on your machine. Riding a motorcycle is not a complicated task but mastering it and becoming a safe rider takes practice and a full motorcycle licence is required in the UK to be street legal. It is also a legal requirement in the UK and good practice to wear a full motorcycle helmet, however, this does present some challenges in a world of ghouls as it muffles the sound of the approaching zombies. A good compromise may be an open faced helmet which enables better all-round vision. It is a question of balancing safety and awareness.

The right motorcycle can be a real benefit to you in your fight to survive. It will enable you to explore long-term locations even if they are miles away, and you will be able to explore other places not possible on foot and maybe link up with other survivors. It is a sound investment if you have the funds and can be more safely stored away from looters than say a car.

Cars

Be it an expensive super car, the family saloon or a suicidal soft top, most zombie survivalists in Britain will have easy access to a car. After all, it is estimated there are now some thirty million vehicles on our roads and most families have at least one and heading towards two cars. So, assuming you don't have the funds to convert your Corolla into the ultimate post-apocalyptic vehicle, there are some practical steps you can take to prepare your car for the coming test as you would any other area of survival preparation. As has been previously identified, investment in any vehicle larger than say a motorcycle needs to be carefully considered against the road chaos you will face. Bear in mind that even with the best preparations, your vehicle may still end up with either being stuck on the drive or worse still stolen by desperate survivors as they try to escape the rampant living dead.

If you decide a car is worthwhile, it is important that your vehicle is maintained and serviced. Ideally, you should complete some rudimentary mechanical training yourself so you can carry out basic tasks. To support this knowledge, you should have a stock of parts for your vehicle. For a guide breakdown of which parts to stock, you should consult your car's regular service requirement so you will be looking at things like spare oil filters, spark plugs and rotor arms.

You should trade in any soft top vehicles or those with only two doors as soon as possible as open top cars offer no protection against the sharp claws of the living dead and two doors will restrict a rapid exit or entrance to the vehicle. Equally, low-level sports vehicles will not be best suited as roads become rougher and potholes develop unchecked. In fact, hardcore zombie survival enthusiasts tend to go for older models such as Ford Fiestas or an old Toyota Hilux. Many of today's modern cars are incredibly complex and often require specialist equipment to maintain them. At least with an older vehicle, you have a chance to keep it on the road.

If you plan to use your vehicle as your main method to escape the zombies then you need to ensure you can develop a specialised bug out bag to be stored in the car. This can be similar to the normal kit but you can pack in a few more items such as blankets for sleeping on the move and spare things for the car. Always keep your fuel topped up, carry spare cans in the back and additional drinking water. Jerry cans and larger storage barrels are the best option provided you adhere to all safety and best practice guidelines as any potential accident or fire could be fatal for all your party. Rotate all these supplies regularly.

Most cars nowadays have toughened glass windscreens and windows but you can reinforce these with a mesh grille to prevent zombies reaching through any shattered glass. Equally, welding any protection to the front of the vehicle will help if you need to cut through dense crowds of ghouls. Any blades on the front of the car should push the battered dead up and over the vehicle rather than down and under, as they will do less damage to areas such as the exhaust pipe.

The question of whether cars will be any use during the zombie apocalypse continues to be debated across survivor forums but most expert opinion in the UK maintains that you will be unable to get your carefully-prepared vehicle very far due to our blocked and congested roads. The possibility of driving through the empty streets, stopping to load up with loot every now and then and returning to your fortress fully laden, is indeed tempting. As is the chance to 'zombie proof' your vehicle with mesh, an anti-ghoul scoop, extra lights and even on-board weapons. But, with time and money being limited, it is just as important that you have an appropriate vehicle, maintain it, keep a small stock of parts and regularly top it up with fuel. Also, be prepared that when the dead rise, it may not be the life-saving investment you imagined.

Coaches and Lorries

When looking for a powerful motor vehicle with good availability and excellent load capacity, it is hard to beat either a lorry or a coach. Both of these categories of vehicles dominate our roads through their sheer size and one can easily imagine how, by welding grilles over the windows and bull bars at the front, you could create a form of transport quite able to punch through any ghouls unlucky enough to get in the way.

As with any vehicles this size, both require a special licence in the UK and each need specialist training to drive. Whilst the police won't be stopping people to check whether their licence includes the relevant categories to drive and manoeuvre one of these leviathans safely, you will certainly need this advanced training. The best way is if you drive one regularly as part of your job. As any experienced driver will tell you, with an amateur at the wheel, these vehicles, which can weigh up to 44 tonnes when fully laden, are more of a liability than a benefit and can do some serious damage.

If you don't have access to one of these vehicles as part of your job, then you are looking at a serious financial commitment to secure one. A decent second hand coach or lorry could easily cost you over £60,000, with new vehicles over £100,000. With training and regular maintenance factored in costs soon become far beyond the reach of most survivalist planners.

If you are lucky enough to have an experienced coach driver within your party, these vehicles can be particularly useful for long distances. Along with other large motor vehicles, they benefit from excellent height, visibility and power but in addition they have up to 45 seats within a single area which can easily be converted to help transport both your party and supplies. Many lorries with trailers lack direct access to the container or load section but a coach, by removing some of the seats, can provide the perfect mobile platform. In addition, the last decade or so has seen massive improvements in the drivability of these vehicles making them easier and less physically demanding to drive along with some significant improvements in fuel economy.

On the downside, the net result of this technology is a far more complex machine which only a trained technician can maintain. It must also be remembered that with low ground clearance, most coaches are very much road machines and have rarely been tested on uneven ground. This also applies to any public buses or coaches and even the traditional London double decker.

With their power and size, you will be able to plough through the hordes of the living dead with your party and supplies safely packed on board in one of these larger vehicles but, to do this you will certainly need the training and in most cases this will mean training for a licence which is not cheap. Having an experienced driver in your party would be invaluable but you will still have the challenge of securing a vehicle and ensuring it is ready to go. However, if you can get these in place, then your travelling range and security will be greatly improved provided you can get out on to the open road.

Camper vans and Light Commercial Vehicles

Zombie survivalists are not generally big fans of camper vans because of their flimsy construction and poorly fitted almost suicidal doors. The chance to have a mobile 'fortress' may be tempting, enabling you and your team to move around the country in relative comfort and with sufficient supplies but recent tests have shown the living dead have few problems scratching and clawing their way in, particularly with the older vehicles. Even the American influenced larger vehicles share the same poor security features often with walls less than a few millimetres thick. Add to this that most decent camper vans, even used ones, retail from about £15,000 upwards, then the option looks less and less attractive.

A hardworking light commercial vehicle (LCV) such as a delivery van or a smaller truck, with their solid construction, powerful engines and metal sides, may present a better option to consider. Ideally, you would need to select a vehicle with direct access through the cabin to the cargo area but with the right improvements, you could create a robust and reliable vehicle well-suited to such a challenging environment. Remember, you do not need any fancy add-ons such as air conditioning as these will only drain your battery so go for an older model and strip out any unnecessary equipment. As to cost, it is possible to pick up a used light commercial vehicle at a very reasonable price and convert it into a fighting vehicle in which you can confidently face the zombies.

Specialist Vehicles

This is a practical guide to surviving the zombie apocalypse in one piece and as such will largely ignore vehicles which are out of reach of most people in Britain. This category includes all military class vehicles, police SWAT team or armoured cars. There are some such as fire engines, security vans or construction vehicles which may be more accessible but much of the advice around lorries will fit equally with this class. There are undoubtedly advantages to securing one of these vehicles if you can but the same issues of training, maintenance and fuel will apply to whatever vehicle you choose.

However, the US-built Hummer is one specialist vehicle which has particularly caught the attention of the survivalist community and so warrants a few words. These large unwieldy vehicles are more common in the USA, mostly driven by men resembling Arnold Schwarzenegger and look like a cross between an armoured car and a pickup truck. They are street legal vehicles with a heritage in the military to go anywhere and do anything. Their principal advantage includes superb off-road capability including good ground clearance and water fording ability. They have powerful engines with a robust body which will keep virtually any ghouls at bay. Although these vehicles are available in the UK and have a growing dealership network, British survivalists have steered away from them because of the cost and horrendous fuel efficiency figures, possibly favouring the less robust Land Rovers. In recent years, Hummer have made significant progress on both counts with prices starting from around £27,000 for new vehicles and smaller models for the European market delivering much more acceptable fuel economy.

For the survivalist, Hummers may seem like a logical choice and they are certainly built to survive the chaotic conditions of the zombie crisis. But the cost is still an issue for most of us and the fear is you simply won't get to use what could be your principal investment if you either can't get it off the drive or it is looted within the first few days. In addition, it may be possible to achieve some of the benefits by investing in a decent sports utility or light commercial vehicle which may not look the part but will still deliver an acceptable level of performance.

Air Travel

Having discounted the option of airports, which along with other transport hubs will become hotbeds of zombie activity as the unprepared panic to escape the ghouls, there are few viable airborne options open to the survivors of a major zombie outbreak. You should immediately discount helicopters and light aircraft unless you are or have a trained pilot in the group and easy access to your local airport or amateur air club. Even if you manage to reach the aerodrome, light aircraft and helicopters require aviation fuel and maintenance and neither will be available for long, if at all. Some will keep private aircraft flying but the numbers will certainly be small. If you are lucky enough to get airborne, your priority should be to head straight for one of your long-term locations. Be very wary of any stopovers to pick up supplies and be sure to have a lightweight version of your bug out bag onboard.

As a low-tech alternative, the microlight offers a world of possibilities in the UK, given that it is relatively cheap, easy to maintain and training is fairly widely available. A decent second-hand machine will cost around £3,000 but of course on top of this you will need to add in all the relevant kit and training. With the right set-up, this option could make limited air travel between bases or airborne scouting an option.

A microlight could enable one or two members of your fledging community to bypass miles of bandit and zombie-infested territory and explore significantly further afield than on foot. You will also be able to carry out fly-bys on possible long-term locations to assess zombie concentration or perimeter integrity. You could even land a scout to establish interim bases for your party as they move towards their long-term location. If you have the resources, an airborne scout could perform an invaluable role flying ahead of your party, and radioing back information on the route ahead and any obstacles.

It must be remembered there are serious weight restrictions and fuel and maintenance would still be a key requirement, however, the humble microlight could be the only way isolated communities stay in touch. Most machines will also need at least a 300-metre cleared landing strip which may be easier to find in commercial locations unless you have a very straight and very clear road close to your home.

The investment of getting a microlight or small fleet of microlights up and running will be significant if your funds are limited. However, the benefits are clear: if your family could all be airlifted to a safe long-term location, you could concentrate most of your resources in this area. The key points will be whether you can secure access to a decent runway and then keep your microlights safe before and during take-off. Remember, neighbours and others will be panicky in these opening days and the sight of you and your family preparing to fly off to safety may create near-riot conditions as they try to clamber on board. Another consideration is your long-term location. Ideally, you will already have a contact there monitoring the perimeter to ensure you are not swamped by ghouls on landing.

After the microlight, the options open for air travel move from the unusual and the experimental, to the plain dangerous and bizarre. Hot air balloons and airships for example may have been around for hundreds of years but neither is a viable option as a form of transport over a country dominated by ghouls. In reality, both require dedicated ground support to keep them aloft for any length of time. Navigation is a challenge in most cases and impossible in others, with the result being a directionless drift potentially bringing you down in a worse location than the one you started out in. Airships are marginally better than hot air balloons but neither presents a realistic method of transport.

Any form of paragliding or hand gliding suffers from many of the same pitfalls. Possibly of use as an emergency getaway, these forms of air transport, along with gliding, offer little in practical application so do not invest vital time and resources. They are great as a leisure pursuit but will not be useful in most survival situations.

It is a sad fact that the development of the personalised jet pack has largely been abandoned after a very promising start, due to significant problems around manoeuvrability and fuel efficiency. A fully functioning and easily rechargeable jet pack of a reasonable size would enable survivors to fly out of sticky situations as and when required. It is a technology which should be monitored for future developments but currently it does not look promising.

Boats and Water Transport

Luckily, most parts of the UK are within reach of coasts, rivers or one of our recently much-improved canals or waterways. Anything more than a puddle can be a real challenge for the average zombie and we have already learnt that they, by and large, avoid deep water where possible and they certainly can't swim. This does not necessarily make any lake or river a ghoul-free zone as we know they will float if in the water and are more than capable of clambering up on to any boat. However, it does mean that if you are lucky enough to have good access to either the sea, or one of our major river or canal systems, then escaping the ghouls by water should certainly be investigated.

Before getting carried away with the idea of a life on the waves, it is important to understand that all types of crafts, bar the very smallest dinghy, will need some degree of specialist training; if not to steer then at least to maintain. Add into this the treacherous currents around our coasts and the problems of navigation, then boats are not something you can just jump into and go. In some areas, rapidly developing technology will be both a benefit and challenge. For example, most modern cruising yachts have advanced GPS to help with navigation but equally, their control panels now look more like a spaceship. Furthermore, some areas of seafaring such as current and sailing skills always need to be learnt; they cannot be picked up in a few hours.

That being said having water-based transport can greatly improve your chances of surviving the zombie uprising and can provide an invaluable escape route, a means for gathering extra supplies and even a secure living space afloat if you have the right set-up. And, if you are just considering say a fibre-glass canoe for foraging, then you will only need a few training lessons then plenty of practice.

This section will review all aspects of using water-related transport to survive the ghouls from using a canoe to patrol our rivers to setting up a permanent settlement in one of the massive cruise vessels moored at our major ports.

Small Boats

As has already been mentioned, easy access to a river or waterway could greatly increase your ability to forage and explore further afield. For example, you could use river transport to reach some key supply locations such as large retail stores or warehouses rather than risking a more dangerous road route.

For reliable and practical river transport, you will struggle to beat a glass fibre two to three-man dinghy which can be bought for around £200 and will provide you with an easy to control craft in which two team members could forage and still have room to bring back valuable suppliers. Robust and hardy, these craft are typically lightweight and could be easily carried to the water's edge when required. For a lighter and faster option, a well-designed strong plastic touring or expedition canoe will cost between £400 and £600 but it is a craft which, although able to carry less booty, is purposely designed for longer-distance travel. Modern canoes and kayaks can come with all sorts of accessories such as special fixed storage containers, etc. What is common to all of these types of small boats is their shallow draught in the water which will enable them to move on most waterways even if they are only a few feet deep.

Whichever craft you select, it is important you get some experience on the river before the dead rise. Thousands of people enjoy canoeing around the country and it is an ideal way to learn the rivers and waterways in your location. It may be that these routes for example offer you a more secure trip to a long-term location, in which case, you will need to think seriously about accommodating your whole party and supplies.

In practice, few homes in the UK have direct and secure access to a waterway so the chances are you will need to lift and carry your boat to the water's edge. It sounds like a small point but in reality this could be a very dangerous exercise. If you are lucky enough to back on to a river then remember you will still need to 'secure' your access with strong anti-ghoul fencing.

As a final note, although there are countless books and courses which can teach you river craft or how to handle your new small boat, few will prepare you for the unique challenges of the zombies. For instance, you must be prepared for the numerous floating corpses which are expected in the aftermath of the ghoul rising and the grim possibility of blocked rivers. Forget any ideas of a pleasant river cruise, there will be the constant threat of floating ghouls clawing at your paddle or dropping from low bridges. You will need to be vigilant and silent as you move through the water. So, if you decide to use a motorised version of your dinghy you need to balance carefully the noise implications against the advantages of distance travelled.

Yachts and Larger Craft

Yachts or any seagoing craft require substantially bigger investment in money and resources than say fibre-glass canoes or smaller craft. The market for private vessels is a significant but a very wide one with prices ranging anything from £4,000 for a used single diesel engine boat which will have a kind of floating caravan feel, to the multi-million pound super yachts of the rich and famous which can include their own pools and be over 160 metres in length. In reality of course, anyone planning to use a larger craft for their survival will need to weigh up these options and decide the best option for them. What larger craft do offer is the security of greater range from the shore and more living space.

The good news is there is a well-established used boat market in the UK with prices to suit most budgets. For example, £4,000 could easily secure you a reasonable 10-metre long vessel around a single cabin and capable of up to six knots. Such a vessel would be quite capable of longer distance travel having 50-litre fresh water tanks and sails to use to manage fuel consumption.

As you move up the price range, new options open up to the zombie survivalist. Even if you mark the luxury yacht market as unrealistic, there is a whole range of medium-price vessels which, although still requiring a serious financial investment, will provide you with one of the most secure living spaces in zombie Britain. One example is a converted commercial whaler which is on the market at around £190,000 – a substantial commitment for most people. This particular vessel is over 25 metres long and offers six cabins along with additional living and storage space. It is a seagoing vessel and a rough calculation on fuel capacity indicates it could do over 24,000 km on one full tank of fuel. It is possible, particularly if you are part of a larger survival team, that you pool your resources as this vessel could easily accommodate 15 to 20 people and opens up the possible strategy of heading to sea for the first few months of the zombie apocalypse and then carefully exploring the coast in the weeks and months that follow.

Apart from the initial cost, the training and the ongoing maintenance of any vessels, there are several other factors to be considered. First, the purchase price of any vessel is only part of the cost. Any boat of a certain size will need berthing when not in use and even with careful planning, this can become very expensive in the UK. For example, it is estimated berthing a 10-metre boat on the south coast could cost you up to £4,000 per year. These fees are often calculated in a fiendishly complicated way based on price per metre, number of days and additional support services required such as engine repairs. It means owning and maintaining a vessel is not a cheap business even without factoring in that the boatyard may not be secure as the zombies start to create chaos. In any emergency, you will either already need to be at the yard with your party or you will be danger of seeing your expensive survival plan and supplies sailing off into the sunset.

One peril which has been very much in the news in recent years has been the ongoing threat of pirates. For the most part, attacks have been in busy shipping lanes around the Horn of Africa or the Malacca straits, which have a long history of pirate problems. However, the zombie apocalypse, along with the accompanying collapse of most central governments, will create enticing new opportunities for these well-organised groups to move into particularly the Mediterranean and then into British waters. As France and Italy are overrun with zombies, thousands of craft will put to sea to escape the chaos and these boats will be tempting opportunities for the pirates. The general breakdown of law and order on land will be mirrored on the sea and survivors in their well-stocked vessels will provide rich and unarmed targets. Without access to firearms, defence against these groups will be a significant challenge and so caution and keeping a low-profile will be the best strategy. As on land, plan and expect for things to get nasty as people on other vessels who may be less-prepared than you, fight to survive, hopefully not at your expense.

There are, however, also lessons that can be learnt from how pirates now and in the past have always operated. For example, it is a common misconception that pirates constantly ply the sea, living on their vessels and searching for victims. In fact, virtually all groups will operate from sort form of fixed land base. Pirates of the Caribbean historically operated from the numerous free ports dotted around the region whereas many of today's modern groups have bases along the lawless Somalian coast. The point is that a secure land base is essential to keep any vessel operating over the long term if only for repairs and resupply. This does not mean you need to abandon any plans to last the 90 days on your boat but it does mean you will need to plan over the long term to have a secure base of operations such as an isolated bay, island or even oil rig.

Living on the Water

The option of living on a ship or boat is worth some serious consideration as a long-term settlement option. The benefits of being able to move away from a shoreline dominated by ghouls or to be mobile enough to move your entire base around depending on the circumstances make any powered boat you can live on an ideal solution to many of the security challenges presented in zombie Britain. You may be able to build your whole 90-day survival plan, training and supplies around a water-based refuge.

Take for example, the numerous pleasure craft available on the Norfolk Broads and the 125 miles or so of navigable water and some excellent remote rural locations to moor presented by this mostly protected location. The older boats often hired out for holidays are like flat-bottomed floating caravans and are designed to take up to 12 people in relative comfort. With dependable diesel engines and a fairly robust build, these craft could easily provide a floating bastion for you and your team. A family holiday fortnight on one of these boats will equip you to manage on the waterways and this should be supported with training to look after the engines and other systems. However, they are designed to be simple to run and easy to maintain. Many have worked hard over the years clocking up thousands of river miles, so with the right skills you can be confident in your boat.

Better still if you can buy and secure a boat before the zombies arrive, you can stockpile fuel and supplies ready for the crisis. You will then be able to head out to a secure bug out location, moor up and see the opening months of the crisis through in comfort and even do a bit of fishing.

Although simple to control, it is still important that you familiarise yourself with both the craft and the waterways. For instance, whilst the Norfolk Broads are lock-free and typically wider waterways, the canals and locks of other areas could provide countless opportunities for strolling ghouls to lumber on board and start doing some real damage.

It should be noted most of the boats on the UK's inland waterways are not designed for the open water of the sea but can, if stocked up, provide an excellent alternative to a fixed land location.

Whilst on the whole, the UK's rivers are wider, deeper and faster flowing than our manmade waterways, zombie outbreak planners point to the fact many will become blocked by the ghoulish remains, some still moving, as our urban centres are overrun. As in every location, there will need to be a constant guard to ensure floating zombies do not catch hold of your boat and manage to clamber aboard.

Other Ships

The advantages of setting up on a boat are not just about mobility. There are hundreds of ships and vessels moored around the UK which are well worth investigating as potential secure living locations. The queens of all these are the massive cruise liners which may be found at various locations such as Southampton and Dover. They often have over 15 decks and many are designed to take in excess of 2,000 guests. With access tightly restricted to normally two or three 'gang planks' when in port because of much tightened security, these huge areas can easily be made secure and cut off and their massive height out of the water make it virtually impossible for any drifting ghouls to get on board.

So, with acres of interior space, in some cases approaching 90,000 square metres and a vast range of facilities, cruiser liners would seem to present an ideal zombie defence location. However, as with every option, there are some drawbacks and one of them is their sheer size. With hundreds, even thousands of rooms and a crew of anything up to 1,000, it is possible your perfect location could easily turn into a real death-trap with floors overrun with ghouls and numerous zombies trapped in locations around the ship. Factor into this whilst many rooms have windows or portholes, anyone who has been on a cruise will be able to confirm most of the corridors are narrow and confusing and will be dark as the power fails. You will need a substantial force, endless patience and nerves of steel to clear out a vessel with anything approaching 1,000 zombies. The reward is if you manage to find a ship with a few ghouls to clear out, you may find yourself with enough food, supplies and fresh water to supply a small army for months.

Any thoughts of moving one of these vessels without an experienced crew should be quickly dismissed. The bridges of these modern ships are more like advanced computer rooms and their control systems unfathomable to those not fully trained and qualified. For power, the biggest ships don't so much have a generator as a diesel-electric power station producing up to 70,000 kilowatts. Again, these centres require a team of skilful engineers to maintain and keep running – something well beyond most survivor groups.

Whilst the giant white cruise liners will probably attract most attention from bands of survivors and any foragers, it should also be remembered there are many other more humble craft berthed around the country which offer some of the same benefits albeit on a smaller scale. Many of the freighters for example have ample cabin space and are mostly well equipped with canteen areas, accommodation, gyms and medical facilities. They are designed to be hardy and have the same restricted access via a gangplank as the cruise liner. All in all, moored freighters and tankers represent many of the same benefits in a more manageable and less glamorous package. With this in mind, it is less likely to attract attention.

Emigration

Emigration has long been a feature in the UK and Ireland and could be an interesting option for survival should the country be overrun. With a transatlantic crossing being impossible for any but the most experienced of seamen, the various islands and our closest neighbour, France, present the most realistic options.

Several factors need to be considered with any international travel. If the outbreak began in the UK, then it is probable the country will have been quarantined very quickly by the rest of the world. This could mean any coastal forces will use deadly force to prevent any landing in their territory. Remember, this won't be a pleasant sojourn, you will be fleeing for your life and even if the UK has not been quarantined, other countries may not look kindly on a new invasion of refugees.

With this in mind, it is essential foreign radio broadcasts are monitored to ascertain the situation, particularly with any channel crossing. Any French language speakers will be worth their weight in gold. There is certainly no point in going to the considerable effort of a channel crossing only to swamped by garlic-soaked ghouls as you arrive in Calais. You need to know or at least have some idea of the kind of welcome you will receive.

The zombie virus is no respecter of international boundaries and the most likely scenario is if a major country such as the UK is overrun, the rest of the Europe and possibly the world would soon follow. So, you should avoid the mindset that if you are on the coast and you have the transport, then you have a ready-made route to safety: it won't be that easy. The various islands dotted around our coast may present a better option and will be considered in the next section which reviews realistic long-term locations.

Long-term Locations

The 90-day zombie survival plan is designed to get you through the chaos of a Zed-Con 1 outbreak. Of course, there are no guarantees but hopefully it has been shown that with the right planning and preparation you can greatly increase your chances of surviving the zombies. However, as the weeks pass after the ghouls emerge, you will need to give serious consideration to your long-term survival.

We have briefly reviewed the key decision on whether to stay in your current location or move to a better site for permanent settlement and this section will examine some of the various long-term locations you may wish to consider. In an ideal scenario, you and your team will have researched at least three alternative sites before the zombie onslaught. If this is not the case, this information will help to guide your thought process. A short list of places to avoid, such as hospitals and airports has already been provided.

Other Houses/Residential

The easiest option to take when considering an alternative location is to look at what is immediately around you and in most cases this will include other residential buildings. There will certainly be homes which have been vacated but also other options such as residential care centres, local hotels and small commercial premises. Many of the principles outlined in the home defence section naturally carry over into any new residential site you choose to occupy. Most residential accommodation will have the same advantages and disadvantages, the same challenges and benefits.

It is important to carefully assess whether a building is occupied by either the living or the dead. For example, a building may be observed from a concealed location before more detailed scouting takes places. Are the windows closed? Are the doors undamaged? Moving closer, you will need to test the doors. If they are locked, it's a double-edged sword. It will mean they have kept any ghouls from wandering in. Equally, there is a risk that any living dead may have been trapped within, lying dormant in a bedroom ready to spring into action at the scent or sound of a human. If there are living inside then you should return to your group and agree any next steps in what could be a first contact situation with another survivor group – remember, never rush things in ghoul town.

Extreme caution is the order of the day and you will need to develop some techniques for clearing even the smallest home. Some of these have been outlined in previous sections but others such as using a cat flap to poke a stick through and making a deliberate noise to attract any zombies are learnt through experience.

In a world dominated by the living dead, any travel will be challenging and dangerous so a nearby location obviously has some real benefits. It is also easy to overlook locations in your immediate area as you get carried away looking at remote islands or the highlands as your refuge. The chaos in the opening weeks of the crisis will see thousands fleeing our towns and cities so finding empty accommodation should not be a problem. As with all things in survival, choose carefully and cautiously. Do not overlook an obvious solution.

General Office Buildings

Next to residential, general office or light commercial buildings will be the most common type of sites close to survivor communities. These include anything and everything, from small one-man offices to large multi-floor blocks. The trend towards greater security in modern offices is a great boon in zombie defence, with most glass now toughened and reinforced as well as potential blind spots being eliminated by good design. Some security features such as cameras or control turnstiles will be of limited use against the living dead but many more including interior shutters and anti-ram posts outside to protect the building from ram raids or stray vehicles, will greatly support your efforts to transform a former humdrum work environment into a protected strongpoint for you and your team.

As with any buildings designed for general use, there are always numerous entrances and exits to cover in any office location and although usually secured, do not assume that because the front doors are locked a rear fire exit or window will also be sealed. However, the real danger in any office accommodation lies in its interior design. The fashion towards open plan office layouts is great for building good morale and encouraging a more open and creative corporate culture but in resisting the living dead, it's quite frankly a nightmare. The inability to seal off parts of floors to any degree means any zombie incursion can quickly escalate to overrun an entire floor. In the worst scenario, you could end up barricaded in one of the artfully designed all-glass buildings as the dribbling ghouls press up against the windows.

Another potentially fatal weakness in most office accommodation but equally applicable wherever it is used, is a tendency to use plasterboard partitions rather than strong brick walls between rooms. Commercial office buildings are often leased as a shell, allowing companies to adapt the location to their needs, and using contractors to partition off quickly any areas they need for meeting rooms or offices. However, the boards used to section off the areas are about as strong as thick cardboard and despite appearance cannot be depended on to hold back the hordes. If in doubt, just knock the board, if it's hollow or plasterboard, it simply isn't strong enough for zombie defence. Although ghouls are not the niftiest of climbers, the suspended ceiling in most UK offices provide an additional vector from which the living dead may attack.

So, whilst the security features make them an attractive option, office building should only be approached in the full knowledge of the weaknesses so common in most offices. Some buildings will suffer none of these shortcomings and if an office building is selected as a long-term location a pre-crisis visit would certainly be in order to check out the status of these key areas.

Retail Parks and Outlets

Retail parks or shopping malls are legendary locations in which to survive a zombie onslaught and have, through movies and books, entered zombie survivor folklore as the perfect long-term survival location. And, on the surface, their reputation would seem to be justified. Now in virtually every part of the country, these parks include a bewildering variety of resources waiting to be used from hardware stores to food sites. The list seems endless. There are also many sites on the edges of urban areas and with reasonably controlled access to both the buildings and the car park area, offering the possibility that you and your party could seal off not only the interior but also a large area of outside space for your vehicles or gardens.

Modern shopping malls such as the Trafford Centre in Manchester are vast operations, catering for well over 30 million visitors a year, however, having over 230 stores can make securing these locations a challenge for anyone but the most organised groups. Indeed, it would take a small army to secure the Trafford Centre and many of the other similar purpose-built shopping centres. Although secure, there are still normally hundreds of doors as well as the thousands of visitors and workers who may be still in the buildings. You could literally be facing an army of the living dead. It is also likely other survivors will have the same idea and flood into any nearby centre. So, if you venture into one in the months after the crisis, expect to find looted shops and broken, open doors. As a general rule, avoid any shopping centre location in the early days of the zombie rising.

So, some strong pluses if you have the resources and are lucky enough to find a centre with even some of the doors still locked and shops stocked. It is also worth remembering that even as the months pass, these central and high profile locations will continue to attract human raiders desperately looking for supplies or shelter so you may need to prepare to defend against both the living and the dead.

Industrial Complexes or Factories

Factories and similar complexes present both a challenge and an opportunity as areas of long-term settlement. Some of these are common to most large buildings, such as securing a larger number of access points. Others, such as dealing with any toxic waste storage, can be more unusual and problematic.

A real strength of these sites is many have a strong external perimeter fence or wall. Most large commercial or factory sites now have some form of on-site security and although the guards will be well gone by the time your party moves in, any barriers, gates and walls can be put to good use in sealing off the perimeter. As with any large building or complexes, if it is viable, then secure this perimeter.

Although it can be quite an effort to secure an external fence which will probably run for hundreds of metres, once you have and have followed up with a clearing exercise, you will be left with an expansive living area which may include large open areas and even green space you can use for growing food. Another benefit is that many of these sites will have dedicated facilities such as kitchens, canteens, and shower facilities. Some locations even have their own water supply fed from substantial roof tanks.

Any office areas are normally a good place to set-up a 'home base' as they tend to be more comfortably furnished than other warehouse or factory floors. The latter can however prove to be an excellent location to secure tools and other useful supplies.

One of the downsides to any large or complex location is the number of corridors, rooms and hidden corners which need to be cleared and the factory is no exception. One important factor to note is any scouting work is the availability of natural light. If the complex has few windows and large areas in darkness then it may be prudent to move on. The risk of trying to clear such a location in near darkness is a significant and dangerous challenge. Most factories have a number of outside buildings which also need to be secured but can provide useful storage or be used to keep any vehicles secure.

Military Bases

Whilst in some countries it is still common to encounter various troop garrisons and military bases with just a standard fence and barbed wire as security, due to the ongoing threat of terrorism, sites across the UK have long been well-fortified and robustly defended. This puts most military sites in good shape to face the zombie hordes with solid steel security fencing and often cleared 'kill zones' so as not to allow any intruders to work on any barriers unseen.

This good level of security combined with the mouth-watering possibility of access to firearms and other goodies make our military bases a logical prospect as a long-term location. The sites are often spacious in addition to being well-defended and have robust internal communications. There may even still be members of the British Armed forces on site, who will work their normal miracles in defending British subjects in peril.

The great advantage of any military locations is however also its downfall. If you see a long-term location ably defended by the British Army then so will thousands of others and no doubt many bases will be swamped in the opening days of the crisis. The army will not be able to cope and will be under pressure itself after receiving a drubbing in its ongoing battle against the ghouls. Order may well have broken down and soldiers will understandably want to defend their own families.

Finally, as has already been noted, the UK has thousands of combat troops committed abroad so it is equally possible that you manage to get to a base only to find it deserted with whatever troops there were long gone. There is no doubt our military will do their best against the ghouls but with the massive challenge they will be facing, the situation may make it impossible for them to take on additional refugees so, don't bank on military bases in a zombie crisis.

Prisons

For fortified buildings with massive security potential including high walls, locked doors, easily sealed-off areas and even firearms, prisons and other secure holding centres present an interesting long-term settlement option for your community. It should be noted that many other sites such as secure mental hospitals, safe storage buildings and even large banks will share many of the same features.

As previously noted, sites lacking sufficient natural light should be avoided unless you are particularly well-stocked with torches and even then clearing darkened areas can be a harrowing experience. Other specific challenges will include overcoming automatically sealed doors, the clearance of individual cells and other advanced security measures.

In the immediate aftermath of the crisis, your local prison will be no place to be. The thin blue line maintaining order in our secure facilities will quickly break down as the living dead begin to take over. Security officers will leave to look after their own families, there will be wide scale riots and escapes. Those unlucky inmates unable to break out or are locked in their individual cells may find themselves at the mercy of the zombies

However, once the initial onslaught has passed, it is certainly worth investigating these sometimes forbidding complexes to assess their suitability as long-term locations for settlement.

The newer prisons tend to be much better for natural light and open plan areas making them easier to sweep than the creepy and dark Victorian buildings across the UK. Both can be large, sprawling and complex buildings so any plans you can acquire either from sifting through the offices or beforehand will be a great advantage. Some of the new generation of super-prisons are being designed to hold over 700 inmates, giving some idea of the scale of the facilities.

Standard procedure is once again a quick scouting operation of the site, starting with the open areas formally used by visitors and guards which can be extensive.

Modern prisons contain all of the facilities you would normally expect in a hotel. Most will have a gym, proper canteen and extensive stores. You will also find breakout areas, plenty of sleeping areas and often a well-equipped medical area.

Most sites will have been 'locked down' during the crisis so expect to encounter a series of sealed-off areas. Explore and expand slowly. Secure an area and fan out from there to sweep key locations. If you find an area of cells infested with zombies, then seal it off and leave it – these areas can always be tackled later.

So, whilst prisons can at first glance look like a foolhardy or challenging option, with the right choice of location and the right resources, they can become excellent bases for permanent settlement. Few modern buildings can rival their protective walls or fences, after all, these buildings are designed with security in mind. In addition, the substantial facilities particularly on a modern site can be very useful as you look to develop your survivor community.

Going Underground

Most urban areas have a veritable labyrinth of tunnels and complexes hidden beneath the pavement ranging from disused Victorian sewage piping to modern state-of-the-art facilities designed during the cold war. Although there are numerous natural cave complexes in the UK in areas such as Derbyshire, a majority of the options available to survivor communities will be these manmade structures. For example, major cities such as London benefit from extensive underground utility networks such as a major postal tunnel complex, in addition to the well-known Tube network.

One major attraction of underground sites is they are perceived as both secure and relatively secret locations. Most have restricted entrances which can easily be secured and offer potential tenants the chance to keep a low profile, possibly with the benefit of avoiding any social unrest as well as attracting the living dead.

Many of the cold war locations dotted around the UK were built in the late 1940s and 1950s and include everything you would need to survive in a sealed-off environment including an air conditioning facility where it still functions. For an example, visit the recently opened Essex County Nuclear War Headquarters bunker in Manningtree which is a massive underground complex across two floors with its own energy and communications centre.

However, any underground option does have some substantial drawbacks which may deter even the hardiest survivors. The biggest is the constant and often total lack of natural light. This can make these often complicated sites a real challenge to clear and in which every shadow becomes a ghoul if only in the mind. In addition, the long-term impact of living a troll existence may also take its toll on your community when it comes to being ‘locked up’ underground for most of the time. Basically, if you start to see members of your group developing large saucer shape eyes, then you have been underground for too long and it is time to move on. Fresh air and sunshine can have a very relaxing effect on people under stress and having them live in dark and possibly damp cave-like conditions may end up damaging already fragile morale.

In general and across the wide variety of underground locations, there are major strengths in security and ensuring your band of survivors keeps a low profile when required. However, the darkness, dampness and size of some locations may make it a challenging long-term option for members of your team. It may be possible to find a complex incorporating some kind of underground facility which could serve as a fallback position but have the living quarters in a location above ground in the light.

National Parks and the Highlands

In contrast to the disorder and chaos of urban areas, our well-established and protected network of some 14 National Parks combined with other protected wilderness seem to offer the chance to see the whole zombie apocalypse show through in safety and at one with nature. On paper at least, access should not be a problem as these parks are scattered across the country from Dartmoor and Exmoor in the south west to Snowdonia in Wales and the Cairngorms in Scotland.

Since the 1940s these protected areas, the largest being the Cairngorms, have been protected and nurtured for the good of the nation and what could be better than these areas becoming sanctuaries for human kind from the wrath of the living dead?

Well, before rushing out to buy maps of these parks, the zombie survivalist needs to face some uncomfortable truths. First, the idea that these parks are deserted wildernesses where you can set-up in an isolated cottage and survive the ghoul onslaught is simply not true. Most of our parks are teeming with human activity even without the bank holiday tourist rush.

For example, nearly 40,000 actually live and work in the Peak District National Park so whilst it may still be an area with a comparatively low population density, it is far from a people-free rural haven. Indeed, some campaigners have complained that the development of holiday homes, hotels and hostels has begun to threaten the very purpose of the parks.

Even the impressive Cairngorms National Park has some 16,000 people living in it but in an area of some 3,800 square km including the UK's only arctic mountain landscape, your chances to survive may be higher. With the right equipment, supplies and good shelter, it may be possible to sit out the zombie crisis, with the added benefit that any sub-arctic conditions will help by freezing any living dead who happen to wander your way. Adopting a kilt and growing long braided hair may also enable to you to cut a dashing "highland" persona in your battle against the ghouls.

A further complication around national parks will be access. Despite being spread across the country, there will be several thousand other survivors with exactly the same rural plan you have. Even presuming you can get a vehicle, it is likely the access routes to these parks from cities such as Manchester and Liverpool to North Wales, Glasgow into the Highlands and most of central England into the Peak District, will be clogged with traffic and those desperate to escape our overrun city centres.

Our National Parks and other less populated locations do present some real benefits in surviving the zombie uprising. Being away from any centres of population is good.

People mean panic and hordes of the living dead, and the further you are away from this the better. In addition, the parks have some delightful period cottages available which, with their small windows and thick walls, make surprising good anti-ghoul bastions. However, the problem of access will make these areas a non-option for most urban dwellers and there are serious question marks over how many survivors plan to rush to these areas which could result in them becoming dangerous as our towns and cities.

Islands

Some estimates put the number of islands scattered around the mainland of Britain to be in the region of 5,000. Now whilst some of them are just rocks sticking out of the water, the best example of this being Rockall off the Orkney Islands, others such as the Isle of Wight on the south coast are the size of counties. The obvious benefit of any island is the fact the living dead or anyone else for that matter cannot reach you easily. Previous sections have already highlighted the potential danger of ghouls drifting on to shores but on the whole you should be safe from the shuffling masses of the living dead that will swamp much of the country.

It is also worth remembering the same applies to locations such as the Isles of Sheppey and Skye which though technically joined to the mainland by a bridge, can easily be cut off provided you have the resources to barricade the bridge.

If you are planning an island refuge and have the transport then ensure you research your target location. Detailed maps are a must and you will need a good understanding of the spread of resources and buildings and a detailed file on the location.

For example, the island of Lundy lies off the coast of north Devon, where the Atlantic Ocean meets the Bristol Channel and is around three to four square miles. It has plenty of buildings and sites around 10 miles offshore. As with any island, it shares the danger of ghouls being washed ashore but presents a very viable option for survival in the zombie world. As an interesting plus, the island has its own ship, the MS Oldenburg berthed locally, which can comfortably take 260 people - perfect for raiding supplies from the mainland, providing you have a trained seafarer with detailed current maps and knowledge of any tidal patterns.

So, by all means check out the numerous island locations but again their distance from most urban locations and access problems will probably be the main drawbacks.

Offshore Platforms

Any offshore platform can provide a viable long-term option similar to islands with regards to living space and defence against zombies. The good news is there are thousands of artificial platforms worldwide and hundreds around the UK ranging from converted Napoleonic forts in the Solent to state-of-the-art drilling rigs in the North and Irish Seas. The next section considers some of the main types of offshore platform.

Oil Rigs and Drilling Platforms

A modern drilling rig is a massively complicated piece of machinery which, although often self-sufficient in electricity and water, would normally have a crew and support staff running into hundreds. They are dangerous places at the best of times but as a defensive location, they are probably as close as you can get to a zombie-safe location.

Although rigs can be hundreds of metres above sea level, there is always a risk the living dead may float towards them and possibly clamber aboard. There is also a risk that a zombie-infested ship could collide with the structure.

Your biggest challenge will be maintaining the rig in a usable condition. For example, the generator must be kept running or much of the station will be unusable. Equally dangerous will be accessing and leaving the rig. They are all equipped with safety vessels and lifeboats but normally most of the traffic to and from rigs tends to be via helicopter. Without access to choppers, you will need to master the dangerous business of mooring in what could be treacherous weather conditions.

All of the workers on a rig typically go through intensive training, particularly with regard to surviving in the sea and the use the life rafts. A modern rig is however well equipped with all the facilities you will need for the survival of your team including kitchens, medical facilities and dormitories.

With the right preparation, an offshore rig can be an innovative solution to surviving in the living dead world but the safety of this kind of settlement must be balanced against the requirements. Some familiarity with the offshore or marine industry is vital as well as having individuals skilled enough to maintain the systems on board. It may be possible to reach a platform, which in itself can be treacherous, if only for a temporary base, but for long term settlement you will need these specialised skills. One zombie survivalist interviewed for this volume pointed to an expert in this field working across the various anti-ghoul forums and simply known as 'Mr Smith'. This experienced source has been advising people on how to survive zombie incidents by making use of the many rigs and platforms around our coasts. If you can find this mysterious expert, then he may be the best place to start.

Costal and Estuary Forts

These military structures are common features around the UK coast having been built at various times in our history to defend our shores. For example, the numerous World War Two forts, particularly those set in the Thames and our other major river estuaries, are near perfect structures from a living dead defence point of view. Unlike floating structures, they require little in structural maintenance but are still surrounded by defensive waters and are often closer to the shore. Many stand up to 20 metres or more above sea-level with living accommodation set up high and secure on massive iron girders.

Access to these forts can still tough and if looking to occupy these locations for any length of time, you would need to consider access. On the plus side, it is extremely difficult for any aqua-ghoul to climb up. Generally, the accommodation is generous but pretty rough. However, this could be sorted out. Some of the forts have more facilities than others as they were used fairly recently as pirate radio stations or hippie colonies. One recent observation noted fish congregated in large numbers around the base of these structures providing an easy food source and having stood since the 1940s, it is safe to say the forts are well established.

You would need to secure small boats or tenders to enable you to forage along the river for supplies and few of these forts have access to their own clean water supply. You also need to consider what would happen if a tender boat was lost and you became stranded.

In summary, many of these forts are in excellent locations and are very defensible. Also, they are much easier to access than the distant rigs. However, on the downside, conditions on most are basic and plenty of hardware would be required to get them up to the specification you would need as a permanent base. Another big drawback may be the sheer number of floating bodies or ghouls in the water. No one can predict whether this number would be sufficient to block our rivers – not a pleasant prospect or the delightful river view you may be after.

Victorian Sea Forts

What did the Victorians know about the upcoming zombie apocalypse? Well, it seems like the answer is plenty as they succeeded in creating the near perfect zombie defence location. The UK is littered with Victorian fortifications from this era when invasion from the continent was a real fear. However, it is these historic sea forts and the Spithead forts in particular which will dazzle the zombie survivalist with what they can offer.

Built in the 1860s to defend the important naval base at Portsmouth, these huge round structures in the middle of the water have probably been spotted by anyone who has ever taken the Isle of Wight ferry.

Factoring in their size, height and defensible sea location, these forts may well be the best location Britain to survive a major zombie incident. Many of them have been fully restored and all feature extensive rooms and a superb defensive location. With solid foundations and 20-ft thick walls, collisions are less of a worry and with sunken wells for fresh water within the forts themselves, they are excellent all-round locations.

These forts were built to last and at massive expense by our countrymen and will be one of the best venues in which to ride out the zombie storm. There may be competition for such a facility and as with any sea location, a tender boat is essential to be able to reach land for further supplies. However, their nearness to land and superb location create a very attractive option if you can get to one in time and defend it.

Long-Term Team Survival Dynamics

So, you and your team are safely in your long-term location, stocks have been built up and your little community has slipped into a regular routine of foraging, patrolling and constant vigilance. The initial shock of seeing the ghouls ravage the nation will have subsided, to be replaced by a grim realisation that the zombies are here to stay.

Whatever the set-up of your team, be it family, friends or an ad hoc group thrown together, or the circumstances you find yourselves in, it will be down to you as "leader" to provide the one element you won't find in a burnt-out retail park – that is the leadership your group needs to stay strong together and hopefully start to rebuild after the grey devastation of the ghouls.

There are countless books on the market which explore different aspects of leadership and it is worth taking the time to research these in your local bookstore. Whilst much of this book has focused on practical steps, books or courses on people management, leadership and specific areas such as team working or problem solving can greatly support the smooth running of your operation. Just remember that in most cases, real survival style courses are better preparation than classroom training so look out for outbound activities as a preference.

Even though your little community may be safely in its fortress and you may even be starting to feel 'safe', you and your party will still be facing some very real challenges. The matrix below outlines some of the areas you as leader will need to consider once the first phase of the crisis draws to a close and the zombies takeover. These are in no particular order but provide a core of the questions which need to be answered if you are to prosper over the long term.

90 Zombie Survival Plan	Team Dynamics	Maintenance
What do we have left from our 90 Day Plan? Is our location fortified sufficiently? Can we defend ourselves if they break in? Where are our bug out locations?	What kind of leadership do we need? Have we agreed a work rota? Is the group capable of solving practical problems? Can this group stick together?	Do we have the skills to maintain our fortress? Do we have the resources? Are we lacking in any key areas? Which kit needs regular care such as generators?
Defence	Sourcing Food	Human Needs
How many active defenders can we rely on? What weapons are available to the team? Can everyone use at least one weapon? Do we have enough fighters to break out?	How can we expand our 90-day stock? How long can we last and where can we source more food? In the long term, can we grow our own food? Do we have access to a source clean drinking water?	Do we have any urgent or complex medical needs? Do we have the skills to keep ourselves healthy? Do we have a qualified first aider? In the long term, what other skills will we need to develop?

An audit of your team's skills is advisable as you begin to plan your long-term survival. Some of our former skills will no doubt be invaluable, such as doctors, dentists and other practical skills. Other skills developed in professions such as the law and accountancy will rightly take their place behind nurses, carpenters and mechanics. Any members of the armed forces will be a useful addition to the team, particularly if you are lucky enough to have any men from one of Britain's elite units such as the Parachute Regiment, Marines or Special Forces. Office bods from the royal paperclip brigade may not be the assets you thought they were.

With good preparation, it is possible each member can develop areas of expertise to contribute to the team. Skills such as basic first aid, food preparation and basic DIY should be underpinned by general fitness training and survival skills. Before any crisis, get every member of your party or family to draw up a list of their skills, remember everybody has something to contribute and these gifts are not always immediately obvious. For example, elderly relatives may be unable to take out two ghouls with a single blow but they may have lived through rationing and have some useful tips on cooking with scarce ingredients. In addition, the frugal years through the 1940s and 1950s created a 'make do' generation, quite used to mending and adapting everyday items rather than rushing to buy a new replacement. This experience and their quiet wisdom will be as valuable as any other skill as you face the challenge to survive in a country of ghouls.

Building your new Society - The Zombie Crisis One Year On

Britain after a Zed-Con 1 will be a very different place – that is certain but zombie experts disagree on the exact scenario which will emerge. Some see the old human world completely disappearing beneath the zombie hordes whilst others suggest there will most likely be scattered survivor communities clinging on in various isolated locations across the country. Whatever the situation, one thing is certain, with the 'authorities' gone, it is vital that you plan for the long-term needs of your community. The old world is not coming back so you need to make plans, in survival speak; your settlement needs to become 'sustainable'.

Obviously, securing a long-term supply of food and fresh water will be a priority after shelter and defence. You and your team will be able to survive for years on canned and preserved goods but you should turn your attention to growing your own food as soon as practicable. Establishing a fruit and vegetable garden is a good place to start but remember to take advantage of any old commercial greenhouse facilities you can find to plant crops. You will eventually need to grow all your own food so the sooner you start learning the better. Clean water sources will be at a premium and you will probably need to establish a robust filtering system for your drinking water. Most rivers and freshwater lakes will still be polluted by rotting corpses but old factories, leaky pipes and other factors will also play a part in making most water unsafe to drink. Most diseases in developing countries are spread through contaminated water so ensure that you have plans for a simple filtration system drawn up well before the crisis.

Once safely established in your permanent location and having secured a source of food and water to meet your immediate needs, you will need to turn your attention to the political development of your community. This analysis will bring into play a range of complex issues around what sort of society you want to rebuild. For example, will you look to expand by taking in other survivors? Will you establish some form of democracy? Or, will you be tempted to establish your own feudal kingdom in which you rule as lord and master?

Whatever the size of your survivor community, it is recommended you implement a fair system of consultation as soon as the immediate crisis subsides. It is vital that either family or 'town' meetings are held to discuss important issues and allow others to vent their opinions. A council of 'village elders' made up of experts and leaders can be set-up to make policy and guide activities in your community. This model has been used throughout history and was the genesis of real democracy in this country and the United States.

A key area you will need to agree early on is your policy towards 'outsiders'. Most experts see the UK population after a major zombie incident at well below four million so there will be far fewer people around but also diminishing resources and some will be prepared to fight to take what you have built. Any newcomers may present challenges to your authority and even a drain on your scarce resources. Whatever you decide, you, your 'village elders' and community should always have the final sanction to banish real troublemakers if the need arises.

However, many newcomers will be wandering survivors, just searching for a safer place to live and you will certainly need to establish numbers if your community is to survive and new arrivals may bring in new skills and insights to help your group flourish. Any visiting Commonwealth or American citizens should be made particularly welcome within your community as this will certainly be the case for any British subjects trapped in these countries during a worldwide zombie crisis.

Your growing community will face more substantial threats from any larger bands of survivors, particularly if these groups have taken to surviving through raiding and stealing from others. It is important that your defences take this threat into account and you will need to consider developing your own 'armed forces' as soon as you are settled. To start with, this will mean regular military training for all able-bodied people to establish a 'militia'. In the longer term, you could even develop full time guards or soldiers. Your first action as leader should be to appoint a 'chief of security' to manage the various aspects of your security policy including defence against both zombies and raiders.

As a final note on life after the zombies, remember your community will always need more than just its basic needs to prosper. Man does not live by bread alone and you should also allocate some resource, no matter how scarce, to regular cultural events or celebrations. Schools will need to be established for any children and training sessions for everyone, to ensure crucial skills are cross-trained to others. Hope is important too. Even if you have not seen a live human for years, there is certain to be other survivors somewhere. Avoid your community feeling it is the last one on earth by reminding them of that. Above all, always remember that you are British, so hard work, fairness and of course a sense of humour will be as important as any tools you have.

Recommended Reading/Further Information

There a wide range of material available to those looking to learn more about subject areas such as emergency preparedness and survival guides. Few directly answer the questions around how to survive a zombie outbreak in the UK but they do offer more in-depth analysis in other areas. This section offers some highlights from the vast library of knowledge out there in books, on DVD and on the internet.

This list is by no means exhaustive but will point you in the direction of some robust and trusted sources of knowledge. A word of warning, however, is that you should use your library or resources to help you prepare for the coming trials, not as a substitute for intensive training or effective preparation. There is no easy way to prepare for the coming of the zombies and there will be no room for armchair generals in the coming struggle for survival. Any bookworms who ignore their practical training will provide easy snacks for the hungry dead long before they can hide their *Star Trek* DVD collection or online gaming passwords.

Books

Listed below is a short selection of recommended reading material:-

SAS Survival Guide (John 'Lofty' Wiseman)
It has been a classic for years and now comes in more varieties than Heinz. Some readers still prefer the vintage 1986 version for its easy reading style and excellent format and layout. He has also recently added an 'urban' version of the guide and there is another 'mountain guide' by a different author. In a section of the market where there are hundreds of different guides, the volumes by Lofty stand out as core texts for the UK audience. They run through with care virtually every emergency situation from security at home to recognising edible from poisonous mushrooms. It may not cover defence against zombies but covers pretty much everything else. If you are limited in time and funds, these books are an excellent choice.

Outdoor Survival Handbook: A Guide To The Resources And Materials Available In The Wild And How To Use Them For Food, Shelter, Warmth And Navigation (Ray Mears)
Based on the BBC2 survival series, this guide outlines the everyday skills required to live in a world without power from the darling of British survival (not a title I would use to his face). Topics range from constructing a natural shelter, building a fire and orienteering, to identifying medicinal herbs. My only comment would be that this book

is aimed more for the person interested in wildlife and enjoying nature than in down and dirty survival training.

Disaster Survival (Collins GEM)
A small, pocket size book giving you practical tips and advice to keep you prepared as far as possible to help protect yourself and your loved ones in the face of any eventuality. The Collins Gem Disaster Survival Guide provides advice on what to do in the event of a range of natural, civil and terrorist disasters. Natural disasters such as hurricanes, volcanoes, avalanches and epidemics are featured, as well as civil and terrorist disasters including fire, chemical incidents and water shortage. A useful primer or reminder but because of its size, limited in detail and depth.

How to Survive the End of the World as We Know it: Tactics, Techniques and Technologies for Uncertain Times (James Wesley Rawles)
All-round hero survivor, Mr Rawles explains in a readable format how to prepare for any 'normal' crisis, from global financial collapse to a flu pandemic. Although it lacks a chapter on dealing with zombies, a gap this volume hopes to fill, it does cover all other key survival topics. A little US-centric, for example the firearms section is of little use to us in the UK - the rest is top notch survival reading.

Emergency Food Storage and Survival Handbook: Everything You Need to Know to Keep Your Family Safe in a Crisis (Peggy Layton)
A very useful survey with a different feel to many of the other survival books on the market. The author is a food expert and as the title suggests this area receives a good deal of focus with some excellent tips on food storage. However, it also covers emergency supplies in your car, grab and go bags and suggested three-month supply lists. Nice one Peggy.

When All Hell Breaks Loose: Stuff You Need to Survive When Disaster Strikes (Cody Lundin)
Survival expert Cody Lundin has written a clear and concise guide on how to survive the next disaster, whether natural or manmade. The chapters are short and understandable to anyone who wants to explore the idea of becoming more self-reliant. It has a good emphasis on the mental preparation for survival and tips on how to avoid 'panic mode'. All in all, as good as it gets without actually mentioning zombies.

The Zombie Survival Guide: Complete Protection from the Living Dead (Max Brook)
The second best book on surviving the ghoul. Beyond a slightly confusing opening chapter, the reader will find a good 80 pages of well-thought through tips to defeating the ghouls. Widely considered to be a bible of the upcoming struggle. I'd be surprised if anyone preparing to fight and survive in any zombie incursion does not have this on

their shelf even if they don't agree with all of the assumptions or guidelines. If a Nobel Prize was awarded for contribution to the zombie debate, Mr Brooks would certainly have a strong claim. A must have.

The Forensics of the Living Dead - Zombie CSU (Jonathan Maberry)
This sounds like an essential title and it still makes the recommended list but hovers uncomfortably between fact and fiction. Some fantastic expert analysis and invaluable case study work is let down by humorous photos of pretend zombies. A great contribution to the growing science of zombiology but be cautious of some of the science.

Papillion (Henri Charriere)
Possibly best known now because of the Steve McQueen film, this book has never been out of print and is a true story of escape, persistence and inner strength like no other. It begins with an amazing escape from an isolated French penal colony and takes the reader across the sea and to South America. Very readable and with a solid follow-up volume called *Banco*. The value of this book is that Henri Charriere constantly seemed to achieve what everyone else would have said was impossible. This is invaluable when you are looking at the zombie holocaust thinking there is no way we can survive. It's the old cliché – nothing is impossible.

The Long Walk: The True Story of a Trek to Freedom (Slavomir Rawicz)
Not to be confused with Nelson Mandela's autobiography, this book is frequently described as 'life changing' and tells the epic tale of a Polish officer escaping from Soviet captivity – a journey of over 4,000 miles. The subject of some controversy in recent years, it contains stories of dedication, suffering and ultimately of survival against the odds. You should think of this as psychology training on the spirit of survival rather than a guide or textbook. An amazing story to be read and kept for when things look bleak.

Five Years to Freedom (James "Nick" Rowe)
Green Beret Lieutenant James N. Rowe was captured in 1963 in Vietnam and from this date onwards his life was dominated by the quest to stay alive. In a Vietcong POW camp, Rowe endured beriberi, dysentery, and tropical fungus diseases. He suffered gruelling psychological and physical torment and experienced the loneliness and frustration of watching his friends die. This story more than any other gives you a real life example of what you need to survive. We are not all superheroes but Nick's book is approachable and there are important lessons for all of us. *Five Years to Freedom* is an unforgettable true story of survival and testimony to the disciplined human spirit. Not to be missed – would make a great movie.

Robinson Crusoe (Daniel Defoe)
Often cited in survival lists and of less value in practical terms but still a fantastic read. An entertaining study in solitude and the part which will ring true to most survivalists is when the main character prepares a positives and negatives list of his current situation to help him draw stock on what's happened. Other entertaining fiction would include the classic *Lord of the Flies* by William Golding. Neither book contains zombies, although there is cannibalism in Robinson Crusoe.

The Death of Grass (John Christopher)
Used to be a standard in schools for GCSE, now seems less popular. A well-written survival story which, if you substitute the zombie virus for the virus wiping out grass and crops, you have a very useful study in the breakdown of society. Interestingly, the whole thing kicks off in China and the reader can see how international events affect the UK. The decline of Britain into barbarism is particularly useful reading. The novel is a much-needed warning against complacency.

Films

There are some key movies in this genre which are regarded by most zombie sources as essential viewing. They should be watched and digested in the same way as a dedicated student prepares for a college or university course with a recommended reading list. The analogy is a good one. These films can paint a picture of a society in breakdown or people in the struggle for survival. Some focus more directly on the zombie menace and how characters respond to the challenge of the living dead

Night of the Living Dead (1968 Romero)
Widely regarded as a reliable source of background information and research. An interesting study of understanding your enemy. The origin of the zombies is a bit dicey but the rest is pure gold.

Dawn of the Dead (1978 Romero)
Arguably the finest zombie survival film ever made. It is virtually a tutorial in survival techniques. Good perspective of the chaos caused by the living dead and collapse of the order, with roving bands of bandits, etc. Don't bother with the updated version, see this classic gospel of zombism first.

28 Days Later/28 Week Later (2002 Boyle)
A film which reinvented zombies into the 'infected' for the 21st century. Whilst excellent and exciting, details concerning rapidly moving zombies have caused massive confusion in the zombie community. It is important to remember this is science fiction, although some scenes such as those of the empty London streets and in particular the church are

accurate predictions. If these movies confuse you, please re-read Dr Ahmed's notes on the Zombic Condition.

Omega Man (1972)
Starring Charlton Heston as the 'last man alive' this vintage survival movie has certainly aged well and apart from the groovy outfits and background music, looks current. A deadly virus has transformed remaining humans into cultish ghouls who are both intelligent and have an objective to wipe out any 'live' humans. Although not strictly speaking about the living dead, it provides a useful tutorial in survivor psychology and the long sweeping camera angles of empty streets builds the atmosphere of isolation. It also develops the concept that lone survivors can almost start to envy their tormentors as they are part of a group – something to think about if you are besieged by ghouls. A "they may be sad at least they are not alone" psychology begins to emerge. Food for thought.

The Last Man on Earth/I am Legend (1964/2007)
Take your pick. Both have inaccuracies but are useful studies of a survivor especially the discipline and routine it takes to survive. However, they also consider the mental impact particularly if you are alone. I prefer the Will Smith version.

Threads (1984)
Widely available on the internet, this is a grim British drama set in the aftermath of a nuclear strike. It is hard viewing but taken as reality preparation, it can be useful. Not many laughs in this one.

Alive (1993)
In 1972 a chartered plane carrying a Uruguayan rugby squad and various family members crashed in the remote Andes. This is a real-life against-all-odds odyssey, most infamous as the survivors ate their own dead to survive. So, you have a true survival story with flesh-eating but again no zombies.

As Far as My Feet will Carry Me (2001)
Based on a well-known book in Germany by Forel, this excellent German language film, tells the story of a German prisoner escaping from Siberia. It provides a fascinating insight into not only what you may have to do to survive but also the costs of survival. The film adds a few extra bits in and cuts out a few real-life events as you would expect but central is the 'will' to survive. If there are any lessons for the zombie survivalist, then it is that if you have this kind of drive, you can survive, no matter how grim the situation.

Survivors (2008) [DVD] (Julie Graham)
The reinvention of the 1970s series which saw virtually the entire population of the UK and the rest of the world wiped out by a plague. The desperate survivors band together and the fun and games of trying to survive starts. The series received a mixed reception from fans but in its updated version, it does present a chilling vision of the UK without people. All you need to do is add the zombies and you would have an ideal primer. Some of the scenarios against other bands of surviving humans are telling. Good viewing all round particularly on team dynamics and if you want more you can always order the older series which is also available on DVD.

Websites

Listed below are just a few websites which you may find useful in your research. There are plenty of sites out there, including many which will confuse as much as inform so, surf carefully and don't believe everything you read.

www.ministryofzombies.com – official home of this handbook with a regular blog and other vital information on the upcoming struggle.

www.zombiesarecoming.com – more articles and survival information than you can shake a stick at, a great site.

www.zombiephiles.com – a very active worldwide forum – excellent reviews and insightful articles.

www.terror4fun.com – few know more about the zombie menace than the creators of this site – they also publish the invaluable Zombie Times e-zine.

www.severedpress.com for great Zombie fiction.

ZOMBIE ZOOLOGY

AN UNNATURAL HISTORY

Severed Press has assembled a truly original anthology of never before published stories of living dead beasts. Inside you will find tales of prehistoric creatures rising from the Bog, a survivalist taking on a troop of rotting baboons, a NASA experiment going Ape, A hunter going a Moose too far and many more undead creatures from Hell. The crawling, buzzing, flying abominations of mother nature have risen and they are hungry.

Available at www.severedpress.com, Amazon and most online bookstores